SEE JANE SING!

A West River Mystery

Jolene Stratton Philo

Midwestern Books

ISBN-13: 979-8-9857175-7-0

Library of Congress Control Number: 1-11733045661

Cover design by: eBook Cover Designs

Published by Midwestern Books
801 W Washington Ave, Polk City, IA 50226

Contact: info@midwesternbooks.com

To Mom.
By telling stories of your one
room school days
and by reading the Little House
books out loud,
you gave me a template for
teaching country school.

CHAPTER 1

I danced in front of the pay phone at the gas station in Belle Fourche—rhymes with whoosh—hopping from foot to foot in a futile attempt to stay warm.

"We hardly saw you. You should have seen Uncle Tim and Aunt Wanda's faces when they came to play cards this afternoon, and you weren't here. They were so disappointed. You should have told them yourself last night instead of leaving me to do your dirty work."

The wind cut like a knife as I counted to thirty to keep my composure. I repeated what I'd told her that morning. "If I'd waited any longer, the storm that's coming might have kept me from getting back to Little Missouri. The roads don't get cleared fast out here. I'm sorry our Thanksgiving visit was cut short, but I'll be back in a few weeks for Christmas."

"Oh, I suppose you're right. It's a long drive from Sioux City." She exchanged her pouty overtones for a drill sergeant ambiance. "Now, you promise to call that switchboard operator in Little Missouri—I can never remember her name . . ."

"Betty Yarborough?"

"That's it. Call Betty and tell her you're on the way."

"I will."

"Promise?"

"Promise."

Mom might have talked longer if she wasn't the one paying for the call. After she hung up, I shivered and dialed Betty's number with clumsy, half-frozen fingers.

"I'w mobiwize the Nationaw Guard if you don't caw in two hours from your apartment," she assured me.

I thanked her, hung up, and hurried to my Volkswagen Beetle. If I checked in with Betty even a minute late, she would call the National Guard. As the new teacher and one of the few young, single women in a town of ninety-two people, I attracted more than enough notice just by being me. My name and picture were in every South Dakota news outlet west of the Missouri River after I pressed charges against a would-be boyfriend who assaulted me earlier in the fall. The news cycle had moved on to stories about the holidays and I was fine with that. I had no desire to be in the spotlight, this time as an East River greenhorn with a small army searching for her because she dinked around when she should have been driving home.

I hit the gas and took Highway 85 out of town, straight into a strong north wind. When I reached the Norwegian Cut-Across I turned onto it without a second thought. The gravel road was curvy and less traveled than the paved highway. It also cut thirty miles off the hundred-mile trip from Belle Fourche to my apartment in Little Missouri. It felt like the right decision right up until the snow began—two hours earlier than predicted. By then I'd driven too far to turn around.

Ice crusted the Beetle's bright red hood. A wall of snowflakes swirled outside. I clutched the steering wheel. My shoulders ached as the car bucked the wind, and I fought to stay on the road. Night fell during the worst of the storm. After more miles than I could count, the snow let up. I relaxed my grip and squinted at the road ahead. It was illuminated only by my headlights. I pressed down on the accelerator a tiny bit.

Big mistake. The front tires spun, the back ones fishtailed, and the steering wheel whirled first one way and then the other. I let up on the gas and pumped the brakes. The car slowed and the steering wheel stopped its impersonation of a tilt-a-whirl.

I breathed a sigh of relief. Before I could let it out, a thunk pitched me forward, and a lurch pitched me back. The car came to a complete halt.

I waited a minute to see if the Beetle was done with its shenanigans. I put on my winter gear, grabbed a flashlight, and pushed the door open. Snowflakes scratched my face and gathered on my eyelashes. Slipping and sliding, I made my way to the Beetle's front end. It was buried in a snowdrift on the wrong side of the road. The wind howled, and the snow was falling in earnest again. The chances of anyone else venturing out in this weather before morning were slim to none, even if Betty sounded the alarm. I wasn't keen on sleeping in my car, but compared to freezing to death on the side of the road, it was as good as a night at the Holiday Inn.

I slogged through the drifts to the rear of the car and

cleared snow from around the exhaust pipe. No need to die from carbon monoxide poisoning during my stay at the Beetle Hotel. I waded back to the driver's side door and climbed inside. My fingers shook.

From cold, I told myself, *not panic.*

I pulled off my gloves and cranked up the heater. The gas tank was nearly full. Mom had packed enough Thanksgiving leftovers to feed a small country. I could hold out for days. Going to the bathroom was going to be dicey. Still, I could do this.

My trembling stilled. I tucked a blanket around my legs and turned off the engine. Then I ate a turkey sandwich. Mom made it the way I like, with a thin layer of Miracle Whip and a sprinkling of salt. I popped open a Cool Whip container, polished off Grandma Josie's tapioca fruit salad, and drank from the peanut butter jar Mom had filled with water. Only a few sips because peeing in the snow was a life experience I could live without.

My thoughts wandered to Beau Kelly who had lost his mother a few months ago. When school dismissed for Thanksgiving he had wrapped his arms around my waist.

> *"Will you be here on Monday, Miss Newell?"*
> *"Of course I will, Beau."*
> *He bit his lip. "Promise?"*
> *I put a hand on either side of his thin face.*
> *"Promise."*

What if I couldn't keep my promise? What would that do to Beau? To my other students? I looked into the darkness outside.

*Listen, God, I'm currently incapacitated and am there-
fore counting on you to take action, though preferably
not by telling Betty to call out the National Guard. This
isn't about me. It's about Beau and my other students.*

I closed my eyes and pictured each one of them. Beau
with the silver butterfly buckle on his belt. Cora Barkley
twirling around the classroom in her sparkly shoes and
her younger brother Bennan steadying her when she
grew dizzy. Stig Borgeson, eyes sparkling, as he sounded
out a word while his big sister Elva coached him. Renny
Berthold inventing one excuse after another to avoid
doing his work, and Tiege Sternquist's enthusiasm
launching him out of his chair several times a day.

A wild rocking roused me. My eyes popped open. The
Beetle lurched from side to side as dim light streamed
in. I sat up and looked out the driver's side window into
a pair of golden-brown eyes half hidden by the slits of a
camouflage ski mask.

Thank you, Betty Yarborough!

"Jane Newell?" my rescuer shouted.

"Yes."

"Open the door."

I tried. "It won't budge."

"It must be frozen shut. You push. I'll pull."

I knelt on the seat and pushed as hard as I could.
The door sprang open and I toppled into the snowdrift.
When I tried to right myself, my feet shot out from
under me.

The man in the mask helped me up and guided me to
a two-tone Ford pickup truck. "Get in."

I did. He did too, so I scooted over until I was next to

a skinny kid in the passenger seat. I removed my gloves and warmed my fingers under the heater.

"Feels good, don't it?" The boy grinned, his black hair flickering an incandescent blue under the dome light.

My rescuer removed his ski mask. His light brown hair crackled with static, and his golden-brown eyes, straight nose, full lips, and clean-shaven cheeks were visible in the early morning light. He held his long, slender fingers beneath the heater.

"Me and Edgar'll dig you out soon as I warm up."

I smiled at the boy. "Do you have a last name, Edgar?"

"Running Horse."

I looked at the man in the driver's seat. "And you are?"

He donned his ski mask and gloves. "Gotta dig your car out." He got out and slammed the door behind him.

Edgar pulled on a stocking cap. "He don't talk much. But he'll chew my tail if I don't help." He jumped out and grabbed a shovel from the truck bed.

I had no intention of waiting for them to dig out my car while I sat in the cab. I left its warmth for the glittering white landscape that stretched to the horizon. I made my way through the snow, pulled my shovel out of the Beetle's back seat, and started scooping alongside Edgar and What's-His-Name.

CHAPTER 2

A half hour later the Beetle was free. I tailed What's-His-Name into town, and we parked our vehicles in the street south of the school. They waded through the snow to my apartment with their snow shovels over their shoulders. I followed the narrow path they'd created.

"We'll clear your sidewalks." What's-His-Name attacked the snowdrifts in front of the trailer that housed my apartment and classroom.

"Thank you. I'll make you some hot tea."

"No need," he yelled over his shoulder. "Call your parents. Betty said they're worried."

Edgar started to clear the stairs and the landing. His puffy, electric-blue snow boots were bright spots of color in the white landscape. My students called them moon boots. I called them ridiculous.

I went inside, turned on the kettle, and set out tea bags and mugs. Then I picked up the phone receiver, and twirled the crank.

"Jane?"

"Betty, thank you—"

"Me and your mother, we been so worried. I'w con-nect you."

When Mom answered, Betty took charge again. "Doris, Jane got home safewy."

"Is she on the line? Can I talk to her?"

"I'm fine, Mom."

"Jane. I am speechless. Absolutely speechless. Your dad and I didn't sleep all night."

I could believe *she* hadn't slept. But Dad? He could sleep through anything.

"If Betty hadn't called me every hour with updates, I would have been a basket case. Do you hear me? A basket case!"

I held the receiver away from my ear. "You're com-ing through loud and clear, Mom." Emphasis on the loud.

"Betty, you were a godsend."

"Happy to be of service, Doris." Betty turned her attention to me. "Who rescued you, Jane?"

"I don't know his name."

"Can you describe him?"

"He had a Ford two-tone pickup truck and kid named Edgar Running Horse with him."

"That's Dick Phiwwips. He works at Fwy Ranch."

"Fly Ranch? Where's that?"

"South of town. I can't bewieve no one towd you about Fwy Ranch. It's where those city boys who get in trouble with the waw get sent. I don't know Edgar, but Dick is a very nice young man."

"Really?" Mom purred.

A knock sounded at my door.

"Someone's here, Mom. I have to go. I'll call you later to talk more."

"No, dear. You have to be worn out. Write us a letter when you're rested. You know how your dad loves getting mail."

"Will do."

As I moved the receiver to the cradle, Mom said, "Betty, tell me more about this Dick Phillips."

Good grief! With the two of them fast friends, Mom now had a direct line on my comings and goings. She might as well live next door. I slammed down the receiver.

The knocking grew louder. I hurried to open the door. Edgar grinned and jerked a thumb at Dick. "He said I could come in for some tea."

I motioned Edgar inside and hollered to Dick, "I'll fix a cup for you, too."

He kept shoveling. I shut the door and went inside. Edgar stood in the entryway, his boots shedding snow on the rug.

"Leave those there and come in." I waited while he took off his ridiculous moon boots. I led him into the kitchen, poured boiling water into three mugs, and handed him a box of tea bags. "Would you plunk one of these in each cup?"

Since Mohammad Phillips wouldn't come to the mountain, I grabbed a mug of tea and took the mountain to him. I set a hot pad on the landing and placed the mug on top. Then speaking in my teacher's voice, to be sure he could hear me, I said, "Here's your tea, Dick."

He kept shoveling.

"Okay, Mohammad. Have it your way," I muttered before dashing inside.

Edgar sat at the table, his eyes closed and his head tipped downward to catch the steam rising from his mug.

I opened a package of Oreos and set it in front of him. "Help yourself."

He opened his eyes, grinned, and took several. "They don't got these at Fly Ranch."

"You don't get cookies? That's not right."

"We get cookies all the time."

I think that's what he was saying. He'd stuffed several Oreos in his mouth and was hard to understand. He chewed and swallowed before going on. "The cooks are always making homemade ones. But not Oreos, like Mom bought back home. I ain't had any since I come to the ranch."

"When was that?"

He stared at the calendar on the wall, his lips moving like he was counting in his head. " 'Bout three months ago, I think. I was messed when I come, so I ain't real sure."

"What's it like living there?"

"Some stuff's okay." He dunked an Oreo in his tea and crammed the whole drippy mess into his mouth.

"Such as?"

He dunked and ate two more before answering. "Three meals a day and the food's real good. I ain't always hungry now."

I glanced at the half-empty Oreo package. How much did he eat when he *was* hungry?

"I got my own bed. No bedbugs. No lice. Clothes that fit. They're clean too. The shop teacher is helping me get my GED." He straightened his shoulders. "I want to go to mechanic school when I get out."

"Is there anything you don't like about it?"

"Too many white people. When we come to town they look at me funny."

"Anything else?"

He stared out the window. I followed his gaze to where Dick Phillips was flinging snow right and left. I glanced back at Edgar who appeared to have collapsed in on himself. I tried to engage him in conversation again, but he refused to open his mouth. Except for polishing off the Oreos. Boy, oh boy, the kid was cruising for a stomachache.

Another knock sounded on the door. When I opened it, Dick Phillips and Merle Laird, my backyard neighbor, stood side by side on the landing.

Dick pushed an empty mug into my hand. "It's time to go, Edgar," he snapped.

The boy sprang up, pulled on his boots, and ran to catch up with Dick. I invited Merle in and surveyed the playground as he shuffled inside. The sidewalk was clear and so was the area where I parked my car. When I turned to wave goodbye to Dick and Edgar, they and the truck were already gone.

"You gonna keep standing there lettin' in the cold?"

I shut the door.

Merle held out two egg cartons and a glass gallon jug of milk with a thick layer of cream on top. "I figured you might be needing these 'bout right now."

"You're too good to me, Merle."

He ducked his head, and I half-expected him to poke a toe against the linoleum and say, "Aw, shucks."

I dragged a kitchen chair to the entryway and patted the seat before taking the milk and eggs. "Take off your things and I'll make breakfast."

"You ain't got things quite right." He sat and pulled off his overshoes. "I'll do the cookin' and you can haul in what's still in your car."

"It's a deal."

I grabbed my keys and moved the Beetle from where it was parked on the street to the spot Dick had cleared. Within the hour the car was unpacked, and we were feasting on scrambled eggs and toast topped with brown sugar and cream. Between bites I gave him the condensed version of my snowbound adventure.

Merle rubbed the hairs on his ear. "Betty tell you 'bout the hunnert and fifty people out hunting for you in the storm?"

The fork fell from my hand. Scrambled eggs flew everywhere. "Where did they all come from?"

"We-ull, Sheriff Sternquist brought a crew from Tipperary. The parents of your students was all rep-ree-sented." He let out a long, schleppy whistle. "Velma Albright threatened to drag everbody else outta bed if they didn't show up."

I burst out laughing. Velma stood barely five foot four and weighed in at a hundred and fifteen pounds. As the school janitor she'd terrorized students for generations. They might be grown and twice her size now, but when she said jump they still asked how high.

Merle stood. "I best git going or she'll be on me 'bout not letting you get some sleep. Besides, you gotta rest up. Since you got home a day earlier than expected, I thought you might like goin' to the Long Pines to cut your own Christmas tree tomorrow. I'll bring a thermos of cocoa."

A chance to thank everyone Velma had bullied into searching for me?

Yes, please!

A tromp through the evergreen forest west of town?

Heavenly!

Hot cocoa made with Snippy's insanely rich and creamy milk?

Yum!

"Count me in."

After Merle left, I unpacked my suitcase and put Mom's box full of leftovers in the refrigerator. Then I started a load of laundry, laid out work clothes for the upcoming week, and got out the ironing board. But when my brain refused to tell my hands how to set it up, I gave up and lay down for a short nap. Just enough to take the edge off my drowsiness so I could power through the rest of the afternoon. Get down the boxes of Christmas decorations from the guest room closet . . . iron clothes . . . set out . . . seat work . . . for . . . Monday . . .

Chapter 3

A ringing began in my ears. Softly at first. Then louder. And louder. It called to me from a velvety blanket of sleep. The phone!

I stumbled to the kitchen, barely able to open my eyes, and answered it. "Hello," I croaked.

"Were you napping? Did I wake you?"

Betty sounded mortified, so I lied. "No."

"Good. The sheriff said you should wock your apartment tonight. A Fwy Ranch kid just run away."

Betty's speech impediment was no big deal when I was fully rested. Half-asleep, it took me a minute to translate "wock" into "lock" and "Fwy" into "Fly."

"A Fly Ranch boy took off in this weather?"

"It happens every time there's a big snow. The sheriff says you met this kid. Edgar Running Horse."

"Thanks, Betty. I'll check the locks right away."

I swallowed the lump that rose in my throat and went from door to door and window to window in my apartment and the adjoining classroom but I couldn't imagine the young man with a penchant for Oreos hurting anybody. I brushed my teeth in the bathroom. Then I crawled into bed, eager for the escape sleep offered. My eyelids drifted shut and I pictured the skinny boy with dark hair and a huge appetite. As the wind howled around my apartment, rattling the windows and forcing the cold in through the cracks, the memory of his ridiculous moon boots soothed me. At least his feet would be warm.

"Oh, Edgar," I whispered as sleep crept closer. "Why did you run?"

***

I slept until mid-morning. Between sixteen hours of sleep, a long hot shower, and a very late and large breakfast I felt fully recovered from my night in the car. I had missed church, which gave me plenty of time to find my long underwear and wool socks and top them with wool pants, and a wool sweater. Merle might mistake me for a sheep while we hunted for Christmas trees. In the entryway I added a down vest, my winter coat and warmest hat, a scarf, mittens, and snow boots to the sheep outfit. My watch said it was one o'clock when I waddled outside.

Merle waited next to his truck. He wore a plaid wool jacket over insulated tan coveralls and the same overshoes he'd had on last night. The flaps of his Elmer Fudd hat were tied securely in place, and gigantic wool mittens covered him from fingertip to forearm.

His lips twitched as he gave me a once over. "Glad to see you got some sense about how to dress in this country. Though in that get up you may need a boost up."

I ignored the dig and, thanks to a snow drift on my side of his truck, crawled into the cab. Not elegantly, but it got the job done.

Merle pointed to a thermos on the seat between us. "It's got an extree dollop of Snippy's cream so we can keep up our strength."

Be still my heart.

He turned the key and the engine roared to life. The truck chewed through the snow that blanketed the road to the Long Pines. The South Dakota map claims the two-mile stretch we were on, between town and the Montana border, was a state highway. It was barely passable, a sorry collection of ruts and potholes that made me grateful for the extra padding provided by my multiple layers of clothing. In Iowa, all state highways were smooth pavement. Well-maintained, smooth pavement.

This wasn't Iowa.

The highway proved to be a warm-up for the bone-jarring logging road into the Long Pines. I cushioned the thermos in my arms, hoping the glass inside wouldn't shatter. Only after Merle pulled into a wide, snowy meadow and braked to a stop did I set the thermos down again.

A dozen or so vehicles rimmed the circular area. There was the Berthold's pickup truck and the Kelly's, too, as well as Dan Barkley's Forest Service truck. That meant at least two of my students, Renny and Beau, were running around somewhere. Maybe Cora and Bennan as well, unless Dan was here for official business.

I didn't see anyone other than two men who were heading up the hill on the far side of the parking area. One wore a green down coat that made him look like a puffy Incredible Hulk. The other guy was in a Daniel Boone get up. I didn't recognize either of them, not surprising since Tipperary County was wide open, with ranches miles apart and towns spaced even farther. Besides, I'd started my job a week after moving here in August. Teaching seven students in three different grades left time for either socializing or solving murders. I'd chosen to concentrate on the latter.

"We ain't the only folks with the Christmas spirit today." Merle took a paper tag from the dashboard and passed it over. "Put that in yer pocket in case one of them forest rangers gets all official and asks to see your tree permit." He pulled a hatchet from behind his seat, gave me the thermos, and we got out.

The scent of pine was like breathing in Christmas. White snow glittered. The sun shone bright in the winter blue sky. The cold was a megaphone, carrying the shouts of children and warnings of their parents on the frosty air. Evergreens covered the buttes. With so many trees to choose from, finding the right one would be a piece of cake.

I was wrong.

We tromped up hills and down into valleys. We examined tens of trees, hundreds of trees crammed together in clumps on the steep hillsides. Every one of them made Charlie Brown's Christmas tree look like a winner.

My legs were aching when we crested a hill. Merle turned in a slow circle and pointed to a less crowded stand of pines a couple hundred yards away. "Don't that look promising?"

"It does. But it's not going anywhere. Are you thirsty?" I held up the thermos.

He took it and sat on a tree stump. He untwisted its cup and filled it with steaming cocoa. Then he handed it to me before pulling a second cup from the pocket of his overcoat and pouring some for himself.

"Scoot over." He did, and I sat beside him on the stump. The cocoa was delicious. I drained my cup and held it out for more. "Tell Snippy she outdid herself."

Merle divided what was left between us and screwed the thermos shut. "This here is a new recipe I been testing for the town Christmas party. You comin'?"

"There's a town Christmas party? When?"

"Saturday night at the dance hall." He licked a smidge of cocoa from the corner of his mouth. "Santa and his elf will be there."

"Count me in!"

Merle finished his cocoa and stood. I gave him my cup. The Bertholds tromped past us toward the cluster of trees Merle and I had spotted, the Kellys following close behind.

"Miss Newell!" Renny whooped and plowed toward me through the snow. "My dad went looking for you in the snowstorm."

Beau shouted, "My grandpa did, too."

I cupped my hands around my mouth. "Thanks, Glen and Burt. You're my heroes!"

Glen tipped his hat and kept walking, but Burt paused. "Anything to keep you safe and sound after all you done for Beau, Miss Newell. Next to me and Iva, you is the most important person in his life."

I wanted to answer him, but that would make me cry. If I cried, my nose would run. And if my nose ran, snot icicles would form on my nose. Instead, I waved and smiled and fell into line behind Merle.

As we climbed the hill, Merle's limp grew more pronounced. My heart dropped to the heels of my snow-covered boots. I had been thoughtless, dragging an old man hither and yon in search of my idea of a perfect Christmas tree. It was time to lower my standards and choose a tree, no matter how scraggly.

I quickened my pace and caught up with Merle. "I'll go ahead and claim a couple trees for us." He waved me on, and I tromped to the stand of evergreens, passing Renny and Beau as they lobbed snowballs at Glen and Burt. As I got closer, a patch of bright scarlet glimmered between two trees. A scarf perhaps, or a down coat. I scrambled up the incline and slid to a stop beside someone lying on the ground. Or rather, a former someone. The pale, lifeless head was wreathed in blood-soaked snow.

It couldn't be a dead body. My eyelids clamped shut, and I waited for the aberration to pass. I opened my eyes again. The body was still there. Despite the gash on the side of his head and the blood on his face, I recognized him.

Edgar Running Horse.

I stood over him, as motionless as he was, until the high voices of approaching children spurred me into action.

"Merle!" I shouted and spun around.

He was right behind me. When he took in the scene, his head reared back like he'd been hit.

"Beau and Renny." Their shouts grew nearer. "They can't see this!"

Merle started down the hill, loosing a stream of words as he went. "You stay right where you is. I'll corral them kids. You git yourself arranged so's that poor fella is hid from view."

I forced myself to say the words that made the truth before me too real to bear. "Find Dan Barkley so he can sound the alarm. Tell him it's the missing Fly Ranch boy."

Chapter 4

I turned away from Edgar and stood between the trees, blocking the view. I watched Merle reach Glen Berthold and gesture up the hill. Glen lit out, kicking up snow until he intercepted the little boys and led them away. Merle traipsed down the hill, hollering Dan's name.

One disaster averted. As for the disaster behind me, all I could do was look away and wait for help to arrive. I shifted my gaze from one snow drift to another. From one family hiking up and down hills to another. From one tree to another as tears streamed down my cheeks.

A length of yarn, variegated brown and green, fluttered in the wind, caught in a cluster of pine needles. My mind was blank as I slid forward a step or two and pulled the yarn free. I stared at it for a moment. My hands were cold. All of me was cold. I put my hands into my pockets, seeking warmth, and the yarn went with them.

My gaze shifted to Edgar's body again. I saw what had

been blocked by the tree trunk before. Edgar Running Horse was barefoot. His electric-blue moon boots were gone. My tears fell faster at the sight of his toes in the snow.

Dan Barkley barged up the hill.

"What you bellyaching about, old man?" he shouted at Merle.

"Me and Jane stumbled onto a real bad sit-ee-ation." Merle led Dan over to me. "Teacher," he spoke softly, "you got to move so Dan can see."

His request made no sense to me. He put an arm around my shoulder as gently as if I were a child, and guided me out of the way. I stepped aside so Dan could take in the scene.

The color drained from Dan's face. "He's just a kid."

"Teacher says he's the Fly Ranch kid that run off the other day."

He scratched his head. "Either of you know his name?"

"Edgar Running Horse." My voice was thick with tears. "He and Dick Phillips found me the night of the blizzard."

"Ah, Jane, I'm sorry." He frowned. "I hate to ask, but are you two okay standing guard while I sound the alarm?"

Merle scratched his nose. "We got any choice?"

"Not really." Dan took off for the parking lot, a spray of snow marking his descent down the hill.

I began to shake.

"Here." Merle wound his scarf around my neck. It smelled of wood smoke and cow poop.

We stood silent and unmoving until Dan returned.

"The sheriff is on his way. He says he wants you two to guard the crime scene until he arrives. He doesn't want people disturbing anything."

Dan unfolded two camp stools and handed us blankets. "Wrap up in these and sit down. I gotta go wait for him and the ambulance. They should be here soon."

The blankets were no match for the cold. The wind picked up as the sun sped toward the western horizon. My teeth began to chatter. Merle's did too. We were a two-person drum line, our teeth pounding out a frozen, toneless tattoo. By the time several sets of flashing lights approached, my jaw muscles ached and my feet were numb.

Sheriff Sternquist and his deputy climbed the hill and went straight to Edgar's body, ignoring Merle and me completely. Only after they had wrapped yellow tape from tree to tree to enclose the crime scene and the deputy pulled out a camera did the sheriff mosey over.

"I apologize for the wait, but we needed to get a look at the crime scene and take pictures before the sun sets."

Merle tried to speak, but he was shaking too hard. His nose was dripping, and his lips were an alarming blue.

When the sheriff noticed, he stuck his fingers in his lips and whistled.

Dan Barkley barged up the hill. "What do you need, Rick?"

"Take Merle to the ambulance to warm up, and then come back for Jane."

Dan helped Merle to his feet and led him away. The sheriff turned his attention on me. "Can you answer a few questions?"

I wanted to shout, "No! I'm too cold. I can't remember what warm feels like. Take me to the ambulance, too." Then I thought of Edgar lying behind me. He would never be warm again.

"If it helps find the person who killed Edgar."

Rick asked me to show him which boot prints were Merle's, which were Dan's, and which were mine. Next, he wanted me to point out where Merle had talked to Glen Berthold and where Glen had intercepted Renny and Beau.

"That's all I need for now. The rest can wait until you get warmed up and the EMTs have checked you over."

I stood and took a step, but my toes weren't where they were supposed to be. I began to sway and pitch forward. Rick yanked me back by my parka collar, put his arm through mine, and led me to the parking lot. The sun sank behind the hills as we went. Grey shadows swallowed the last of the light, intensifying the cold around me and inside me. I began to shake uncontrollably as we neared the crowd huddled inside the circle of vehicles. Dan walked from person to person, writing in a notebook.

My eyelids drooped as I watched the Incredible Hulk and Daniel Boone glide away into the shadows. I wanted to enter the welcoming darkness too. My knees buckled and I surrendered to sleep.

"Oh no you don't." Rick put his arm around my waist and gave me a shake. "Just a couple more steps and we'll be there."

He dragged me to the ambulance and banged on the doors as a second ambulance drove up, lights flashing and sirens screaming.

The noise roused me from my stupor. "Why are they here?"

"To bag the body and take it to the morgue in Rapid City."

My stomach flipped as the door of the first ambulance swung open. Merle's cocoa, which had tasted like a celebration an hour ago, rose like bile and spewed out of me right onto Rick's parka. He wrinkled his nose and pulled away. Someone jumped out of the ambulance and caught me as I lost my balance. I looked up to see who it was. At the same time, the dregs remaining in my stomach rose in rebellion and hit Dick Phillips square in the chest. Everything went black.

Chapter 5

"Wake up, Jane."

The voice was familiar, but came from miles away. I tried to work out who was calling me. The voice grew louder. Closer. Someone shook my shoulders.

I batted at the unwelcome hands. "Go away. Let me sleep."

"You can take a nap after we've checked you over. Can you roll onto your back?"

I did, and a foul odor wrinkled my nose. "Who threw up?"

"You did."

"No." I opened my eyes and saw Mary Borgeson kneeling beside me. Mary? Why was she here? "Not me. Rick and I were walking to the ambulance when—"

The scene as we neared the ambulance came rushing back. I groaned. I'd distributed Merle's cocoa liberally. A little for the sheriff. A little for Dick Phillips. And, if my nose was telling me the truth, I'd kept a little for myself.

I let my head flop onto the pillow. Today might be a good day to die.

Mary Borgeson wrapped a cuff around my arm and took my blood pressure. How she could hear through the stethoscope with the ambulance rattling down the road was beyond me.

I licked my lips and grimaced. They tasted awful. "Are we going to the hospital?"

She wrinkled her forehead and undid the blood pressure cuff. "The ambulance isn't moving."

"Then why is it rattling?"

"It's not. But you're shaking with cold. And shock." She wiped a thermometer with an alcohol swab. "Put this under your tongue."

She laid more blankets on top of me, as well as another pillow under my head and one under my feet. My shaking subsided a titch, but Mary frowned when she read the thermometer. "Dick, can you give me the box of hand warmers when you finish with Merle?"

What was wrong with Merle? Had his hip given out? I shouldn't have made him traipse all over the Long Pines looking for Christmas trees. I rose up on my elbows. "Where is he? Is he okay?"

Mary pushed me down gently. "Stay under the blankets."

A whistly inhale came from beyond Mary. "I'm right here, Teacher. And I'm doing a sight better than you is."

Dick's face appeared over Mary's shoulder. He handed her a box. After she tucked warmers along both sides of my torso, in my hands, and under my feet, she stuck the thermometer under my tongue again.

"Don't move." She held up the box. "I'm going to put this away."

Once she was gone I could see Dick wrapping a blood pressure cuff around Merle's arm. Merle smirked and spoke into Dick's stethoscope. "Teacher's gonna have to toughen up to make it in this country, ain't she?"

Dick winced and yanked the stethoscope out of his ears.

"You and me," Merle thumped on Dick's chest, "we got to agree not to tell Betty about Jane baptizin' you with sick. If that gets out, nobody'll drink my cocoa at the town Christmas party."

Dick blushed. "Stop talking and cooperate for a change, would you? I need to take your blood pressure and get your temperature." He waved a thermometer under Merle's nose.

Dick's brusque manner made me uneasy. I closed my eyes and tried to pinpoint what was troubling me. The image of Edgar's cold, lifeless body formed behind my lids. I sat up and gasped. The thermometer fell out of my mouth and shattered on the floor.

Mary leaned over me. "Jane, what's wrong?"

I wrapped my arms around Mary's neck and clung to her. "How can Edgar be dead?" I sobbed.

She rubbed my back until I grew calmer and then pressed a wad of tissues into my hand. "That had to be a terrible shock. Now get back under the blankets and let the hand warmers get to work." She took a whisk broom from a cubbyhole and swept the bits of broken glass and balls of mercury into a dustpan.

Merle took the thermometer from his mouth and gave it to Dick. "Teacher." The word squeaked out of

Merle, and he sounded like a chastised mouse. "I didn't mean to worry you so. I was aimin' to keep your mind off what we seen, but I done the opposite. Can you forgive an old man who don't know how to keep his mouth shut?"

"Merle, it wasn't anything you said. Every time my eyes close, I see Edgar's body in the snow. There was so much blood around his—"

Dick's head snapped up and his eyes drilled into mine. Those were the eyes I'd first seen peering out from his camouflage ski mask. I burrowed under the blanket to hide from them. A fist banged on the ambulance door and I flinched.

"It's okay, Jane." Mary put her hands on my shoulders. "Take some deep breaths. In for three and out for three. In, two, three. Out, two, three." She counted until I settled into the rhythm. Then she opened the door.

The sheriff sat in the jump seat and looked from Dick to Mary. "How are the patients doing?"

Mary answered. "They're starting to warm up."

"Do you think they're up for a few questions?"

She crossed her arms. "Don't even think about it. The only things they're up to between now and tomorrow are hot showers, hot soup, and warm beds."

"In that case, I'll question them tomorrow."

Mary's eyes narrowed. "What's the big hurry?"

"The longer a murder investigation takes, the less chance we'll catch the killer."

Murder? Had he said murder?

"Sorry, Sheriff. Jane and Merle spent a good long time guarding the dead for you, and they're in tough shape. So why don't you call Betty and tell her to have somebody waiting for Merle and Jane when they get home? They should bring hot soup and overnight bags. Once you've done good by the living, write yourself a note to call Jane and Merle tomorrow afternoon"—The sheriff tried to speak. Mary held up a warning finger.—"and not a minute sooner."

I rose up on one elbow. "How do you know it's murder?"

The sheriff eyed Mary. "Do I have your permission to answer her or does that have to wait until tomorrow afternoon too?"

"Don't act smart." She thawed an iota. "You can answer."

"He died of a knife wound. Not self-inflicted."

Dick dropped the thermometer he was disinfecting with an alcohol swab. Shards of glass scattered everywhere. Tiny balls of mercury rolled on the floor like silvery Christmas ornaments in search of a tree.

Merle poked at the floor with his boot. "This ain't a good day to be a thermometer."

"It was an even worse day to be Edgar Running Horse." I stared at Dick. He stared back. I didn't look away. He did.

CHAPTER 6

Mary brandished the whisk broom at Sheriff Sternquist. "Right about now is when you should call Betty and warm up the patrol car. When it's good and toasty, you can collect Merle and Jane."

Rick opened the door and jumped into the snow. "Give me twenty minutes. I need to talk to the crew at the crime scene." He swung the door shut.

"Mary, you been givin' Rick Sternquist what for since you babysat him as a kid." Merle removed his Elmer Fudd hat and ran a hand over his wispy, white hair. "You ever give any thought to tryin' a different tack?"

"Now and again." She bent and swept the remains of the thermometer into a small dustpan. "He was one of those kids who wouldn't stop asking questions. Now he's a man who does the same thing. If I hadn't gotten after him, he would be pestering you and Jane on the drive home. Neither of you are up for that."

She emptied the dustpan into a tiny wastebasket. "Dick, you help Merle get ready to leave. I'll see to Jane."

Dick turned to Merle and blushed.

What was the deal with him? Either he was the shyest man on the planet, or he had something to hide.

Mary folded back my blankets and piled the hand warmers next to me. "Stuff some of these in your pants pockets and boots. Put the rest inside your mittens."

"Aren't you worried I'll melt?"

"Nah. As low as your body temperature dipped this afternoon, the most we can hope for is a slight thaw." She pulled my stocking hat over my ears and tied my scarf around my neck like she was my teacher and I was a kindergartner. "Getting chilled on the way home won't do you any favors." She arranged a blanket around my shoulders and fastened it under my chin with a safety pin while Dick did the same for Merle.

When Rick arrived, he and Mary walked with us to the patrol car and tucked us in the back seat. Rick climbed into the driver's seat and shut the door. Before he could leave, Mary rapped on his window.

He rolled it down. "Yes?"

She shook an index finger at him. "Not one question. Now shut the window and stop letting in cold air."

Rick drove toward town in silence. Mary had banned him from asking questions, but not me. I made the most of her oversight.

"How long do you think Edgar's been dead?"

Rick kept his eyes on the road and his voice expressionless. "I can't comment on an ongoing investigation."

"Oh, come on, Rick, we found him. Doesn't that count for anything?"

"I want to do everything by the book. There can't be

any room for a judge to declare a mistrial. You know that."

Did I ever. The week before Thanksgiving, I'd given a deposition against Junior Wentworth, the man who had killed Beau's mother in a hit and run accident. Junior's big time lawyer got the hit and run charges dismissed after poking holes in how the case had been handled. Not that Rick had done anything wrong. I was the one who decided to color outside the lines. Holding me at gunpoint is what finally landed him in jail. The assault charges stuck because Merle and Rick's depositions corroborated my testimony. That case was going to trial and had a good chance of sending Junior to prison. Still, he would never pay for what he'd done to Beau and his mom, and that truth made me see red. Rick was right. The evidence against Edgar's murderer had to be airtight.

"What's your deputy doing at the crime scene?" I asked.

Rick slowed to negotiate a sharp curve. "He's taking molds of prints in the snow."

"Will that do any good after so many people were in the forest?"

Rick reached the straightaway and accelerated. "It's probably an exercise in futility. I'm just following standard procedure."

"What else will the deputy do?"

"Search the area for anything out of place."

"Like what?"

"Oh, telltale signs of evidence that's been removed or ruined. Defense lawyers jump all over that kind of stuff."

He drove into Little Missouri and glanced in the rear-view mirror. "You didn't take anything, did you?"

Merle shook a finger. "You gotta take back your question, Sheriff. Otherwise, I gotta report you to Mary Borgeson. What'll it be?"

"It was a rhetorical question. You two know better than to remove evidence from a crime scene."

"We're here," Rick announced. He pulled in behind my Beetle and told us to stay put while he made sure people were waiting to help us. "I'll see who Betty got to stay with you and be right back."

When the sheriff returned, Merle looked as sour as an old lemon. "Rick Sternquist, I ain't never needed a nursemaid, and I don't need one tonight."

"You probably don't," Rick agreed. "But Dale Cunningham has already milked Snippy and has the cream separator put together all wrong. He's going to mess things up bad unless you get in there quick."

"What the hell?" Merle bolted out of the car. "If he done anything to hurt ol' Snip, I'll use a piece of my mind to choke the bastard—" A string of curse words trailed after him as he railed against the postmaster.

I got out and stood beside the sheriff. "Poor Dale. He's in for a long night."

Rick took my elbow and walked me to my apartment. "Yours may be on the long side too." He cleared his throat. "Velma Albright's staying with you."

"What?" I shook my arm free and reached for the door handle. Velma was a good and true friend. She was also overzealous, crusty as dry bread, smelled of cigarette smoke even when she didn't light up, and was old enough to be my grandmother. She'd stayed overnight at my apartment about a month ago. I had yet to recover from that slumber party.

"Why would Betty call Velma of all people?"

Rick started to reply, but I cut him off. "Never mind. I'd better go before Velma throws out all the art supplies and spreads newspapers everywhere." When I went inside, she was lining the apartment entryway with layers of old papers.

" 'Bout time the sheriff brung you home." She spoke without looking up. "You take those boots off before you track mud all over this nice, clean floor. Then you ladle up a bowl of soup and cut some bread from the fresh loaf I brought."

I yanked off my boots and let them fall. Velma grabbed them almost before they hit the floor and set them next to the wall. When I took off my coat and unwound my scarf, she snatched them and hung them up.

"Betty said not to give you any grief tonight. She's been carrying on about you finding a dead body to anyone who'll listen. When she's done calling the entire population of South Dakota, she'll be on the horn with neighboring states."

What if she calls Mom and Dad?

My pulse quickened, and I dashed for the phone. "Betty!" I shouted into the receiver. "Are you there?"

"Miss Neweww, is Vewma with you?"

"She is. Betty, have you—"

"Did she bring hot soup?"

"She did. But Betty, have you—"

"Did it hit the spot?"

"I don't know."

"Why not?"

"I haven't had any yet. Have you talked to my parents? Did you tell them about me finding a dead body?"

"I'm sorry, Miss Neweww, but between tawking to the
sheriff and the EMTs and every Tom, Dick, and Harry
who wants to know what's going on in the Wong Pines, I
haven't had time. I can caww them now if you don't feew
up to it."

"No!" My voice cracked and my entire body went
weak. I spoke more quietly. "They've had enough to worry
about this weekend. I don't want this news to keep them
from getting a good night's sleep. The best way to handle
this is for me to tell to them Saturday after the sheriff's
investigation is done and things have calmed down."

"My wips are seawed. And Miss Neweww?"

"Yes?"

"You are a wonderfuw daughter."

Wonderful daughter?

No.

Complete coward?

Yes.

"Thank you, Betty. Goodbye."

Velma thrust a bowl under my nose. "Sit down and eat."

"Not until I've used the bathroom."

Moments later I was wolfing down chunks of chicken,
carrot rounds, and homemade egg noodles floating in a
rich broth. It was warmth and safety ambrosia. Velma
cut a slice of fresh bread and slathered it with butter. I
wolfed it down too and ate a second slice while she tested
the water temperature in the shower. Then she insisted
that I take two aspirin before I got in. I stood under the
hot spray until the bathroom resembled a sauna. My eyes

were so heavy when I came out of the bathroom wearing my warmest pajamas that I suspected Velma's aspirin were sleeping pills. I fell asleep when my head hit the pillow and didn't stir until Velma pounded on my bedroom door in the morning.

"Them students of yours'll be here in an hour. You better get up, 'cause I ain't gonna teach 'em."

I rolled out of bed, dressed in wool pants and a fuzzy sweater, and went out to thank her. She was gone, but a bowl of steaming oatmeal was waiting for me. It was dotted with raisins and walnuts, dusted with brown sugar, and swimming in cream. A mug of hot coffee had been poured, and a note was propped against it. I ate and read simultaneously.

I hope your week is a darn sight better than your weekend was. You sure got a knack for finding excitement. Don't touch them newspapers I put in your entryway. You mighta found that poor kid, but that don't give you the right to track snow and mud on my clean floors.

I carried my bowl to the window and watched Velma make her way across the playground, cigarette smoke haloing around her head. I now understood why Betty had called Velma, of all people. The crotchety old janitor knew exactly what I needed—chicken soup, a hot shower, uninterrupted sleep, oatmeal for breakfast, and a reminder that finding a dead body was no excuse for making a mess.

I leaned my forehead against the cold window. On the other hand, stumbling upon the body of the kid who found me in a snowstorm was a good reason to make his killer pay for taking his life.

Chapter 7

Velma's oatmeal was good to the last drop. The same could not be said about her coffee. I liked mine strong, but hers was a sludge so thick it coated my tonsils on the way down. I poured the disgusting mess into the sink and ran to the bathroom. Even after gargling and brushing my teeth, I could still taste it.

I hurried from the apartment side of the school's double-wide, double-long trailer to the classroom side. I glanced over my lesson plans and made sure the children's seat work was in order before my students arrived.

Elva and Stig Borgeson were the first to burst into the cloakroom swathed in hats, snowsuits, gloves, and boots. They were accompanied by swirls of frosty air and their mother.

Mary gave me an appraising look. "Did you sleep last night?"

"I did. And I feel great."

"Glad to hear it." She held out a shiny, foil-wrapped

casserole dish. "It's lasagna. I thought you might not feel like cooking yet."

Soon the cloakroom was crowded with kids wriggling out of snowsuits and mothers pushing casseroles into my hands. I shuttled the pans they'd labeled with care—Pam Barkley's egg bake, Trudy Berthold's chicken and rice hot dish, Iva Kelly's scalloped potatoes and ham, Cookie Sternquist's beef and noodles, and Mary Borgeson's lasagna—to the freezer.

The kids stuffed their hats and mittens in their cubbies and hung their snowsuits on the hooks beneath them. They lined up their boots on the newspapers Velma had laid on the floor.

"Look at them," Cookie said as the seven children went to their desks and started their seat work. "How do you get them to do that?"

"I don't know."

Pam Barkley squeezed my elbow. "Cora and Bennan told God they would do their best work in exchange for your safe return. Now they're keeping their end of the bargain."

Cookie pulled on her gloves. "When Tiege heard you were missing, he was bound and determined to hop on the snowmobile and start looking for you—and that was before you found the body of the Fly Ranch boy."

Not one of the women blinked an eye at the mention of a seven-year-old on a snowmobile.

Trudy lowered her voice to a loud whisper. "Glen said the snow was thick with boot tracks behind Round the Bend on Sunday morning." The Bend, which she and her husband owned, was Little Missouri's biggest business.

"He thinks that Fly Ranch boy was looking for something to eat in the garbage cans."

The mothers—all but Cookie—took their leave, heads shaking, tongues clucking, and admonishing one another to take the keys out of their vehicles to be on the safe side. When they were gone Cookie wrapped me in a huge hug.

"When we heard you were missing I started praying. I told God in no uncertain terms that these kids were depending on you. Not that he has to do what I say. Still, when Betty called to say you were safe, I was relieved that he and I had the same plan in mind." She put her hands on my shoulders and held me at arm's length. "You've seen your fair share of trouble this weekend. You know you can call if you want to talk about it, right?"

"Right."

I watched her leave, wondering how this rancher's wife I'd known for a handful of months had become my dear friend. I was still puzzling over this unexpected joy when I entered the classroom.

Seven heads sprang up in unison. Elva Borgeson raised her hand.

"Elva?"

"What was it like to spend a night in your car?"

Her question was like the breaching of a dam, and the rest of the students joined in.

"How did you get stuck?"

"Were you scared?"

"Did you have to go to the bathroom?"

"How did you get dug out?"

"Did you really find a dead body?"

"How bloody was it?"

The children wouldn't be able to concentrate until they had some answers. "Let's say the pledge"—I motioned for them to stand and put their hands on their hearts—"and then we can talk about Thanksgiving weekend."

I spared no details regarding their night-in-the-car questions. However I made my dead body responses vague and boring, all the while keeping an eye on Beau in case it brought up unwelcome memories of his mother's death.

"Now it's your turn to tell everyone about what you did over Thanksgiving vacation." Their hands shot up with the grace of synchronized swimmers. "Renny, would you like to go first?"

One by one, they described their adventures in mind-numbing detail. I struggled to stay awake, though the children paid rapt attention to one another. Tiege laughed so hard at six-year-old Stig's account of operating the blade on their snow truck and plowing their lane, he nearly fell out of his chair.

I roused from my stupor and announced it was time for reading class. Instantly, we all settled into the groove of our classroom routine like the needle of a record player. They worked on spelling and English until morning recess. I snuck into my apartment and brewed tea to keep me going.

The sheriff called while the children were outside. "How did the sleepover with Velma go?"

"Better than expected. Except for the coffee she made. Have you ever tasted her coffee?"

"It's like drinking battery acid."

"That's a charitable description." I waited for him to

say something. He didn't. "Are you calling about Velma or about the investigation into Edgar's death?"

"The investigation." His voice deepened, and he grew serious. "Can I stop in after school to ask some questions?"

"Could you wait until fifteen minutes after dismissal? My students are already way too curious about Edgar's death, and seeing you will feed the beast."

"That's reasonable. See you later today."

The rest of the day passed without incident. After locating mittens, cramming legs into snow pants, zipping coats, and shoving feet into boots before each recess only to reverse the process minutes later, my love-hate relationship with winter moved firmly into the hate camp.

The phone rang as I shooed the last child out the door. Liv, who taught upper grade students, was calling from her classroom in the double-wide, double-long tan trailer that ran east to west along the north side of the school yard.

"You got a few minutes to talk? We got to get going on the Christmas program."

"Sorry, but no. The sheriff will be here any minute to get the gory details about what Merle and I found in the Long Pines yesterday afternoon. I'd much rather be talking to you."

"Can we meet for breakfast in the morning? For some cockamamie reason, I promised my students that I would hand out parts tomorrow. I'll bring pancakes and bacon at seven if that's not too early. You make the coffee."

"It's a deal."

I hung up with a whoop and a holler. Between friends fixing my breakfasts, a freezer full of casseroles, and the rest of Mom's Thanksgiving leftovers, I might not have to cook until Christmas. I whooped again and added a jig for good measure.

"Where's the party?"

I turned around and found the sheriff standing in the entryway. When had he come in?

I straightened my sweater and began tidying my desk in an attempt to look professional. I almost pulled it off, but then the barrette holding back my hair snapped in two. Its halves flew through the air and landed at the sheriff's feet. My hair went bonkers. A mass of curls fell across my eyes. I tucked them behind my ears, but my hair had tasted freedom and refused to be restrained.

"Uh . . . hi." I batted at my hair and dragged the only adult-sized chair from the low, kidney-shaped table near the chalkboard closer to my desk. "Use this instead of a kid's chair. It's no fun to sit with your knees up to your ears."

He waited to sit down until I'd taken my seat at the wooden teacher's chair behind my desk. Then he took out a notebook and pen. "Are you ready to get started?"

"I'm ready to get it over with."

"Fair enough." He clicked his pen. "Could you tell me what happened yesterday afternoon after you and Merle finished your cocoa?"

"Why are you so sure we were drinking cocoa and not coffee? Or something stronger?"

"Do you want me to embarrass you by describing how hard it is to remove a rancid chocolate stain on a parka?"

I took a small stuffed teddy bear from my desk and threw it at him.

He ducked and continued. "Also, Merle insisted on copying out the cocoa recipe for me while I interviewed him."

He listened intently as I told of spotting the stand of pines, going ahead of Merle to claim our trees, seeing the red against the snow as I got closer, and finding the body.

He asked me to describe the pattern of blood around Edgar's head, the position of his parka and hood, and wrote something down. "Did you notice anything else that might be significant?"

"As a matter of fact, I did." I pushed away the curls that were in my eyes again. "Edgar's snow boots were missing."

Rick straightened. "How can you be sure he'd been wearing snow boots and not shoes or cowboy boots?"

"I can't be a hundred percent certain." I fiddled with a lock of hair. "But when he and Dick Phillips found me the night before, Edgar was wearing puffy, electric-blue moon boots. They were hard to miss and looked brand new."

"You've got an eye for detail, Jane." He wrote in his notebook again and stood. "If you think of anything else, call my office."

I wished there was more to tell him. A description of a pair of boots wasn't much. Rick had said I had an eye for detail. Maybe I should use that skill and the box of items from my brief foray into a criminal justice major in college to start my own investigation into who had murdered Edgar. Mom had ordered me to get rid of the carton full of contraband after she coerced me into changing my major to education. Instead, I moved it with me to Little Missouri.

I was about to haul my stuff from the closet when a voice of caution intervened.

No, no, no, Jane. Don't you dare interfere with the sheriff's investigation. You did that before and ruined the murder case against Junior. Don't do it again. You want to know how to help Rick to catch Edgar's killer? Stay out of his way.

Chapter 8

Liv arrived the next morning at seven on the dot. I took the pan she held. "Let me put this on the kitchen table." The aroma rising from it made me drool.

"Be right with you." She pulled off the black galoshes covering her scuffed cowboy boots and left them on Velma's infernal newspapers in the entryway before entering the kitchen. She pushed unruly brown bangs away from her weather-beaten face and striking dark eyes. Out of breath, she said, "I got to get overshoes that go on and off easier."

Liv and her husband Axel ranched north of town. Born and bred in Tipperary County, Liv's idea of dressing up was a corduroy blazer over a western shirt and new Levis. Today she wore a brown sweater over a western shirt and worn jeans.

I handed her a mug of coffee. "Let's dig in."

While we ate, she gave the lowdown on the school Christmas program. "It's scheduled for the evening we get out for Christmas vacation. So we've got just shy of four weeks to practice." She shuffled through the papers in front of her.

"Four weeks isn't very long."

"We can do it." She handed me a sheaf of papers. "Here are the plays we can choose from."

I paged through them, reading the titles aloud. "*The Littlest Star. The Littlest Christmas Tree. The Littlest Elf. The Littlest Angel. The Littlest Sheep. The Littlest Christmas Bell.* Do I detect a common theme?"

Liv laughed. "We usually pick the one that matches how many kids we've got between us."

We did quick nose counts of casts and kids and decided *The Littlest Christmas Tree* was the best match. Next we assigned parts and looked over the music.

I frowned. "I can plunk out the melody to teach the songs during music class, but me accompanying the students during the performance is out of the question. Who can we bribe to do that?"

"Cookie Sternquist has done it ever since Rick was in first grade."

A vision of the sheriff—young and fresh faced, clad in an elf suit, tights, and slippers with a bell on each curly toe—floated before my eyes. At least until the sound of Liv's voice pulled me into the present.

"I know it'll be awkward to have Corinne Wentworth make the costumes after that business with Junior, but she's done it for years. Would you like me to call her?"

Corinne and I had been on the way to becoming friends before her son assaulted me. She accepted my decision to press charges against him with grace and said she hoped to renew our friendship someday. I had the same hope, but thought it would happen in a few months rather than in a few weeks. Yet here we were, with a children's Christmas program forcing the issue.

Blast Junior! I'd had enough of him yanking my chain—and his mother's too.

"I'll do it." I stood and picked up our breakfast dishes. "She doesn't deserve to pay for what her sorry jerk of a son did."

Liv gathered her things. "In that case I'll hustle over to my room and correct papers until the kids arrive." She said goodbye and left.

Before I could procrastinate, I picked up the phone receiver and gave it a crank. "Betty, would you connect me with Corinne Wentworth?"

"It must be Christmas program time," Betty caroled. "Putting your caww through right away."

Corinne picked up immediately. She agreed to make the costumes without any hesitation. We were soon chatting about what kind and how many of each to make.

"I think I have enough fabric and trim to get started. Can I stop by the school tomorrow afternoon and take measurements?"

"I'll let Liz know. Can we pay for the materials?"

"No." Her reply broached no argument. She hesitated before speaking again. "There is something you can do."

"Anything to repay you for your time and trouble."

"Come over on Saturday and sew with me."

"I'd love to."

Junior's ability to yank my chain came to a swift and irrevocable end.

Car doors slammed and children shouted outside.

"The kids are here, Corinne. I've got to go. See you Wednesday." I hung up and went into my classroom.

The school day was as ordinary as dirt until the children received their parts shortly before dismissal. Cora and Elva were delighted to be elves in Santa's doll-making workshop. Beau, Stig, Bennan, and Renny accepted their roles as reindeer with aplomb. Because, as they told anyone who would listen, reindeer are the second best animal after horses. Except for Christmas Eve when reindeer are best.

Tiege couldn't hide his dismay at receiving the title role of the littlest Christmas tree. "I wanna be a reindeer with the other guys."

"Did I forget to tell you?" I improvised as I went along. "You'll wear a flashing yellow star on your head during the entire show."

I imagined Tiege wearing his flashing light. Surrounded by a couple dozen Christmas-crazed kids. Being watched by the entire adult population of Little Missouri and its surrounding area. Heaven help me, what had Liv and I done?

"Give this note about the program to your parents right away." I passed out slips of paper. "Have them jot down your clothing and shoe sizes and bring the paper back tomorrow."

After the children left, I bundled up and drove to the post office.

Dale Cunningham stood behind the wide counter. "Hello, Miss Newell." His voice was as crisp and precise as his military haircut and official uniform.

"Hi, Dale." I admired the tidy lobby with its wall of ornate post office boxes. The smell of disinfectant and floor wax wafted up from the shiny tiles beneath my boots. I inserted the key into my box and removed a handful of letters. "What's new?"

"Other than you getting stuck in a snowbank and finding that dead body, this town's been right quiet lately."

I cringed. I didn't want to be the most happening thing in town.

"Oh, there is one thing. The price of a first class stamp is going from thirteen to fifteen cents next year." He rapped his knuckles on the counter. "You heard it here first."

I turned and bumped into Dick Phillips. Or he bumped into me. I'm not sure which. He turned bright red—honestly, he acted like the guiltiest man on earth—and muttered something while he jabbed his key at the lock on his post office box.

Dale flipped up a hinged section of counter, pushed open the half-door under it, and took the key from Dick. "Let me give you a hand."

Dale opened the box. Dick withdrew its contents. He jammed everything into his parka pocket and crossed to the door. Not once did he make eye contact with either Dale or me.

"Hang on a minute." Dale hurried behind the counter and came back with a small package. "This is yours too. It's another one of those that comes from Alaska. Regular as clockwork they are."

Dick covered the return address with a gloved hand and wedged the package under his arm. He left without saying thank you to Dale. And without apologizing to me.

"Trying to have a conversation with him is like pulling teeth." Dale returned to the other side of the counter and began sorting mail.

"Only more painful." I put my mail in my purse. "Have a good weekend, Dale."

"Same to you, Miss Newell."

On my way out, something on the floor caught my attention. I knelt down. It was a piece of yarn, the same color as Dick Phillip's ski mask. Dale kept his post office in immaculate condition, so I picked it up, intending to throw away the offending bit of trash. The movement triggered a memory. Fragmented images flashed in and out of focus. Edgar's motionless body. Snow stained red. A tree branch. Bare toes.

My heart thumped wildly, and I slid my free hand into my parka pocket. My fingers found a small, fuzzy lump lodged there. In an instant, I remembered what the shock of Sunday's horrible discovery had driven from my memory until now. A tangle of yarn.

Chapter 9

I walked home in a daze, clutching the yarn from the post office floor in a cold, gloveless hand. My other hand remained in my pocket. I held tight to the tangled ball of yarn hiding there, as if I feared it might disappear again.

At home I put both pieces on the kitchen table. To the naked eye, they were identical. The semester of criminal justice classes I'd taken said they were not. An examination under the microscope I'd brought when I moved might tell a different story.

I pressed my lips together. *No. Don't screw it up any more than you already have.*

I got my tweezers from the bathroom and gave them a thorough cleaning under the tap to avoid contaminating the evidence more than I already had. With the tweezers, I transferred each bit of yarn into its own zipper bag. Then I wrote where the yarn was from on bits of masking tape and stuck the labels on their corresponding bags.

I took a deep breath to screw up my courage and picked up the phone. After Betty's greeting, I said, "Please connect me with the sheriff's office in Tipperary.

"He's not there."

"How do you know?"

"I just rang his office for someone else—don't ask me who, Jane, you know that's confidentiaw information—and no one answered."

Well, that was that. I hung up the phone and regarded the precisely labeled bags. Every minute they remained in my possession hindered Rick's investigation. He didn't have a complete picture of the case without the samples, and the chance of Edgar's killer escaping increased. The first piece of yarn might be useless after spending a week in my pocket. The yarn from the post office would mean nothing to the sheriff, no matter how fast it was handed over, but it might lead to a new line of questioning.

One thing I knew for sure—Velma would throw both bags in the burn barrel if she spotted them. I took them to my bedroom and buried them in my undies drawer. Not too many weeks ago, I'd almost hidden the silver butterfly buckle Junior Wentworth had taken from Beau's mom in the same spot. Thank goodness I'd opted for a locked drawer in my classroom file cabinet. It turned out Wentworth had a penchant for pawing through women's panty drawers. Velma could be nosey, but I doubted she had that particular proclivity. The bags would be safe where they were until I could get them to Rick. After that, I made a hot turkey sandwich with the last of Mom's Thanksgiving leftovers and ate it at my desk while I corrected papers and recorded grades.

Wednesday I gathered notes from my students and

handed them to Corinne when she arrived in the afternoon. One by one, the children went to the back of the room where Corinne took and recorded their measurements. Then she went to Liv's room and did the same thing all over again.

Practice began in earnest on Thursday. I worked with Liv's students on their songs during music class while Liv had gym class with my kids. Friday I introduced the same songs to my students. When they put on their coats and boots at the end of the day, they were belting out *Silent Night*.

Their singing was as raucous as Merle's old rooster. Nonetheless, my hopes for a Christmas program worthy of the season rose. So did a foul stench.

"The boys are passing gas." Elva pinched her nose. "Tiege says it's to make electricity for the blinking star on his costume."

I teacher-stared each boy in turn. "Hold your fire, fellas. Don't you ever let loose at school again unless you want to write notes to your parents about it at recess. Is that clear?"

They gulped and nodded.

"Good. Now, everybody out. I'll see you on Monday."

My hopes for a respectable program fell as they trooped across the snowy playground. So did my definition of respectable. With the star of the show entering the gas market, all I wanted for Christmas was a fart-free performance. And the arrest of Edgar's murderer.

Really, I asked the true star of the Christmas season, *is that too much to hope for?*

Once the playground was clear of children, I went to my apartment and exchanged my wool sweater, trousers, and nylons for comfy sweats. Plastic crinkled as I pulled a pair of warm socks from my undies drawers. Oh my stars! I'd been so wrapped up in the Christmas program for the past few days, I'd forgotten to call Rick about the yarn.

I finished changing clothes, went to the phone, and asked Betty to ring the sheriff's office. This time Rick was in. Better yet, he picked up on the first ring.

"Rick, I have something you should see." My words tumbled out, trying to make up for the delay in turning over the evidence to him. "I've had it since—"

A click stopped me mid-sentence. Someone was listening in on the party line. Not good. "It would be better to talk to you in person," I said. "Can we set something up?"

"Unless it's urgent, not until next week." He sounded tired.

"It's not really urgent, but it is important. Very important."

"Okay. I'll call or stop by on Monday." He hung up.

Once again, the only comfort in our brief conversation was the assurance that I'd done what I could. Now, on to the weekend. I kicked off the Friday night festivities. First, I recorded grades and compiled my students' work packets for the following week.

Drudgery.

Next up was polishing off Mary Borgeson's lasagna.

Delicious.

The finale was anticipating a day of sewing with Corinne.

Delightful.

No doubt about it, I'm a woman who knows how to party.

Chapter 10

In the morning Merle's rooster made sure I welcomed the dawn. In December that's much later than it sounds, so I didn't threaten to slit the rooster's neck while getting ready to go to Corinne's. After breakfast I buckled my sewing machine into its carrying case and took it outside.

Sunlight bounced off the white snow, making my eyes squint and water. The insides of my nostrils stuck together. How cold was it?

The Beetle growled as it cranked over. I ignored its protestations and chugged out of town to the east a mile or two before turning down the lane to the Wentworth ranch.

Once there, I parked in the driveway of the tan brick ranch-style house where Corinne and her husband Richard lived. I carried my sewing things onto the front stoop and rang the doorbell—one of those bong, bong, bong pretentious affairs. I hoped Richard wasn't home. I almost said a little prayer, but decided against it. No

need to overload the system. A fartless Christmas program and the arrest of a murderer took precedence over
a day without Richard the First. That was my pet name
for Junior's dad.

Corinne opened the door. She was a little over five
feet tall and wore an elegant, beautifully pressed wool
jacket and matching trousers. I guessed she had made
them herself. Her brown eyes were wells of sadness and
peace, her short white hair a series of tight curls.

"Come in, Jane!" She picked up the sewing machine
case. "Let me take that."

I entered and sat on the bench in the foyer to remove
my boots.

"My goodness, it's cold. Let's get some hot chocolate
before we start."

I rubbed my hands together. "Only a fool would say
no to that."

She led the way into her perfectly appointed kitchen.
Its turquoise appliances and light peach walls had been
the height of fashion when I was in kindergarten. I sat
down at the built-in booth beside a cheery bay window.

Corinne took a pitcher from the refrigerator and
filled two mugs. She put them into her Amana Rada-
range, pushed buttons, and stepped aside. "The salesman
said the microwaves can't escape, but I'd rather be safe
than sorry."

In less than a minute we were sipping from mugs
of steaming hot chocolate while we went through the
costume list and decided how to proceed. Only then did
we move into her sewing room, which rivaled the state-of-
the-art home economics wing of my high school. Not that
I'd frequented the school's sewing room. When Mom saw

I'd added a home economics class to my sophomore year schedule, her response was swift and absolute.

"You tell the guidance counselor that you are to take college prep classes and nothing else." She waved the course schedule in my face. "You're going to college and that's that. I can teach you everything you need to know about cooking and sewing."

A few years earlier my older sister Jeanette had waged a similar campaign to take a high school art class. I watched Mom squash that idea and decided not to put up a fight. Instead I daydreamed about imaginary weekends creating trend-setting wardrobes in a perfect, make-believe sewing room.

My dreams were coming true today. Granted, we were creating ten green felt Christmas trees, eight sets of brown felt reindeer antlers, five elf suits in red and green lamé, and matching Mr. and Mrs. Santa costumes for Mr. and Mrs. Santa instead of a high schooler's imaginary wardrobe. But we were making them in Corinne's sewing room with its cutting table, cubbies and cabinets filled with fabric and notions, and natural light streaming through huge windows.

I whistled the melody of *Here Comes Santa Claus* and spread green felt for the Christmas trees on my side of the cutting table. Corinne smoothed out red velveteen for the Mr. and Mrs. Santa suits on hers. We arranged pattern pieces and pinned them in place.

I picked up my shears and began cutting. "I'm going to the town Christmas party at the dance hall tonight, but I'm not sure what to bring."

Corinne tilted her head. "Why bring anything?"

"It's a potluck."

"No, it's a complete Christmas dinner. The volunteer fire department cooks everything. All you have to do is bring a donation and an appetite."

"Are you coming?"

"I should . . ." She lowered her gaze and concentrated on cutting out Mrs. Santa's skirt. "I know what they're thinking. They have every right to be disgusted with Junior. But I can't bear to see it in their eyes."

The wall phone beside the door began to ring. Corinne went across the room and picked up the receiver. She listened for a second and held it out. "It's for you, Jane."

"Who would call me here?"

"Your mother."

I stabbed my pins into the pin cushion and went to the phone.

Corinne handed it over and whispered, "I'll go to the kitchen and fix us a snack while you talk."

I nodded and she left. "Why did you call me here, Mom?"

"When you didn't answer your phone, Betty said she thought you were sewing with Corinne Wentworth." She lowered her voice. "Isn't she Junior's mother?"

"She is."

"What possessed you to spend your Saturday sewing with the woman who raised that terrible young man? Stay as far away from her as you can."

"It's hard to avoid someone in a town with only ninety-two people. Corinne is a lovely person, and she's been sewing costumes for the Christmas program for years. I couldn't very well say no when she asked me to help make them, could I? You raised me better than that."

"When you put it that way, you were right to say yes. But after this, you tell somebody before you make your merry way into that house."

"I think Betty's got things covered."

"Thank goodness for that."

"Why did you call, Mom?"

"Oh, yes. Your father and I were watching the news last night, and there was a report about a murder in Tipperary County. I couldn't believe my ears. Neither could your father. They mentioned the Custer National Forest and the Long Pines. Isn't that where we went hiking last summer with your windbag of a neighbor? What's his name?"

"Merle Laird."

"That's the one. I wish you'd quit hanging around him. Those old coots will scare off every nice young man in a three state area."

"So you called to talk about Merle?"

"Will you pay attention, Jane? I called to ask if you're involved in this murder investigation."

"Mom, do you really think the sheriff is going to ask for my help? Even if he did, which he won't, I would say no. Because Liv and I have to pull a Christmas program together in three weeks." I wasn't lying to her. I simply chose not to tell her about the evidence in my underwear drawer. My intent was to get the yarn samples out of my hands and into the sheriff's at the first opportunity. Which would have been yesterday, if it were up to me.

"I'm glad to hear it. You concentrate on the job that earns your salary and leave the rest to the professionals. You don't want to get a reputation for stumbling onto dead bodies or some such thing."

Too late for that.

"Do you want to talk to your dad? He's taking a nap, but I can wake him up."

"No, don't. Corinne and I have a lot to do." I hung up.

Corinne brought in a plate of fruit. We snacked on it as we cut out the remaining costumes. We took a short break for lunch and then continued sewing.

Around four o'clock Corinne stood and rubbed her neck. "We should stop soon so you can get ready for the Christmas party."

A pile of unfinished costumes loomed between us. "We're not even close to being done. I don't want to leave you in a lurch."

"Piffle. Richard's in the Black Hills for the weekend. I can sew as long as I want. I'll bring everything to school Tuesday afternoon for fittings."

Corinne carried my sewing machine to the Beetle and stowed it in the back seat. Then she handed me an envelope. "Would you drop this in the donation basket tonight?"

"Of course. See you Tuesday?"

"With the costumes in tow."

I glanced in the rearview mirror as I drove down the lane. Corinne was waving, small and slight, cold and alone. Her solitary frame saddened my heart, and tears pricked behind my eyes as she shrank in the distance.

Chapter 11

The dance hall, which also served as an indoor basketball court, was crowded and noisy when I arrived. A Christmas tree, strung with frantically blinking lights, stood on a raised platform at one end of the room. People hung their winter coats on the backs of chairs arranged around the round tables that dotted the dance floor. Sound bounced off the bare floors and windows and walls. The clompy snow boots worn by almost everyone added to the din.

I searched the crowd in hopes of spotting Rick and persuading him to stop by my apartment to collect the evidence after dinner. He wasn't there, but the rest of the town was. Liv and Axel McDonald were standing at the free throw line with Brock, Rosalie, and Keeva, their three children. Axel's parents, Frost and Fannie, who owned Little Missouri's gas station, were with them. Frost waved me over. I waved back and elbowed my way toward them. The Bertholds from Round the Bend and the Kellys from the grocery store greeted me on the way.

"Hey, look!" Tiege Sternquist's clear, high voice cut through the low murmur of adult conversation. "Miss Newell is here!"

He led a stampede of students over to greet me. Next the boys blazed a trail onto the raised platform. Elva Borgeson and Cora Barkley pulled me up the stairs and stopped in front of the Christmas tree.

Beau Kelly squatted beside the pile of gifts beneath the tree. "These isn't all the presents."

"Santa Claus brings his bag after supper every year. It's this big." Stig Borgeson spread his arms as wide and round as he could. "Full of presents for all us kids."

"The Little Missouri Santa gives good presents. But he isn't the real Santa." Cora squeezed my hand. "The real one comes on Christmas Eve."

Mary Borgeson came over. "It's almost time to eat, kids. Go find your parents." The children stampeded away, and Mary pointed at two men filling cups from big coffee urns. "There's someone you know."

The man nearest to us stood out in his brown leather jacket, a white button down shirt open at the neck, and blue jeans. His curly hair was the same shade as his jacket. Not a cowboy, but I couldn't place him.

Behind the stranger was Dick Phillips. He was filling cups and setting them in neat rows. He looked up. I smiled. The guy in the leather jacket said something to Dick and gave his arm a friendly punch. A blaze of red crept up Dick's neck. His expression went blank, and he stared at the floor.

A dinner bell sounded. Glen Berthold, wearing a fire hat trimmed with tinsel and mistletoe, raised his voice to be heard above the crowd. "It's almost time to dig in. Soon as you all find your seats, Father Dan will say grace." He moved a wad of chewing tobacco from one cheek to the other as he and the priest climbed onto the raised platform.

Liv motioned me over to her table and pointed to an empty seat between Brock and Keeva. The dinner bell sounded again as I slipped into my seat.

The room quieted and the priest asked us to bow our heads. "Bless us, oh Lord, and these thy gifts, which we are about to receive from thy bounty. Through Christ, our Lord. Amen."

Glen sent the first table to the serving line before the priest finished making the sign of the cross. A few minutes later Glen approached our table. "Go on up."

We joined the line. I put my donation and Corinne's into the basket. Cookie Sternquist's husband Bud, father to Tiege and the sheriff, thrust a heaping plate of turkey, green bean casserole, and mashed potatoes and gravy at me. I returned to our table and pulled out my chair when someone jostled my arm. My plate tipped. Brock's hand shot out and steadied it.

"Pardon me, ma'am, pardon me." I turned around and found myself nose-to-nose with a short, round-faced man. His grin consisted of more gaps than teeth. As he spoke, spittle flew from the spaces between them. "I is just the clumsiest old fool. Hank York, ma'am." His head bobbed up and down as he introduced himself. "Pleased to meet you, I am. And you is the new school teacher, isn't you? I know ever'thing that goes on in our town, I do. Nothing slips by Hank York, no siree."

Beside Hank, a woman nodded vigorously. Her graying hair escaped its pins and fell in wisps around her face. Her dark eyes and high cheekbones hinted at Native American ancestry. Her hairstyle was decades out of date, her clothes were clean, neatly patched, and hinted at both poverty and pride.

"Pleased to meet you, Hank." I smiled at the woman standing behind him. "And this is?"

"My wife Ruby. We been hitched since after the war. Yes, we have. We sure have."

"Nice to meet you, Ruby. I'm going to get something to drink. Can I bring anything for either of you?"

The light left Hank's eyes. "No siree, Mrs. Teacher. Nobody waits on me and Ruby. I'm a worker, I am. I got me a deal with the city to clean up the dump. Ask anybody."

He walked away with Ruby trailing him. I stared at them as they went. Not because of their threadbare clothes. Not because their plates were piled so high I feared their food would fall off. Hank York was wearing a pair of electric-blue moon boots.

In a daze, I walked over to where Dick Phillips was filling a cup from a large urn labeled "hot chocolate." I picked up my cup as he turned around with the one he'd just filled. His knocked into mine and the contents of both splashed on my plaid wool shirt.

"Watch what you're doing," he snapped and turned away.

The man in the leather jacket gave me a dish towel. "Blot up what you can with this and soak the shirt in a pan of warm, soapy water when you get home." He carried a fresh cup of cocoa to my table and pulled out my chair while I worked on the stain. Dan Barkley walked by and raised his eyebrows.

That's where I'd seen this guy!

I snapped my fingers. "You're the Incredible Hulk!"

He set my cocoa on the table. "Pardon me?"

"I mean, I know you're not the Hulk. But you had on a big, puffy coat at the Long Pines Sunday. You were with Daniel Boone—"

"Daniel Boone?"

"Not really Daniel Boone. You just reminded me of the Hulk and Daniel Boone." I was babbling like Hank York. "I had a lot on my mind."

The Hulk raised an eyebrow.

You might as well go for broke.

"I'm Wonder Woman." I gestured at my long sleeved shirt and wool pants. "It's too cold for my normal uniform."

"I'm Vince Douglas. When you're not Wonder Woman, what name do you go by?"

"Jane Newell." His grip was firm when we shook hands. "There's an empty place at our table. Would you like to join us?"

"I'm supposed to be pouring hot chocolate, or I would. I apologize on Dick's behalf. Something's been eating him since Sunday."

He returned to his job and I paid full attention to my food. The turkey was moist, the gravy flavorful, the mashed potatoes fluffy, the rolls freshly baked, and the green bean casserole the perfect mixture of creamy and crisp. Everyone at our table ate with zeal.

Keeva was the first to set down her fork. "Want to go with me to pick out our pie, Teacher?"

I wiped my face with a napkin. "You know it."

We chose our favorites. Pumpkin for her. Cherry for me.

I was savoring mine, as delicious as Mom's—and that's saying something—when the dance hall door burst open with a jingling of bells. The young kids squealed with excitement. The older ones leaned back and tried to look nonchalant.

"Ho, ho, ho! Merry Christmas!" Santa and his skinny elf wove amongst the tables and climbed the steps to the platform. Santa wore a luxurious red suit with shiny black boots and belt. He carried a bag as big as what Stig had described. Santa's helper sported a red felt hat and green felt suit resplendent with sequins and red tights as well as glittery green felt shoes. Bells jingled on the tip of each slipper's curly, pointed toe. I took in the elf's wiry build and defensive stance.

Velma Albright. In sequins and glitter. Santa handed presents to Glen Berthold. He called out names and handed the gifts to their young recipients. Once Santa's bag was empty, he boomed a final, whistley, "Ho, ho, ho" and hitched his way to the door.

Merle Laird.

When Santa opened the door, Velma jumped high in the air and clicked the heels of her elf slippers together. Then she scampered into the cold, dark night leaving a sparkly trail of pixie dust in her wake.

I got up and circled the table to where Liv sat. "The next time Velma gives her glitter ultimatum, let's launch this big gun."

Liv responded with a high five backed by years of calf-wrangling, ranch woman muscle.

Ouch.

Chapter 12

Sunshine greeted me when I crawled out of bed on Sunday morning. I went into the living room and shaded my eyes. When they adjusted to the light pouring through the east windows, I drank in the brilliant, cloudless sky.

A day this beautiful begged to be enjoyed. There was just enough time to dress, coerce my tangle of curls into a presentable mess, and walk to church. I zipped my coat, slung my purse on my arm, and walked outside as the phone rang. Whoever it was could call again later. I let the door shut behind me and filled my lungs with crisp, cold air. The skin in my nostrils glued itself together, my cheeks went numb, and my lungs felt like lumps of freeze-dried flesh. I retreated into my apartment and banged the door shut. Forget church.

The phone rang again and I picked up.

"Jane, I'm gwad I caught you. Pastor Petersen asked me to spread the word that church is cancewed. His car battery is dead."

"How cold is it, Betty?"

"Thirty bewow by our thermometer."

No wonder Tipperary County was so sparsely populated. Anyone with a lick of sense would refuse to live here. If the school principal had told me how low temperatures dipped here, I would have refused the job and stayed in Sioux City.

Then again, thirty below in a town far from Mom's watchful eye wasn't so bad.

"This is a good day to heat up Iva's scawoped potatoes and ham. She and Burt raised that hog and smoked the ham. It's dewicious."

I thanked Betty for the suggestion and hung up with a shiver. Thirty below under Betty's watchful eye was mighty cold.

I put the casserole in the oven and wrote lesson plans, prepared seat work, and ran off worksheets until the food was ready to eat around noon. It was as delicious as Betty had said, comfort food so powerful that eating it was like mainlining Christmas.

I consulted the wall calendar to count how many days were left to make presents for my students and family. Edgar Running Horse was seven days gone today. Despite my good intentions, the yarn from the crime scene was not yet in Rick's possession.

Tomorrow. He promised to get together with you tomorrow. There's nothing you can do until then.

It was time to ditch frustration and dive into Christmas. I stacked all my Christmas albums onto the record player and set up my sewing machine in the living room. Christmas music accompanied me as I cut out and sewed book bags for my students' Christmas presents.

When I was hungry, I made an egg sandwich. When I was thirsty, I brewed tea. When my eyes grew heavy, I checked the clock and discovered it was time to put this bitterly cold day to bed.

The weather was harder to ignore on Monday. The temperatures meant inside recess. Jumping jacks and running in place weren't enough to dispel the cooped-up energy of seven students. At dismissal time they shot out the door like an Apollo rocket. When Corinne brought the costumes on Tuesday, the kids were so antsy they abandoned their social studies assignments like last year's Christmas toys. It took a great deal of coaxing—though threatening may be a more accurate term—to focus their attention on their lessons again.

Corinne took the children one by one to try on their costumes in the back of the classroom, starting with Tiege. He frowned at his plain green tree. "Where are the lights and the blinking star?"

"I won't add those until this part's done." She slipped it over his head and made a few marks with tailor's chalk.

Elva and Cora were enchanted with the strips of silver sequins on their elf suits. Cora jumped up and down in front of the mirror. "Elva, look at what the sequins do!"

"It's like they're taking a hundred pictures all at once!" Elva squealed as sequins sloughed onto the floor.

"Come here, girls, before they all fall off." Corinne pinned the sequin strips in place. "I'll sew these down when I get home."

Next she showed the four boys how to step into their reindeer costumes and secure the Velcro fasteners on their hooves.

Renny pawed at the little pile of sequins on the floor. "Look at the silver snow!"

Bennan galloped over and sent sequins flying in all directions. "We're snowplows!"

"Whoa, there, reindeer." Corinne blocked Beau and Stig on their way to join the fun. "Would you make a straight line so I can be sure your fur fits?" Once they were done, she waited while I dismissed the children. Then, I joined her to survey the reindeer damage.

Before the town Christmas party, a single sequin on the floor would have put the fear of Velma in my heart. I would have run for the Hoover and vacuumed with the zeal of a fanatic. But after Velma's exhibition during the town party, I ignored the sequins and made coffee. I handed Corinne and Liv steaming cups as we sat down to talk about the Christmas program.

We were finishing up when Velma arrived. One look at the sequins and her face turned mean as the reindeer who wouldn't let Rudolph join their games.

"All three of you know I do not allow falderal like this in the school. What you got to say about yourselves?"

Liv stood. "Just this." She jumped and clicked her heels together in midair, then sat down with a smirk.

"Hmph." Velma clamped her mouth shut. Even so, its corners twitched as she marched to the closet and grabbed her cleaning caddy. It was as close to a good mood as she was going to get under the circumstances.

"I met Hank and Ruby York Saturday night." I said.

Liv picked up her coffee cup. "That was the first time you saw them?"

I nodded. "Does he really have a deal with the city to clean up the dump?"

Velma attacked the bookshelves with a dust rag. "That's what the town council tells him. He's too proud to take handouts, but not too proud to pick through garbage. Betty calls around when he's on his way to the dump with his wheelbarrow so people can drive out ahead of him to leave clothes and what not."

I rubbed the side of my cup with a thumb. "Where do they live?"

She sniffed. "You know the lot across the alley west of the Methodist Church? The one with wooden fence around a dirt patch and the tarpaper shack?"

"Isn't that an old outhouse?"

Velma sprayed cleaner on the top of Bennan's desk. "No, that's where they live. They got a wood stove, a propane refrigerator, no electricity, and about twenty cats."

"I haven't seen them for months." Corinne drained her coffee and stood. "How are they doing?"

Liv crossed her legs. "About the same. They both had a week's worth of food piled on their plates at the party."

Corinne packed her tailor's chalk and pin cushion in her sewing case. "Hank worked for us almost twenty years after he came home from the Second World War. He and Ruby lived in the old homesteading soddie Richard's grandparents put up. We offered to build them a little place, but they said the soddie with a garden was all they needed."

"Why did they leave?"

Corinne sighed. "Every month or so, Hank would pick through junk at the dump, like Velma said. I thought it was quaint, but the more successful the ranch became, the less Richard liked it." She buckled the sewing case shut. "He asked Hank over and over to stop his scavenging. Finally, Richard threatened to fire him if he did it again."

"I don't know why he said that." Corinne shook her head. "Hank exploded, swearing and swinging his fists. Richard and Junior had to hold him down until the sheriff arrived and put him in jail for a week, mainly to keep Ruby safe until he calmed down. We found a lot for them here in town. They don't know we had any part in that, and Hank doesn't have anything to do with us. He's a man of great pride and violent temper."

"Do they get enough to eat?" I looked from Corinne to Liv to Velma.

Velma put the caddy away and took out the vacuum. "Merle and a bunch of us pay Hank in food for doing odd jobs." She plugged in the vacuum cleaner. "That's enough about that. Pardon me, ladies, but I got work to do even if you don't." She turned on the Hoover.

After Corinne, Liv, and I mouthed our goodbyes, I went into my kitchen and stared at the wall calendar. I'd waited an extra day for Rick to stop by or call, and he had yet to do either. Edgar's murder was now almost a week and a half old. I went into the guest bedroom closet and stared up at the box on the top shelf.

I'd originally stored the box behind some art supplies in one of the cupboards in my classroom. Then Tiege discovered it during an indoor recess.

"What's in here, Miss Newell?"

I raised my head as he undid the flaps. "Leave it alone," I ordered in a tone the children had never heard from me before.

Tiege snatched his hands away as if they'd been burned. The eyes of my other students widened, and the room went silent. I walked over, picked up the box, and set it on my desk.

"I'm sorry." Tiege's lip quivered.

I went back and sat on the floor beside him. "Did I scare you?"

He nodded without meeting my eye.

"I'm sorry for snapping at you. It's just that it contains some things I want to stay in good condition. I should have put it somewhere else."

After school that day, I moved the box to the top shelf of the guest bedroom closet. Now I dragged a kitchen chair and climbed onto it. As I reached for the box, the chair tipped forward. My forehead smacked against the shelf, and a sharp pain brought me to my senses.

I steadied the chair, climbed down, and ran to the bathroom to assess the damage. The mirror revealed a goose egg at my hairline, small enough for my bangs to hide.

That's what you get for thinking about messing with evidence, Jane. Why don't you think of something that won't compromise Rick's investigation?

I was icing the goose egg when the "something" came to me. I could create my own suspect list. I took a yellow legal pad from my bedroom closet, flipped to a new page, and drew a line down the middle. In block letters, I labeled the first column "suspects" and the second "reasons." In rapid succession, I listed Hank York and Dick Phillips as suspects. After Hank's name, I wrote "boots" and "violent behavior." For Dick, all I could muster were "yarn matches his ski mask (maybe)," "he blushes," and "antisocial."

Doggone it! Rick would laugh me out of his office if

he saw what I'd written about Dick—and rightly so. Furthermore, what I'd written about Hank would make him the focus of the investigation. The evidence was stacked against him. I refused to believe that a man so proud he preferred digging in the dump to accepting charity would commit murder to steal a pair of boots. The best thing I could do for Hank was to deflect Rick's attention by producing a more viable suspect. I didn't know how I was going to do it, but ignorance hadn't stopped me before. It wasn't going to stop me now.

Chapter 13

The phone rang, and I almost hit the ceiling. My heart raced as I ran to the bedroom and put the legal pad in my underwear drawer. Until I was certain Velma had left the building, I wasn't taking any chances of her seeing what I knew about Hank. When I picked up the receiver, a wet, schleppy inhale tickled my ear.

"Hello, Merle."

"How'd you know it was me?"

"Call me clairvoyant."

"I'll stick with Teacher if you don't mind. You hungry?"

I was, but Iva's leftover scalloped potatoes and ham, a cut above Merle's bachelor cooking, was calling my name.

"I ate an early supper and I'm stuffed," I fibbed. That might make me a terrible person, but I'd declined Merle's supper invitations before with complete honesty and witnessed his disappointment. Lying was the kinder option.

"Might you be hungry tomorrow evening? I got something for you."

We'd engaged in supper battles before. He was not one to accept defeat. Quick surrender seemed the wiser option. "What time should I come over?"

"Five-thirty. And Teacher?"

"Yes, Merle?"

"Don't wear your chore sweatshirt. It's so ugly it scared the chickens last time you was here."

The gall of the man! First, coercion and then fashion advice. I banged the receiver into the cradle without saying goodbye.

Other than the deliciousness of Iva's cooking, the remainder of the afternoon and evening was ordinary in every way. So was the next morning, though the temperature had moderated in the night. That meant the children could go outside for recess. Hooray! I dressed in brown wool trousers, a rust-colored turtleneck, and forest green blazer. If I didn't spill my soup at lunch and none of my students threw up or squirted glue on me—teaching is a dangerous business—I'd wear it to Merle's too.

My clothes made it through the day unscathed. By the time I was done correcting papers and readying the classroom for tomorrow, it was almost five-thirty. I bundled up, walked to Merle's house, and banged on the door.

"You don't gotta knock. Just git in here." Merle hollered.

The odors of fresh milk and manure greeted me when I stepped into his mudroom. The smell transported me to a different state and different time. I was eight years

old, standing in my Minnesota aunt and uncle's mudroom.

*They greeted me and went outside to talk to my parents.
Getting Dad and his wheelchair into their house was too
much work. My cousin Karin rushed into the mudroom
holding a ball of twine. "Come on! Let's make string
houses."*

*We ran to the grove, giddy with excitement. We
spent the afternoon building the play house, stringing
twine and our little girl dreams from one tree trunk to
another.*

My thoughts jumped from string to twine. From
twine to yarn. From yarn to ski masks. From ski masks
to Dick Phillips. Blast it! He had no right to invade my
daydreams.

Merle came to the doorway between the mudroom
and his grimy, cramped kitchen. "I got someone for you
to meet." He turned to the man sitting at the table. "I call
him Reek Dupee, but that ain't right."

I recognized him. "You're Daniel Boone."

"No." Merle shook a wooden spoon, dripping waffle
batter onto the counter and his overalls. "That ain't right
either."

Reek, or whatever his name was, bore a striking
resemblance to the actor who played Boone on the old
television show. Our family watched it religiously on
Sunday nights during my childhood. Even more so up
close than when I'd seen him from a distance in the
Long Pines. He had the same dark eyes and dark hair, at
least what was visible under his coonskin cap.

That's right. A coonskin cap.

Daniel stood and doffed his cap in a perfect imitation of my Sunday night hero. "You're not the first person to make that observation. My name is Rikard DuPeuss, but I go by Rique. R-I-Q-U-E"

"Rique DuPeuss." I said it Reekay Doopwee like he did. "Is it French?"

"French Canadian." He shrugged as if the difference was inconsequential. "And you are Jane Newell, correct?"

"That's me." I snuck a look at Merle. His expression, equal parts eagerness and embarrassment, explained everything. The old coot was playing at being a yenta. And Daniel—or Rique—was the big surprise he'd alluded to on the phone.

"Reek done you a big favor this afternoon. You and him can take what he brung to your apartment while I finish up these non-skid pancakes and bacon."

Rique put on an army parka, not buckskin. That was more of a disappointment than I wanted to admit. We walked to the garden fence where two Christmas trees were propped.

The sharp smell of pine tickled my nose. "These are for me?"

"One for your apartment and one for your classroom. Merle and me cut them for you in the Long Pines today. I thought we should ask you to come with us to pick them out, but he swore up and down he knew which ones you wanted."

I forgave my neighbor for playing matchmaker. He had known that the shock of Edgar's death hadn't diminished my need—and my students'—for Christmas traditions this year. Rique and I dragged the trees to their respective rooms where we put them into their tree stands and watered them. Then we traipsed to Merle's kitchen where supper was waiting.

After we'd eaten our way through Merle's non-skid pancakes, known to the rest of the English-speaking population of North America as waffles, I asked Rique how long he'd been in Little Missouri.

"Two weeks."

"What brought you here?"

"I'm state trapper for several West River counties. Tipperary County is one of them."

"What does a state trapper do?"

"Ranchers call on me when predators attack their livestock. My job is to supervise trapping operations on their private land and monitor it on government land."

"You mean the Long Pines?"

"And other national forest reserves in the region, too. I also oversee annual wildlife counts and the stocking of ponds and public lakes. What I enjoy most"—his face came alive—"is holding trapping and fishing classes for kids."

"You must have to travel a lot."

Merle broke in. "Reek come up with quite the solution for that. He's got one of them campers on his pickup truck. When he gets to wherever he's goin', he stays put until it's time to move on."

"Where are you staying now?"

"About a block over that way." He pointed to the southwest.

"How long will you be there?"

Merle started to clear the table. "Him and me pulled the camper off his truck and propped it on cee-ment blocks a couple weeks ago. He's hunkered down for the winter. I been fixin' to make introductions ever since on account of you being both being single and all."

Smooth, Merle. So smooth. My face went hot. I jumped up without looking at Dan—I mean Rique. As I washed the dishes, I realized Rique's camper couldn't have running water. How did he wash his hands after using the bathroom? And what did he use for a bathroom? I stacked dishes on the drainboard and made up an excuse about having schoolwork to finish. It was my second fib to Merle in two days, but I had no interest in being set up with a man who not only looked like Daniel Boone, but also lived like him.

Merle's door swung shut behind me and icy air slapped my cheeks. I shivered. Not from the cold, but from the memory of the first time I'd seen Rique. He'd been slipping into the forest after the discovery of Edgar's body like he was trying to hide. I shivered again.

CHAPTER 14

I was extra vigilant, or compulsive, depending on your point of view, about checking the apartment and classroom locks that night. I was miffed at Merle because he'd provided Rique with an excuse to enter my apartment and angry with myself for allowing him to come in. The more I replayed the incident, the more it and the man at the center of it gave off a bad vibe I couldn't shake.

I was equally miffed with the sheriff who still hadn't called or shown his face. I was done waiting. During my morning recess break, Betty connected me to the sheriff's office. While the phone rang, I rehearsed the diatribe I intended to let loose the minute he picked up. Only he didn't pick up. His mother did.

"Tipperary County Sheriff's Office," she said.

The diatribe shrank down to a single word. "Cookie?"

"Jane?"

"Is Rick in a meeting?"

"In a manner of speaking, yes."

"Is it possible to interrupt him? We've been trying to

get together for almost a week. It's really important I talk to him very soon."

"I'm sorry, dear. He's on his way to Pierre for meetings he lined up with the higher-ups at the state crime lab. He's got one after another for the next few days. He won't be back until late Friday."

The knuckles on the hand holding the receiver turned white. I wanted to scream. Bang my head on the wall. Stamp my feet like a three-year-old. Instead I spoke as clearly and quietly as my gritted teeth allowed.

"If he calls, would you tell him I need to talk to him in person without any further delay?" Then I hung up without another word for fear of launching into my dandy diatribe. Cookie didn't deserve that.

Despite my disappointment, the next few days passed quickly. The students memorized the songs for the Christmas program. Other than that, nothing noteworthy happened at school for the rest of the week. Until Friday after school when I succumbed to temptation and removed the yarn samples from my underwear drawer. I laid them and a lamp from the living room on the kitchen table. After retrieving a magnifying glass and drawing pad from the box in the guest bedroom, I switched on the lamp and sketched what I saw. Then I compared the two drawings. Both contained twig and pine needle debris. The one from the post office also had fragments of what looked like straw and seed heads.

My stomach growled and I checked my watch. It was well past the supper hour. I went to the kitchen, put Trudy Berthold's hot dish in the oven, and set the timer. Then I got my legal pad from the closet. I stared at the paper a long time before adding Rique DuPeuss' name to the suspect column. In the second column, I added "familiar with the Long Pines" and "avoided questioning" as reasons. Not much to go on, but they stacked up better than two of the three notes next to Dick's name.

My stomach growled again, so I put the legal pad away and ate supper. The hot dish was delicious, and I made a mental note to ask Trudy for the recipe. Then I started a load of laundry, washed my dishes, vacuumed, and went to bed.

After breakfast the next morning, I carried my sewing machine to the Beetle and drove to the Wentworths'. The temperature was a balmy thirty-five degrees. Icicles were forming along the edge of the roof of Corinne's house like a row of jagged, dripping teeth.

She opened the door before I reached the front stoop. "Come in, Jane. This break in the weather is a real treat, isn't it?"

"Yes, it is."

She hung my coat in the foyer closet. We went straight to the sewing room and got to work. Corinne had completed the alterations, facings, and seams. I added Velcro fasteners while she added decorative bits. Then we moved on to hats for Mr. and Mrs. Santa and the elves, which went together easily. The reindeer antlers and Tiege's blinking star slowed us down.

Corinne added a reindeer headpiece to the pile of completed ones and stretched. "Let's break for lunch."

We went to the kitchen and talked about sewing, Iowa, and ranching while we ate. What we didn't talk about was Junior. In her case because she was a kind woman who knew better than bring up her son in my presence. In my case because my mother always said that if I didn't have anything good to say, I shouldn't say anything at all. I was finishing the last bite of the cheese and spinach quiche—pure heaven—when the sound of an airplane buzzed overhead.

Corinne rose and went to the window. "Someone's landing on the airstrip."

"You have an airstrip?" I joined her at the window.

"Nothing fancy. Just a long strip of gravel with a wind sock on one end and a hangar on the other. Richard has a pilot's license and flies all over the state, weather permitting. We keep it plowed all winter in case there's a medical emergency."

A small plane landed west of the ranch and taxied to a stop in front of the hangar about a quarter mile away. The pilot jumped down, opened the hangar door, and maneuvered the plane inside. Then he got into a pickup truck parked beside the hangar and drove along the lane that connected the airstrip to the ranch house driveway. He cut the engine, got out, and walked toward the house.

It was Vince Douglas. Corinne went to meet him. I followed close behind her and peered over her shoulder. She opened the door and took a step back. Which is why she bumped into me. Which caused me lose my balance. Which I regained in time for Vince and me to catch Corinne as she lost hers. Which is why the three of us ended up in a Vince, Corinne, and Jane sandwich.

Vince wiggled his eyebrows, Groucho Marx style, above his aviator sunglasses. "We've got to stop meeting like this."

The only thing missing was the cigar.

Corinne and I began to giggle. Hard. My limbs turned to jelly. I clung to her and Vince to keep from collapsing in a heap. "Are you okay?" I asked her after regaining my composure.

"I'm fine." She took a hankie from her pocket and dabbed her eyes. "Though I have neglected my manners. Vince Douglas, this is Jane Newell. She's the new teacher in Little Missouri."

Vince took off his sunglasses. "We met at the community Christmas party last Saturday."

"Oh, good. Richard said you were going to the Hills with him Monday and leaving your truck at the hangar. I didn't realize you were flying back today."

"Your husband said it was okay to store my plane in the hangar this winter. Is he around?"

"No. He's still in Rapid City with"—she hesitated and looked away—"our son."

"No problem." Vince acted as if her discomfort wasn't noticeable. "When you talk to him, let him know my plane is here and that I appreciate the hangar space."

Corinne nodded.

"Then I'll say goodbye to you and Wonder Woman and get going." He gave Corinne a slight bow and went out the door.

Corinne shut it behind him. "Wonder Woman?" she asked on the way to the kitchen.

I took our lunch dishes to the sink and told her about the nickname I'd given Vince at the Long Pines and our conversation at the Christmas party. She chuckled, but her face grew pensive when we returned to the sewing room.

"That poor, dead boy." She pinned antlers on a brown headband. "I don't imagine his life was easy. Do you know why he was at Fly Ranch?"

"All I know is that boys run away from the ranch when the weather's bad." I began assembling a pair of antlers.

Corinne picked up a needle and thread. "There's more to Fly Ranch than that. It was started by a Catholic priest who was also a pilot. He worked with boys who were in trouble with the law and gave them flying lessons to grow their self-confidence. Some bigwig who owned a whiskey distillery heard about him and bought land for Fly Ranch a little south of here. One thing led to another and now the ranch is the liquor industry's pet charity."

The antlers in my hands fell into my lap. "Are you serious?"

"It's hard to believe, isn't it? People around here say its guilt money. That may be true, but the ranch helps boys from all over the Midwest. It employs plenty of people in Tipperary County, too. I haven't heard anyone complain about where the money comes from when they cash their paychecks." She tied off a knot in her thread and snipped it close to the headband. Then she waved it in the air. "Done."

"Me, too."

For the remainder of the afternoon we ironed costumes, paired them with headbands and hats, and arranged them on hangers bearing each child's name. Then we carried them, one armload at a time, to the Beetle and stuffed them inside.

She handed me Tiege's costume. "That's the last one."

I added it to the pile in the back seat and straightened. "Will you come to the program?"

She looked away.

"The children will be so disappointed if you're not

there." I got in the driver's seat and started the engine. "You can sit in the wings and leave during the last song."

"I'll try." She watched me drive down the lane. In the rearview mirror she appeared as small and slight as she had the previous Saturday.

"Please," I begged as her reflection disappeared. "Please come."

CHAPTER 15

The first order of business was to hide the costumes in my apartment. Christmas fever was heating up in our classroom. If the children saw their finished costumes now, they would crash and burn. I hung the suits and reindeer hides and trees, along with hats, antlers, and Tiege's yellow star, in the guest room closet.

Before shutting the door, I delivered a stern warning. "If you so much as think about jingling, prancing, or twinkling until it's time for the children to see you, I will remove every iota of merry from your Christmas—"

You're threatening inanimate objects, Jane! Snap out of it.

I could blame my behavior on winter. Or the upcoming Christmas program. Or the evidence still lurking in my underwear drawer. Or on too much time spent in the presence of children.

Oh, I liked that one. It meant I needed adult conversation. Not with people old enough to be my grandparents like Corinne and Merle and Velma. But with people my age who preferred Carol Burnett over Gracie Allen, the Beatles over Glenn Miller, and *Jesus Christ Superstar* over *The Wizard of Oz*. The Little Missourians in that crowd spent their Saturday nights at Round the Bend.

I zipped into my coat and shouldered my purse. My first thought was to take the Beetle, but the temperature was bearable and the air was still. I decided to walk instead. I entered the café and scanned the room. The Sternquists and Borgesons were crowded around two tables shoved together end to end. The Barkleys occupied the front booth. Frost and Fannie McDonald sat in the booth behind them. And who was huddled at the corner table closest to the kitchen but Rique DuPeuss.

My first inclination upon spotting him was to leave before anyone noticed me. However, my presence had already been detected. Dan and Pam Barkley waved for me to come over. Cora and Bennan were there. Sitting with them would necessitate talking to children. Not my first choice for the evening, but it was better than talking to Christmas costumes. Plus, the Barkleys were sitting as far from Rique DuPeuss as the tiny café allowed. That sealed the deal. I returned their wave and went to join them.

Cora and Bennan bickered about where I should sit. Dan ended the argument by sitting between them on one side of the booth. I slid in on the other side next to Pam. The kids weren't wild about it, but the arrangement tick-led me. My back was to Rique. Out of sight, out of mind.

Trudy brought a menu, but I waved it away. "I'll take my usual."

She scribbled on her pad. "A cheeseburger, fries, and Diet Coke coming right up, Miss Newell."

The Barkleys and I talked about the Christmas program until our food arrived. Pam ran through the varieties of cookies she and the other moms would be serving between the end of the show and the arrival of Santa.

"They all sound delicious." I meant it. "How am I supposed to choose just one?"

Pam whispered in my ear. "You didn't hear this from me, but we're making sampler plates for you and Liv to take home afterward."

"Oh good." I forgot to whisper back. "I won't show up in Sioux City on Christmas Eve empty-handed."

Dan whistled. "That'll be a long drive on your own. What time will you take off?"

"Around four-thirty that morning if the weather cooperates."

Cora sat up on her knees. "Me and Bennan ask God every night to keep the snow away until you get home. Will you call us when you get to your mommy and daddy's house so we can tell him to make it snow so Santa can come?"

I crossed the pile of mush that was my heart. My words fought their way past the lump in my throat as I promised to do what Cora asked.

This. This was why I spent hours and hours a day with kids.

When Trudy brought my food, I doubted it could bypass the lump. One whiff of cheeseburger—there is no aroma more decadent than one hundred percent ground Black Angus on a bun except for Christmas cookies— and the lump vanished along with my doubts.

Conversation was sparse until our hunger had dulled.

I dipped a fry and considered how to ask Dan something while the kids were listening. "Have many people been cutting Christmas trees in the Long Pines?"

He wiped his mouth with a paper napkin. "Not as many as a couple weeks ago, but a good number. The roads are open again and people can go wherever they want in the forest, so I expect traffic to pick up."

The crime scene was no longer sealed. Why hadn't the sheriff let me know? Didn't finding a dead body come with a few perks?

"The top of our tree touched the ceiling before Daddy trimmed the trunk. And it's still this big." Bennan held one arm above his head and the other below the table.

"It twinkles." Cora turned to Pam. "Mommy, we should have Miss Newell come to Sunday dinner tomorrow so she can see it."

"That's a wonderful idea, Cora." Pam smiled at me. "What do you say, Jane?"

There is only one thing for a teacher, who had chatted with clothing an hour ago, to say when invited to dinner by a child who had Christmas stars in her eyes.

"Yes. If I'm going to spend most of Sunday at your house"—I winked at Bennan and then at Cora—"I need to skedaddle to get school things ready for some boys and girls I know."

"That's me and Cora!" Bennan sprang out of the booth and pointed to the other children in the café. "And Tiege and Elva and Stig! Renny and Beau aren't here, but you should make work for them too."

I scooted from my seat and gave him a hug. "I'll be sure to do that. See you at church tomorrow." Then I paid my tab at the cash register and stopped for a short chat with the Borgesons and the Sternquists.

"You best bundle up good," Frost said as I passed the booth where he and Fannie sat. "The forecast says the wind's supposed to pick up tonight."

I zipped up my coat and yanked my hat over my ears. The door was swinging when I reached it, and I walked outside. Rique DuPeuss was a few steps ahead of me. His parka and buckskin leggings were visible in the glow of the street light, as was his bare head.

The wind ruffled his shaggy, dark hair. He took a camouflage ski mask—Where was his coonskin cap?—from his pocket and pulled it over his head. A hole in the back of it yawned wide, its edges a mass of unraveling yarn. A strong gust tore a length of yarn loose. It sprang free and danced away.

Chapter 16

I stood in the middle of the street trying to process what I'd just seen. Once it fell into place, I entered the circle of light where Rique had been. One step at a time, I placed my feet in the footprints he'd made. After each step, I paused and swept my eyes across the surface of the snow.

There it was! I knelt beside the piece of yarn that had fallen from Rique's ski mask. Another gust of wind sent it skittering. I snatched it in midair and ran home as fast as a person in clunky snow boots on a slick road could. Without shedding coat or boots, I took out another plastic zipper bag and deposited the yarn inside. I wrote "Daniel Boone" on a bit of masking tape and stuck it on the bag. I lined up all three bags on the kitchen counter.

Three suspects. Three yarn samples, but still no evidence compelling enough to take Hank York out of the running once Rick heard about the moon boots. On the other hand, what I knew combined with whatever he knew might lead him to the killer. I needed to see the sheriff immediately. Make that last week.

I was done sitting around doing nothing. It was time to take action. I went to the guest room, dragging a chair behind me. After checking it for wobbles, I climbed up and eased the box from its shelf. With an air of reverence, I carried the box to the kitchen, gently lifted out the microscope, and set it on the table. Then I slipped the yarn samples from their bags and examined them in the order they'd been collected.

After sketching each of them, I examined first one end of the yarn fragment from the post office and then the other under the microscope. Both were frayed, as if they'd been torn rather than cut. Next, I completed the same examination of the fragment from the crime scene. Its ends were also frayed, more significantly than the new fragment. The twigs and pine needle debris in the crime scene sample revealed no more under the microscope than the magnifying glass had. The same was true for the straw and seed heads from the yarn shed by Dick at the post office.

My eyes felt like sandpaper and my neck was hurting when I slid the yarn from Rique's hat under the microscope. Its ends showed fraying similar to Dick's. When I glimpsed tufts of fur and dried flesh caught in the yarn from Rique's hat, my stomach did a somersault. I ignored the nausea and put the samples into their respective bags. Next I got out my legal pad and wrote "yarn from his ski mask" in the column after Rique's name.

I took stock of the items on the table. When my underwear drawer had contained two little bags of evidence soon to be handed over to the sheriff it had been an adequate hiding place. Slightly creepy, but adequate. Now there were three baggies. One piece of yarn came from the hat of a man who had been in my house not long ago. I also had sketches and a growing list of suspects on the legal pad. They needed a better hiding place.

I tucked everything in a manila file folder and took it into the classroom. The metal filing cabinet had a lock. One that was easy to jimmy. Still, if past experience was any indication, the evidence would be safe here. After all, Junior had ignored the file cabinet and gone straight for the underwear drawer. Perhaps Rique and Dick's brains worked the same way.

I locked the drawer and tugged on it. It didn't budge. Good. I carried the key into my apartment and hid it under the ice cube tray in the freezer. Then I packed up the microscope, put the box on its shelf, changed into pajamas, and went to bed.

Rick and Tiege Sternquist took center stage in my dreams. They played the biggest and littlest Christmas trees. Neither had memorized their lines. I chased the sheriff in a vain attempt to finish his costume. Just when I had caught up to him and had begun sewing plastic zipper bags filled with yarn onto his costume, Liv rang a bell to signal the opening of the curtain. It didn't budge. Liv rang the bell again. And again. And again, sounding for all the world like my alarm clock.

It *was* my alarm clock. I rolled over and silenced it before crawling out of my warm bed. The furnace clicked on while I made breakfast and again while I got ready for church. The cold snap Frost McDonald had warned about had arrived. That wouldn't keep me from stretching my legs by walking to church. I dressed in long underwear, plaid wool trousers, a blue cable knit sweater over a white turtleneck shirt, and two pairs of socks. When I left the apartment, I was sweating.

Bits of my dream floated into my thoughts as I walked. I pushed them down. They kept popping up until I entered the church foyer. Cookie Sternquist was talking to Hank and Ruby York. On the far side of them, a group of kids was playing Rock Paper Scissors. Dick Phillips and Rique DuPeuss stood in a far corner with Rick Sternquist. Their expressions and body language hinted at a weighty conversation. My eyes narrowed. I would corner Rick today. Even if it killed me. Even if it made the whole town talk. I didn't care what anyone thought, as long as Rique, Dick, and Hank didn't know we were discussing Edgar's murder.

Someone tugged on my arm. I tore my gaze from the three men to see who it was. Tiege stood there, his face as serious as those of the men across the room.

"Cora and Bennan say you're going to their house for dinner after church."

"That's right."

"Do you like them better than you like me?"

I knelt down. "Why would you ask that?"

"Because you ain't been to our house since the day I drove off and left you to walk all the way down the hill to our house." Tears brimmed in his eyes. He had never cried in my presence before. "I'm sorry for what I did. Will you forgive me?"

I knelt beside him and put an arm around him. "Tiege, I forgave you the minute it happened. And I'd love to visit you again."

He knocked me over and bounded away. "Mom," he

yelled in what we teachers call an outside voice, "can Miss Newell come for dinner next Sunday?"

Cookie rushed over and helped me up. "Are you okay?"

"Fine." I filled her in on Tiege's apology.

"That child! I never know whether to scold him or squeeze him." She brushed at some dust on my trousers. "There's a Ladies' Aid meeting after church next week, so Sunday dinner won't work. Could you to come for supper around six instead?"

Before I could ask what to bring, Pastor Petersen arrived. Cookie went into the sanctuary and took her place at the piano. Dick Philips crossed the foyer in my direction as Pam Barkley caught my attention and pointed at the pew Cora and Bennan had claimed. As I went to join the Barkleys, a flicker of irritation entered Dick's expression and his face reddened. He entered the pew ahead of Cora and Bennan where Rique DuPeuss and the sheriff were already sitting.

This was going to be interesting. The church service held my attention as it never had before. Pastor Petersen asked the Barkleys to come to the front for the Advent ceremony. Dan lit the candle while Pam coached Cora and Bennan as they read about how the candle represented hope.

Pastor Petersen's sermon expanded on the same theme. "God's goodness is all around us. But our world is not all good. Our loved ones become ill. People hurt one another, sometimes to the point of death."

I shuddered. Dick's neck flushed beet red. Rique DuPeuss shifted in the pew. He ducked his head. The sheriff watched them, his face impassive.

The pastor continued, oblivious to the stir he'd caused. "We are entering the coldest, darkest month of the year. The days are short. The nights are long. This is the month when the light of a single candle can bring great hope. This Advent Sunday, we cling to the hope of the Messiah who will bring peace and justice to the world." He gestured at the Advent wreath. "Look to the light. Hold on to hope."

Instead of bowing my head during the closing prayer, I gazed at the candle and prayed. "Shine your light into the darkness of Edgar's murder and let justice be done."

After the service, Hank York pumped the pastor's hand. "Reverend Mister, don't you worry 'bout who's gonna shovel snow around the church. Me and Ruby, we live across the alley, and I always takes care of it. You can count on me, Reverend Mister. I'm a worker, I am."

My eyes went to Hank's feet. He wore leather work boots with holes in the toes. His socks peeked through and the soles flapped when he walked. Strange choice for a morning as cold as this one.

Out of the corner of my eye I saw Rick heading for the door. He was not leaving without talking to me. Not a chance. I dodged past the pastor as he reached to shake my hand and elbowed Dick Phillips out of my way. "Rick!" I shouted.

A warm hand slipped into mine and swung my arm back and forth. "Mommy says me and my brother gotta share you on the way to our house," Cora said as Bennan took my other hand.

I wanted to shake them off and run after Rick. Only the anticipation on their faces and the memory of Tiege crying before church stopped me. I wasn't about to make a habit of bringing children to tears before lunch.

Cora and Bennan led me to their parents' Bronco. When we arrived at their house, they begged me to play with them in the basement.

"Right now I want to help your mom in the kitchen. There will be plenty of time for playing after we eat."

Pam set fresh vegetables next to a chopping board beside the sink. "You can make a green salad." She opened the oven. "How's the Christmas program coming along?"

"Not too bad. Ask me again after the first big practice on Tuesday." I washed and chopped veggies. "Corinne and I finished the costumes yesterday. That's a relief."

Pam lifted a roasting pan from the oven and set it on the counter. "Dan, you can carve the ham."

He took a steel from a drawer and sharpened the butcher knife while the ham cooled.

"How's work?" I asked him.

"Good, for the most part."

I tossed the salad and put it on the table. "And the part that's not so good?"

Pam handed me a gravy whisk. "He stumbled upon some funny business in the Long Pines." She took a potato masher from a drawer.

Don't sound too eager, Jane.

I counted to three before responding. "Funny business?"

"Yeah." Dan arranged slices of meat on the serving platter. "Someone's been setting illegal predator traps in the forest. Whoever it is knows how to hide them in inconspicuous places."

"Do you have any idea who it is?" I whisked the gravy as it came to a boil.

Pam added milk and butter to the potatoes. "It started shortly after Rique DuPeuss arrived. He may be the state trapper, but Dan's keeping an eye on him."

I stirred harder as my brain played tug-of-war with the news. On the one hand, Dan's misgivings about Rique delighted me. On the other hand, Rique had spoken of his job with great passion. Accusing him of illegal trapping was a hard sell. Then again, Dan was the person who had seen the traps.

"The potatoes are ready." Pam began spooning them into a serving bowl.

"So's the gravy." I turned off the burner and poured it into the gravy boat.

The next few minutes were a flurry setting food on the table, hand washing, and sitting down to eat. Cora and Bennan stuck to me like glue through the meal and the board games afterward. There was no shaking them off and no chance of hearing anything more from Dan. At least not today.

Dusk was falling as I walked home. My phone rang as I unlocked the door, so I kicked off my boots and ran to answer. "Hello?"

"I've been calling you every fifteen minutes for hours. Betty had no idea of where to find you. Were you on a date?"

"It's nice to hear your voice too, Mom."

"Of course it's nice to talk to you, Jane. That goes without saying."

True, but I still wanted to hear her say so. "The Barkleys invited me to dinner after church."

"Not a date then. That's too bad."

"Sorry to disappoint you. What's up, Mom?"

"I just called to see how your week went. Betty and I got to chatting when you didn't pick up. She said the investigation into that boy's death is going absolutely nowhere. Is that true?"

"I have no way of knowing. The sheriff hasn't talked to me since the day after Edgar died."

"I'm glad to hear it. Now don't you get impatient and start snooping around yourself."

"Didn't we have this conversation last weekend, Mom? With the Christmas program less than two weeks away, there's less time to spare than ever. And it's cold. Below zero cold. You know I won't go outside in this weather for no good reason."

"Your father will be relieved to hear it. The pastor's here or you could tell him yourself. Oh, the coffee water is boiling. I'd better go."

She was gone before I could say goodbye. I set the receiver in the cradle, hung up my coat, and retrieved the legal pad from my office. I added "illegal trapping" after Rique's name. Now that was a nugget I was eager to share with the sheriff. As soon as the courthouse was open tomorrow I would call him. If he didn't agree to meet me that day, I would drive over and visit him at his office whether he wanted me to or not.

CHAPTER 17

Monday morning's weather was as dingy as old socks. The clouds hung heavy, obliterating the sun and blue sky. Liv stopped by my classroom before school. "The weather'll be unpredictable from here on out. As long as it's above zero, the kids need to go outside for recess. And we should have practice whenever there's school. I think we should rehearse every day from three to three-thirty starting tomorrow."

"It's my first Christmas program. I'll do whatever you say."

Liv went to her room, and I went to call Rick. Betty made the connection. He picked up on the first ring.

"Sheriff Sternquist here."

"I can't believe you answ—"

A blood-curdling scream came from the playground. I glanced out the window. Two boys from Liv's room crouched in the snow, facing one another. There were textbooks and lunch boxes scattered every which way. The first fight of the year, and it had to happen now?

"Gotta break up a fight. Catch you later." I hung up and muttered as I threw on my coat and ran outside.

Liv and I got to the boys at the same time. Her face scrunched into a scowl, and she hauled them up by the scruffs of their necks. "Gavin Wick and Flan Connary, what is going on?" She looked at me. "Give me a couple minutes to sort them out before you ring the bell." The boys dangled like a couple of bullheads caught on fishing hooks as she carried them across the playground and plopped them on the landing in front of her classroom. They listened wide-eyed and motionless during her talking to. They should have known the foolishness of raising the ire of a woman whose muscles rivaled Popeye's.

I waited to ring the bell until Liv was done. When my students came inside, the fight between the two big boys was all they could talk about.

Elva set her boots on the newspaper in the entryway. "Flan started it, but Gavin egged him on."

It's time you changed the subject.

Elva went on. "He shouldn't have called the state trapper a cuss word."

Then again, maybe not. I stepped behind my file cabinet where the kids couldn't see me though I could see and hear them.

Bennan unzipped his coat. "Me and Flan heard his dad say it. He doesn't like that trapper guy."

Elva whirled around and stared at him. "How do you know that? You're only a first grader."

He stood tall until he was nose to chin with Elva. "My dad works with Flan's dad. I was hiding in Dad's office while they were talking about the trapper. They said he was a sudspishus character. I don't know what sudspi-shus means, but I don't think it's nice."

Renny spoke up. "My dad says there's some ranch-ers been finding nasty traps and truck tracks and boot prints right across their land in the Long Pines. They think the trapper's doing it. Gavin sticks up for the trap-per guy 'cause he pays to camp on his dad's lot."

"My brother says we ain't supposed to talk about peo-ple behind their backs." Tiege elbowed his way past the others. "I'm gonna tell Miss Newell on you."

I came out from behind the file cabinet. It wouldn't do to be outed by a third grader. "Get in your seats, kids. School started a little late. We'll have to skip show-and-tell unless you'd rather skip recess."

They voted to keep recess. While they worked on their morning assignments, I chewed over what Bennan and Renny had said. It matched what Dan had mentioned about traps, though he hadn't mentioned truck tracks or boot prints. If he and Flan's dad had reported their findings to the sheriff, maybe I didn't need to. Or was I rationalizing for fear of Rick's reac-tion when he saw the evidence I had?

During recess, I tried to call the sheriff again. The phone rang and rang until Betty said, "I think he's not there."

I banged the receiver into its cradle for the second time that morning and stomped over to my apartment. I picked up that phone and placed a long distance call. Mom was at work, and this was my chance to get Dad's advice instead of hers.

The phone rang ten times before he picked up. "Har-old Newell speaking."

His words were crisper than usual. "Hi Dad. It's Jane."

"Are you okay?"

"Yes, everything's fine. It's just"—I nibbled at the inside of my cheek—"I'd like to run something by you."

"Shoot."

Quickly, I summarized what had transpired since the discovery of Edgar's body. "I've been trying to turn over the evidence I've found for over a week, but Rick keeps shutting me out. By my way of thinking, I should drive to his office when school lets out today and turn over the information. But if he's not there, I need to do some poking around, even though Mom made me promise not to."

"What I'm about to say goes against your mother's wishes, Janie-Jo, and I don't like doing that. The rug got pulled out from under her when I got sick. Now her top priority is keeping you kids safe. You know that."

Boy, did I. Mom was equal parts aggressive bulldog and scared rabbit. I'd seen her make neighborhood bullies cower. Liv had nothing on her in that department. I'd also seen Mom paralyzed by indecision when she encountered risks that exposed her kids to the slightest whiff of danger.

"She never learned how to let you kids decide for yourselves. That's why she doesn't want you involved in this sort of thing. But you're an adult now, Sweetie. You should do what you think is right."

"I don't know what that is."

"Yes you do, Janie-Jo. You just have to work up the nerve to do it."

"Okay, Dad."

"Drive carefully on the way to the sheriff's office. If

he's not there, do what you have to do. Bye now." He hung up.

I stared at the receiver. Before losing my nerve, I asked Betty to call the Tipperary courthouse and ask someone there to tell the sheriff I was coming to see him after school.

A bell jangled, and I heard my students running to line up. I hurried through to my classroom and brought them inside. In minutes they were back at their desks. I called them up grade by grade for math lessons, and the remainder of the morning passed quickly.

They were busy with seatwork when Beau brought his math paper to my desk. "Miss Newell?"

"Are you having trouble with a story problem?"

"Not exactly."

"Then what?"

"I'm hungry."

"Hang on, buddy. We'll be eating in—"—I checked the clock and stood—"Oh, my word, kids, we're late for lunch!"

They set a new hand washing speed record before grabbing their lunch boxes from cubbies and running to eat at their desks. Running inside was usually forbidden, but not today. With recess duty ten minutes away, I ran to my refrigerator for my lunch and wolfed it down at my desk.

Somehow my students and I made it outside before the older students did. Not a miracle at the loaves and fishes level, but close. Partway through recess, light snow began to fall. The children ran around trying to catch flakes on their tongues without much success. When we traipsed inside, their cheeks were rosy with cold and exercise.

"Are we getting out early?" Cora unwound her scarf and ended up in a tangle.

"No." I helped her out of it. "It's not snowing hard enough."

The snow fell harder as the afternoon progressed. The wind began to howl, making it hard for the children to concentrate on social studies. Instead of cracking the whip, I told them to put away their textbooks and take out their scissors and glue. We spent the rest of the afternoon listening to Christmas music on the record player and making paper chains and ornaments for our Christmas tree. By dismissal time, we were all surprised to see how hard it was snowing. The vehicles lined up on Main Street to take students home were barely visible. Parents met their children at the door and guided them across the schoolyard.

"It's bad out there," Mary Borgeson yelled over the wind. She took Elva by one hand and Stig by the other. "Don't go out unless you have to."

A gust ripped the door from my grasp. I struggled to pull it shut. I pounded the door with my fists. Stupid weather! My trip to the sheriff's office had been blindsided by a blizzard. Outside the snow was falling and swirling into eddies and drifts. Try as I might to do my duty as a law-abiding citizen, the weather had bested me. But not for long. Tomorrow I would drive to Tipperary after school, come hell or high water—or to be more accurate, come blizzard or blocked roads. If Rick wasn't there, I would break the promise to Mom and take matters into my own hands.

Chapter 18

Sunrise revealed a cloudless sky. A snowplow cruised along Main Street, and Rique DuPeuss shoveled the school sidewalks. Merle stood on my landing and supervised.

Give it a rest, Merle.

I leaned my forehead on the cold window glass. Rique can shovel snow to the moon and back, and it won't change my mind. My investigation or the sheriff's could prove beyond a shadow of a doubt that Rique wasn't Edgar's killer, and I still wouldn't give him the time of day.

I showered and put on red wool trousers, a white turtleneck, and a navy blue blazer. Then, I checked the school yard again. Merle and Rique were gone. The snow was gone from the sidewalks too. Even murder suspects and matchmakers can serve a good purpose.

The town kids made it to school on time, though the ranch kids straggled in one by one. Tiege was the last to arrive. We had just finished the Pledge of Allegiance when he entered the classroom with a flourish. "Never fear," he announced in booming tones, "the littlest Christmas tree is here."

The kid's comedic timing tickled my funny bone. I held my breath and swallowed the giggle threatening to take flight. It rose like a hot air balloon and burst out of me. I doubled over, helpless with laughter.

Tiege paraded to the front of the room. His classmates hooted, clapped, and joined the parade. Before I knew it, he was leading them around their desks and into the entryway with the panache of the Pied Piper. If I didn't get a grip on the situation, I fully believed Tiege would lead his classmates out of town never to be seen again.

"Go to your desks!" I barked. "Now!"

They obeyed, but for the rest of the day my normally cherubic students acted like fallen angels. They showed no inclination to rejoin the heavenly choir when Liv and her students trooped across the schoolyard for program practice.

Liv's students pushed my students' desks against the walls to create a rehearsal space. Tiege ran to the center of the room, twirled, and announced, "The littlest Christmas tree has arrived!"

If I'd had an ax, I would have chopped him down to size. Instead, I leveled my fiercest teacher scowl at him. He didn't notice.

Head reindeer Gavin Wick laughed and began to chant, "Tiege, Tiege, Tiege!"

That, Tiege noticed.

He launched into a cartwheel. I caught him mid-cart and pulled him to the sidelines. At the same time Liv took Gavin to the cloakroom and gave him a lecture. What I heard of it scared me silly, though the children remained unfazed.

Rehearsal continued its downhill slide. The kids didn't know their lines. I couldn't find the right starting notes on the piano, so every song was pitched too high or too low. While Liv and I gave stage directions, the reindeer chanted Tiege's name under their breath. The elves formed a rumba line in the corner. Mr. and Mrs. Santa bickered like they'd been married for forty years. The Christmas trees swayed and hummed *O Tannenbaum* as Tiege directed them like the conductor of the Boston Pops Orchestra.

"Enough!" A commanding male voice cut through the cacophony.

Everyone went still. They knew the owner of that voice. I closed my eyes and winged a short thank you to God, along with a postscript for him to please, please, please keep Rick from arresting me when I told him about the yarn. And that he would believe that I hadn't been trying to get involved in the case. Or withhold evidence. Or tamper with the crime scene.

The sheriff stood in the entryway, his arms crossed, his expression thunderous. "Unless the lot of you straighten up and listen to your teachers, I might haul you to jail for causing a riot. You"—he aimed his index finger at his brother—"are under house arrest until further notice."

By then only five minutes of rehearsal time remained. Liv motioned for her students to line up, which they did without any funny business, and led them to their classroom. My students shoved their desks back into place without a peep. They remained subdued while putting on their coats, hats, gloves, and boots. With the sheriff keeping tabs on them, what else could they do?

An arm crept around my waist. I looked down.

"I'm sorry, Miss Newell. I'll be better tomorrow. I promise." Tiege looked contrite, but then again, who wouldn't in the presence of a lawman who was also your big brother?

I handed him a script. "Take this home and work on your lines. It'll help you pass the time during house arrest."

He crammed it into his bag and scurried outside. His trademark bounce was missing as he ignored his brother and made his way to his parents' truck.

I shifted my gaze from Tiege to Rick. "I assumed you were here to pick him up."

He scratched his neck. "That was my understanding, but I guess me and mom got our wires crossed."

"Your crossed wires saved me a trip to Tipperary."

"Listen, Jane. You can come to my office. You can call. You can leave me urgent message after urgent message, but I am not consulting with you about this investigation."

I wanted to smack him. I wanted to wipe the sanctimonious smirk off his sanctimonious face. I also wanted to stay out of jail. So I stepped forward and jabbed at his chest with an index finger to punctuate each word I spoke. "I don't want to be consulted. I just want to give you what I've found."

"Okay!" He backed away. "I hear you and would like to call a truce. Can we sit down and talk?"

"Can you spare me the time?"

His sanctimonious smirk crumpled into contrition. "I deserved that. And I'm sorry."

Ever the gracious winner, I accepted his apology and offered to make us coffee. "Let's talk in my apartment?" We went into the kitchen and sat at the table once the coffee was made and poured.

He took off his parka and pulled out a notebook and pencil. "I've gone back to the crime scene with my team several times and we haven't found much. Either we overlooked something or people don't realize they saw something important. So what about you? Did you see anything at the Long Pines that you overlooked before?"

Chapter 19

My hands refused to behave when I lifted my mug for a drink. I set it down, interlaced my shaking fingers, and laid my hands in my lap.

"A few things actually."

"Go on."

"This is probably no big deal, but you know how I almost fell asleep while you walked me to the ambulance?"

"Yes."

"I think I saw Rique DuPeuss sneak away while Dan Barkley went around talking to people. I was half-dreaming, so it may not have happened at all. But you could check with Vince Douglas. In my dream or whatever it was, he saw Rique leave."

Rick raised an eyebrow. "Interesting. What else?"

"The other things are in my classroom. I'll go get them." I took the key to the desk drawer from the freezer. I retrieved the manila folder from its hiding place and brought it to the kitchen. I opened the folder and laid the zipper bags on the table.

"What do you have in these?" He picked up the baggie that held the sample from the crime scene and eyed it quizzically. "Yarn?"

"Yes. It's from the branch of a tree near Edgar's body. I picked it up without thinking while Dan and Merle went for help and put it in my pocket. Once they returned, my brain shut down and I forgot about it. Last week I found it again. I called you right away. But there were people listening on the party line. You said you would come over, but you didn't because you were out of town. I was going to drive over yesterday, but the weather was bad, and everyone said to stay home unless it was an emergency so I—"

"And this one" Rick picked up the second sample.

"Is from Dick Phillips. He has a ski mask that color too, and he blushes every time he sees me."

"He blushes."

"Like he's nervous. Or guilty."

Rick raised an eyebrow.

"Stop looking at me like that. I knew you wouldn't take his blushing seriously."

"Then why tell me?"

"Because when I saw Dick at the post office a week ago, he blushed again. After he left, I found that yarn on the post office floor. It wasn't there when he came in."

He held the bags side by side and compared them. "You're sure it wasn't there before?"

"For crying out loud, Rick, you know how clean Dale Cunningham keeps that place!"

He pointed at the remaining bag. "And the yarn in this one?"

"It's from the torn ski mask Rique DuPeuss was wearing Saturday."

"At the post office?"

"No, at the café."

"Did he blush, too?"

"Didn't you call a truce a few minutes ago?" My voice rose. "The rangers at the Forest Service don't trust Rique. Neither do the ranchers around the Long Pines. Once I heard that over the weekend, I decided to drive to Tipperary after school yesterday since you were avoiding me. My plan was to give you the samples and tell you what I knew. The weather didn't cooperate, so I postponed it until today. Then you showed up unannounced and here we are."

Rick exploded, and pointed at the bags one by one as he spoke. Make that yelled. "Let me get this straight. You found the first piece of yarn more than two weeks ago. The second one almost a week ago. And the third one four days ago."

"I tried to tell you."

"Try using your brain instead of your mouth, Jane. Did you even think about sending the labeled samples to me in the mail? Because if you had, the state lab would already be working on the yarn you found at the scene and in the post office."

"But I—"

"And I could have told you the gossip about Rique DuPeuss wasn't worth repeating. Most every tip we've gotten was about him. And they're all dead wrong. We can account for his movements from before Edgar ran away right up to when you found his body. I can't go into details, but I can tell you this. Rique DuPeuss is completely, unequivocally in the clear. If you want to do something worthwhile, concentrate on your little Christmas program and leave the investigating to me. Unless you have more to tell me." He slipped the baggies into his inside jacket pocket.

"No." I tore my gaze from the file folder where my sketches and suspect list were hidden. He wasn't going to get a look at those and make Hank York one of the suspects.

We parted without saying goodbye. I carried our coffee mugs to the sink where I rinsed his and set it in the dish drainer. Then I poured myself a fresh cup and sat at the table, rotating my mug in a slow circle. Hearing that DuPeuss was in the clear had been a disappointment. Being accused of not using my brain was infuriating. In my opinion, sending evidence through the mail was a risk. At every turn, Rick had discounted my efforts as too little too late. The too late was as much his fault as mine. The too little was something I would start remedying immediately.

Once I found a way to clear Hank and had a handle on who Edgar's killer might be, Rick would see that I was as smart as he was. One way or the other, he would never underestimate me again.

CHAPTER 20

When Tiege arrived at school on Wednesday morning, Beau's mouth gaped. He dropped his coat on the floor and ran to where I was writing on the chalkboard.

"Miss Newell," Beau said. "I thought he was under arrest."

If there was a boy whose heart should stay innocent forever, it was Beau. You know that, don't you God?

I laid the chalk in its tray and looked Beau in the eye. "The sheriff put Tiege under house arrest. That's not the same as jail. Tiege has to stay in his house at night until he knows his lines. But he can come to school every day."

I followed Beau as he ran to the cloakroom and wrapped his friend in a bear hug. "I'm glad you wasn't in jail last night."

Tiege pulled away. "Mom and Dad acted like I was. They made me sit in a hard chair and practice my part from when I got home until bedtime."

"Without any supper?"

"I got supper. But not dessert." Tiege handed me a plastic container. "My parents said I got to give this to you."

"What is it?"

"An apple dumpling. They said you earned it after the way I acted yesterday."

"I'll be right back boys." I took the container into the kitchen and lovingly set it on the counter. *Cookie Sternquist, you are the best!*

I rejoined the boys and the other students who'd arrived during my brief absence.

Tiege was a model student, remaining calm even when Renny announced his big news during show-and-tell. "My dad found more boot prints around the garbage cans behind the café. He says they look like the ones he seen before."

Boot prints? My pencil snapped in two.

Beau's hand shot up. "My grandpa and grandma saw boot prints around our garbage cans, too."

Cora bounced in her seat. "There were a bunch around the Forest Service garbage cans, too."

Elva sprang out of her chair and ran to her brother. "Stig has a bloody nose. It's a gusher."

I grabbed a handful of tissues, shoved them under his nose, and guided him to the sink. When the bleeding wouldn't stop, I told Elva to call her mom.

After Elva hung up, she joined us. "Mom says to tip Stig's head back and pinch the bridge of his nose until she or the nearest EMT gets here."

I pinched. The tissues turned bright red. My fingers cramped. I stopped pinching to exchange the bloody tissues for fresh ones. Blood gushed from Stig's nose and pooled in the sink. The kid was bleeding to death before my eyes. Wait, could that really happen?

A knock sounded. Elva ran to the door and returned with Dick Phillips.

"I'll take over." Dick put his fingers above mine on the bridge of Stig's nose. His slid down as mine pulled away and our hands brushed. He didn't blush. I did.

Dick knelt beside Stig. "Miss Newell, could you get hand towels, ice, and a bowl?"

When I returned Dick had me wrap some ice in a towel and press in on the bridge of Stig's nose. Then he put the bowl under the little boy's chin.

"Now, lean your head into my hand, buddy. I've got you." Dick's words were calm and tender. Stig relaxed and the fear left his eyes.

By the time Mary arrived, Stig's nosebleed had ended. She took him to the restroom to clean up his face and help him change clothes. Dick found Velma's cleaning caddy and scrubbed the area around the sink with a rag.

"Is Stig okay?" Bennan's voice quavered. "He's my best friend."

I went to his desk and rubbed his back. "He's fine." Then I addressed the next question to all the children. "That was a little scary wasn't it?"

They nodded.

"Thank you all for staying in your seats and being quiet. I'm so proud of you."

Dick wrung out the rag and walked toward the exit when he was done. I smiled and mouthed a thank you. He blushed and went outside.

The rest of the day was uneventful. Program practice was an oasis of calm populated by children eager to get on Santa's nice list. Or the sheriff's. Or both. Thursday was much the same minus the blood and the blushing.

Liv came to my room after school. "I can't believe how well practices are going. The kids usually go bonkers when a storm's moving in."

"Another storm? When's it supposed to hit?"

"Sometime tomorrow."

"After school, I hope. The program's improving, but it has a long way to go."

Liv opened the door and the cold rushed in. "And only a little more than a week to get there. With that happy thought, I'll leave you to your work."

***

Friday dawned clear and cold and bright. The clouds rolled in during lunch recess. The wind freshened and the temperature dropped, but the snow held off. Renny Berthold sang his solo, the first verse of *Silent Night*, with the pure tones of an English choir boy. As the other children joined him for the second verse, the snow began to fall. The flakes lazily floating from the sky were framed in windows behind the children. Their sweet voices coupled with the snow to create a longing inside me. I couldn't identify what I was longing for, but it was real. Of that I was sure.

Gavin Wick looked over his shoulder and ran to the window. The other reindeer broke ranks to join their leader. The elves, the trees, as well as Santa and his wife, were about to follow.

"Get back here or the sheriff will put you all under house arrest. That's worse than rodeo season with a busted saddle." Tiege's bellow stopped the children cold. "I oughta know."

The reindeer pranced to their places and rehearsal resumed. The children were singing *We Wish You a Merry Christmas* when the phone rang.

Liv answered and spoke into my ear after hanging up. "That was the principal. She said the wind's bad in the country, and we'd better send the kids home as soon as their parents get here."

Normal dismissal time wasn't for twenty minutes, but already the street was lined with vehicles. Liv hurried her students to their classroom. I helped mine pack up their homework and put on their winter gear. Only after every student had been picked up did I begin correcting the papers piled on my desk.

The phone rang while I was recording grades. "Little Missouri School."

"Hewwo, Miss Neweww."

"Hello, Betty. How are you?"

"Not good. I have a confession to make. I put your weww-being at risk earwier this week."

"That's hard to believe. You always take good care of me."

"That is true, but even the best of us can swip up now and then. Word come Tuesday evening that a Fwy Ranch boy ran off. I cawwed fowks right away. When the weather turned bad this afternoon I thought to mysewf, 'I suppose another kid is gonna run in this storm.' That's when I reawized I hadn't cawwed you Tuesday. They haven't found the boy who run yet, but I keep hearing about strange boot prints—"

The boot prints! I'd forgotten to follow up on them.

"—around garbage cans, so I wanted to remind you to wock your doors and windows for now. I'm sorry for my oversight."

"It's okay, Betty. No harm done."

Several more reassurances were required before she would hang up. I immediately locked the outer doors to my classroom and apartment, all the while berating myself for once again forgetting to take a look at the boot prints around town. Between Stig's bloody nose and working on my students' Christmas presents and another snowstorm, it had completely slipped my mind. After grades were recorded, lesson plans written, and seat work run off on the mimeograph machine, I unlocked the file cabinet and took out the legal pad. The evidence against Hank York was damning. The squishy nature of moon boots made their prints distinctive from others. A look at the boot prints around town might have cleared him, but I'd bungled that chance.My stomach growled. I tore the sheet off the legal pad, folded it, and put it in my pocket. Then I locked the file drawer again and went to the kitchen to put Pam Barkley's egg bake in the oven only to discover I hadn't taken it out of the freezer to thaw earlier in the day. At this rate, I wasn't going to get through everyone's hot dishes and casseroles in the week remaining before Christmas vacation.

Use the situation to your advantage, Jane. Think.

I sat down at the kitchen table and took out my notes. The only way to knock Hank off the suspect list was to do something about the moon boots before Rick found out about them. Hank hadn't been wearing the boots the last time I'd seen him. Maybe he didn't have them anymore.

The casseroles, Jane. Think!

My eyes widened as an idea took shape. I set the paper on top of the refrigerator and opened the freezer section. Then I moved the only casserole that was in a disposable aluminum pan to the refrigerator. Once the storm ended tomorrow, I would take Cookie's beef and noodles to Hank and Ruby, telling them that they were doing me a favor by taking it off my hands. That wouldn't be a lie. Plus, it would give me a chance see if Hank still had the moon boots. What to do after that was a mystery. For now, I would take things one step at a time.

My stomach protested again. I made an egg sandwich and fried a couple slices of crisp bacon. In homage to the guilt Mom had instilled in me when I refused to eat vegetables as a kid, I heated some of her home-canned green beans and only poured a tablespoon—okay, two tablespoons—of bacon grease over them for flavor. So good. So, so good.

After supper I turned on the television and appliquéd the students' names on their book bags. The television and the sewing machine were no match for the howling wind. I lifted my foot from the pedal and stared out the window into the darkness beyond. The missing Fly Ranch boy was out in the storm. Would he be desperate enough to try to break into someone's house? Into my house?

I got up and wedged furniture against every door in my classroom and apartment. I sat down at my machine again and sewed late into the night. Every time I looked up, I expected to see the Fly Ranch boy's face pressed against the window. Instead, I imagined Edgar's still body lying in the snow. When I was too tired to sew anymore, I went to bed. I closed my eyes, and there he was again. His skin pale. His feet bare. His dead body a silent plea for someone to care enough to find his killer and seek justice.

Chapter 21

The storm blew itself out in the night. Drifts were piled in some places and patches of exposed earth peeked through where the ground was scoured bare. I decided it would be best to wait to visit Hank and Ruby until the plows came through.

After a quick breakfast, I stacked my record player with Christmas albums and decorated my tree. I switched off the music to vacuum the tinsel that preferred lounging on the floor to shimmering on the tree, and switched it on again while I did laundry and ironed school clothes for the next week.

John Denver and I were belting out *Silver Bells* when the phone rang. I turned down the record player's volume before picking up the receiver.

"Good morning, dear."

"Good morning, Mom." I inhaled sharply and waited for the hammer to fall.

"Betty said you might be snowed in."

Betty must not have said anything about the missing

Fly Ranch boy, or Mom would have led with that. I exhaled slowly and relaxed my shoulder muscles.

"Oh, it wasn't a bad storm." I tucked the phone under my chin and folded laundry while we talked. I told her about school and program practice. My mouth watered as she described the meals she would cook during Christmas break. All was well until—dag nab it—I slipped and mentioned Rick's visit on Tuesday.

"Do you mean to say the sheriff hasn't solved that case yet? How hard can it be to whittle down the list of suspects in a town as small as Little Missouri?"

"It's a small town in a huge county. The murderer has plenty of room to hide."

Mom squawked, "Good heavens, someone's at the door. I'll hang up." Short pause. "No, wait. Your father's saying something." Another pause. "He says he wants to talk to you. Here you go, Harold."

"Janie-Jo?"

"Hi, Dad. Is Mom out of earshot?"

"Affirmative."

"You are checking up on me?"

"Affirmative."

"Well, I gave the yarn to the sheriff. All I got in return was a piece of his mind."

Snort and chortle.

"I'm glad you think it's funny." I tried to sound exasperated, a tall order for a daughter delighted after making her father laugh. "I love you, Dad."

"Affirmative. Goodbye, Janie-Jo."

His receiver dropped into the cradle with a deafening clunk. I hung up and threw together a chef's salad. Feeling virtuous about my healthy meal, I decided to

get some exercise too. I pulled on my coat and boots,
grabbed the snow shovel, and went outside. Sunlight
bounced off the snow. The brightness made my eyes
blink and water. I blinked again as they adjusted to the
glare and looked at the playground in amazement.

Someone had already cleared the sidewalks. How had
Rique and Merle managed to do it without me noticing
them? I carried my shovel around the corner to my car.
The driveway had been shoveled, and berm left by the
street plow was gone, too. Merle's skill in selecting men
of interest to me was deplorable, but I had to admire his
persistence.

I took the shovel to my apartment and exchanged it for
the casserole. Still determined to get some exercise, I left
the car where it was and walked to Hank and Ruby's shack.

Once I reached their tiny, fenced fortress behind
the Methodist church, I had no idea how to breach it.
I walked west beside their tall, wooden fence. When it
turned a corner, so did I. The shack came into view, and
the door burst open.

Hank hurled a cat into the snow. "I've had enough of
yer belly achin', I have! Git outta here until me and Ruby
lets you in!"

His scowl was so fierce, I nearly dropped the casserole
pan. When he saw me, his fierceness transformed into
a smile. "Ruby! We got company. The teacher's come to
visit." The scowl returned when he saw what was in my
hands. "No ma'am, me and Ruby, we don't take no charity. I'm a worker I am. I got me a deal with the city to—"

"Hank," I interrupted. "I need a favor."

"Well, you shoulda said so." He raised his chin and
squared his shoulders. "You come to the right place. Me

and Ruby, we are workers, we are. You come right on in and tell us what you need."

When I stepped inside, the scent of wood smoke and unwashed bodies assaulted me. Above all, over all, and permeating those odors was the stench of cat urine and feces. Its source was as ubiquitous as the smell. Cats were everywhere—on the table, in the sink, under the quilt on the bed, perched on the refrigerator—even on the chair Ruby pulled out for me.

"Sit down right here, Teacher, and tell us what you need." Hank swept the cat onto the floor and patted the seat. A cloud of cat hair rose from the chair.

Ruby took the pan as I sat down. "My students' parents all brought meals over after Thanksgiving. I can't finish them before Christmas break, and they'll be freezer burned when I get back. Do you know someone who could take this casserole off my hands?"

Ruby smiled and started to speak, but Hank beat her to it. "Well now, Teacher, we sure can. Ruby, you warm it up in the oven right now so it's good and hot for the family I got in mind."

While she slid the pan into the oven of the wood stove, my eyes flitted from one dim corner to another in search of Hank's boots. There they were, tucked under two threadbare coats hanging from pegs near the door. Inside each boot was—what else?—a cat.

"The kitties look cozy."

Ruby giggled, but Hank stomped over and kicked at them. "Get outta my new boots, or you'll get throwed in the snow too."

A cat lover I am not. Even so, Hank's violence made me want to rescue them.

"Where did you get your boots?" I sneezed, and my eyes began to itch.

Uh-oh. Cat allergies.

Hank glared at me. "How come you're asking? I got 'em fair and square."

"It's just that they look very warm and blue's my favorite color. I'd like to get a pair." Another sneeze.

"Well, I got this deal with the city to clean the dump. I was working for them the day I come across these. I only seen this one pair."

I sneezed again. "How long ago was that?"

He scrunched one eye shut and counted on his fingers. "Two weeks ago, maybe two-and-a-half."

Another sneeze. My nose began to run.

Ruby touched my arm. "You catching a cold, Teacher?"

"Maybe so. I'd better leave before you catch it, too." I stood and went to the door. "What kind of thank you would that be?" I went outside and gulped at the fresh air to clear my lungs. I fished a tissue from my coat pocket and blew my nose.

"Teacher?"

I turned around.

Ruby stood shivering in her cotton house dress and patched sweater. "Hank said you might like some of my pickled beets." She held out a quart jar.

I accepted the gift. "Thank you."

"And Teacher, Hank found his boots sooner than he said just now. He come home with 'em the day after you was stuck in that snowbank." Ruby shivered and glanced over her shoulder. "He won't like that I told you."

"He never needs to know." I held up the pickle jar and gave it a pat. "Thanks again. They look delicious."

Which was a lie. The mere thought of eating pickled beets made me gag. My promise to Ruby was also a lie. In light of what Corinne had said about Hank's temper and now what Ruby had said, I wondered if I'd been too quick in discounting him as a suspect. I didn't want to tell the sheriff about Hank's moon boots, but maybe the time had come.

I shifted the mason jar from one hand to the other and saw something floating in the rich, red liquid. I lifted the jar up to catch the sunlight. The brine was swimming with cat hair.

Eww! My grip slackened. The jar fell on the frozen ground. The glass cracked. The rich, scarlet liquid leaked out and stained the snow. The image of Edgar's head surrounded by a wreath of blood-soaked snow filled my vision. I shuddered and bent to pick up the broken jar. As I straightened, a hand clamped my shoulder.

"Who gave you that?"

Chapter 22

The jar fell to the ground again. This time it broke into jagged halves. Beet pickles rolled out and littered the snow like misshapen Christmas baubles. Their vinegary odor assaulted my nostrils.

I shoved the hand away and whirled around. "What do you think you're doing? Do you want me to get cut?"

Dick Phillips glared at me for a long second. He towered over me in his puffy, down-filled parka zipped up over a snowmobile suit. A stunning scowl was his lone accessory. His resemblance to the abominable snowman was striking. I matched him scowl for scowl and glare for glare.

He blinked and took a paper bag from his pocket. He knelt down, grasped one of the broken pieces between the thumb and forefinger of his gloved hand, and slid it into the bag. Then he did the same thing with the other piece. When he stood again, his face went bright red. He stepped closer to me. Too close. Way too close. He leaned in like he wanted to kiss me.

Not in my lifetime! I whipped my head to the side. His nose bonked into my ear, and he sniffed me. That's right. He sniffed me.

I pushed him away. "What is wrong with you?"

His eyes narrowed. "Were you at the Yorks?"

"That's none of your business."

He crossed his arms. "You smell like you were at the Yorks."

The man was impossible. All I wanted was to make him go away. "I took them a casserole."

"How'd you get Hank to accept it?" He sounded surprised.

"I said they were doing me a favor. I have too many casseroles in my freezer."

"How was Ruby?"

"Fine."

Dick relaxed and uncrossed his arms. He almost smiled, and his resemblance to the abominable snowman waned.

"I was on my way home to throw out the pickles."

This time he did smile. "You saw the cat hair?"

I nodded. "But I wanted to return the jar."

"I've got a jar. Let me get it." He clomped across the road to his truck in the biggest pair of snow boots I'd ever seen. Dad could have fit both his feet into one of them. He considered his dainty feet a suitable topic of conversation when visitors stopped by.

"Just call me Twinkle Toes Newell." He would sweep a jerky arm toward his low-heeled boots with the finesse of a shoe model. "I'm a respectable nine-and-a-half medium in thick socks. Can you beat that?"

Most men could, but Dad didn't give them a chance to say so.

"How about a game of hearts? Or cribbage? Hold on a sec while I grab the board." He wheeled to the desk, took the board from the drawer, and set it on his lap. Then he wheeled it into the kitchen and slapped it on the table. "You want to deal for yourself first or for me?"

With that, the game was on. Card games mattered less to Dad than did company and conversation. His favorite topics, other than the size of his dainty feet, were football, farming, and food.

Trucks were not on Dad's list of worthwhile things to talk about, though Dick's truck might prove to be an exception. It was the same truck Dick had been driving when he and Edgar found me in the snowbank. Dad had heard that story already, but he would want to hear it again, along with a full description of the truck's cracked windshield, dinged body, and the snow shovel planted like a flag in a snowdrift in the truck's bed.

"Here." Dick thrust a grimy quart jar filled with spider webs and who knew what else at me. "It needs some cleaning up."

"Uh, yeah." I pinched the rim between thumb and forefinger and held it at arm's length. "Thanks." We stood there until the pause became uncomfortable. At least it was uncomfortable for me. I don't know about him.

He broke the silence. "You didn't notice anything unusual at Hank and Ruby's then?"

"The cats, the stink, the wood stove, their poverty. It was all pretty unusual to me."

"Was anything cleaner than other stuff? Nicer than they could afford or better than what they would find at the dump?"

Now why would he ask me that unless he was fishing for information? He knew I'd seen Edgar wearing his moon boots. If I admitted to seeing an identical pair at the Yorks' shack, Dick would know I could connect Hank to Edgar's murder. Why would he want to know that? To frame Hank and remove himself from suspicion perhaps?

I looked him straight in the eye. "Not that I can think of." Then I pretended to shiver. Which led to a genuine shiver. "It's too cold to stand out here. Could you please move? I want to go home." I stalked off, the jar still at arm's length.

The behaviors Dick and Hank had exhibited this afternoon raised my suspicions regarding both men. Whoever had murdered Edgar knew about Hank's deal with the city. That person could have planted the boots at the dump for him to find. Based on the third degree I'd been subjected to by Dick, he could have framed Hank. Then again, the old man could have killed Edgar and taken the boots.

I scanned the sky and was surprised to see the sun setting already. Meeting Dick in broad daylight had been no big deal. The thought of him following me around after dark gave me the creeps. I shuddered and decided to break a personal rule I held dear. For only the second time since I'd moved to Little Missouri, I began to run.

CHAPTER 23

Merle hallooed and waved as I raced past his place. What was he doing out here when it was almost time to milk Snippy? I was in no mood to talk and kept moving. Until a stitch began in my side. This, I recalled as it bent me double and I dropped the jar, was one reason I hated to run.

"Who lit a fire under you?" Merle gimped over and took my arm. "You better come on in and catch yer breath."

"No." I gasped for air. "Need to get home."

"Home ain't goin' anywhere and neither is you by the look a things." He led me inside, through the mudroom, and into his kitchen. He plunked me into a chair. "You sit there for a bit." He wrinkled his nose and scooted away. "You been over at Hank and Ruby's place?"

I pressed a hand against my side and waited for the pain to subside. I didn't answer until I was breathing easily. "You're the second person to ask me that. Did Betty broadcast it all over town?"

"She woulda if the Yorks had phoned her, but they don't got one." Merle cracked opened the window above the sink. "Some fresh air'll cut the cat pee perfume you dabbed behind your ears."

"It's that bad, huh?"

"You best wash everything you got on when you get home or yer apartment won't be fit to live in." He dabbed at his eyes with a hankie. "If you stay here much longer, I'm gonna have to fumigate."

I rose and walked through the mudroom. Merle followed me and held the door open. "You wait outside for a smidge, and I'll git yer eggs and milk."

"I don't have any money, and I want to get home before dark."

He squinted at the sky. "You got time. I'll be quick."

He banged the door shut and returned with a carton of eggs and a gallon jug of milk. "You can pay me when you smell better."

I tucked the egg carton under one arm and put the milk jug in the crook of the other. I started for home, but stopped when my boot clinked against something. It was Dick Phillip's grody jar. I couldn't leave it there. Merle or I could run over it and puncture a tire.

I took the milk and eggs inside my apartment after unlocking the door, grabbed my flashlight, and ran outside again. Even with the flashlight, it took a while to locate the jar. By the time I did, the sky was completely dark. I was tempted to run back to my apartment, but I'd learned my lesson. With the flashlight illuminating the path, I walked home, climbed the landing stairs, and went inside. As I pulled the door shut, a hand clamped over my mouth. An arm encircled mine and pinned them to my torso. Dick's jar fell from my hands. It bounced off my boot and skittered across the entry room floor.

My attacker pressed his mouth against my ear. "Keep your mouth shut and I won't hurt you."

He loosened his grip on my torso and pushed me toward the kitchen table. "Sit down over there." He gagged. "I don't want to smell you."

I obeyed and sank into the chair on the far side of the table. Then I raised my eyes and looked my attacker square in the face.

Chapter 24

He was a kid with a barely visible line of reddish-blond fuzz above his top lip. His blue eyes were as bright as my younger brother Jeff's. He looked as furtive as my brother had when he snuck out of the house on his first day of high school. He didn't want Mom to see his tie-dyed tee shirt and raggedy cut offs.

There was nothing summertime about this boy or his clothes. His lips were tinged blueish. A thick crust of snow covered his hat and coat. When he sat down, his jeans and tennis shoes crackled, showering splinters of ice onto the floor. His hands were chapped and raw. He looked hungry and cold.

My heart raced, and I took a deep breath to calm myself. Big mistake. The stench coming off him made me sick. He had a lot of nerve complaining about me when we were more or less a matched set. I had to get the kid out of here so I could wash my foul-smelling clothes. Otherwise, our combined stink would permeate the apartment walls.

"How long since you had a decent meal?" I asked. "Can I make you something to eat?"

He jumped up and blocked the passage to the entryway. "Don't try to leave. And don't think you can call anyone. I cut the phone line."

This kid was smart.

"I won't try to leave." To prove the point I rose slowly, took off my coat, and draped it over the back of my chair. Then I took milk and bread from the refrigerator, peanut butter and cocoa from the cupboard.

Body tense and eyes wary, he watched me make peanut butter toast and hot chocolate. I set his plate and mug on the table. He waited until I sat down to lower himself into a chair. He wolfed down the food and drained the mug in a few gigantic gulps.

"Would you like more?"

He slid the plate in my direction, staring at it as if waiting for the food to materialize. Over his bent head, I saw Velma Albright pressing her face against the window of the door to the landing outside the entryway. Her eyes widened as she took in back of the snow-covered figure across from me.

I tended to the kid. "How about eggs and bacon this time?"

He nodded. His teeth began to chatter and his body shook.

I poured him more cocoa. "Drink this while I get you an afghan."

He held the warm mug against his cheek while I fetched the blanket and draped it over his shoulders. When he began to gulp down the cocoa, I pivoted and met Velma's gaze.

"Fly Ranch boy," I mouthed.

A brief shake of her head and she was gone.

The boy snapped to attention. "What was that?"

"I didn't hear anything." I'd *seen* Velma disappear. "Probably the furnace. It's noisy, but I'm used to it."

He remained tense and watchful, so I narrated my movements to put him at ease. "The frying pan is in the bottom cupboard next to the stove. I'm going to bend down and pull it out. It might be sort of loud." My prattle continued until his food was cooked and the full plate was in front of him. I waited until the plate was emptied to speak.

"What's your name?"

"Russ Hansen." He held out his mug for a refill.

I poured the last of the cocoa into it. "Where are you from, Russ?"

"Fly Ranch." He burped. "Excuse me."

"You're excused. Where did you grow up?"

The snow on his hat and parka had melted. He peeled off the damp things and dropped them to the floor. First the coat, then the hat. Long bangs fell across his face. "Sioux City."

"Are you kidding? I'm from Sioux City. What part of town?"

He pushed the hair out his eyes. "Riverside."

"My parents live in Morningside, but my mom teaches at Riverside Elementary. She's been there forever. Maybe you know her. Doris Newell?"

He froze.

I'd touched a nerve.

He thawed. "She was my third grade teacher. Before the Christmas program that year, the school nurse cleaned me up and cut my hair. Your mom gave me a suit and dress shirt to wear. Even a tie. She said her son had outgrown them."

I remembered the day Mom took that suit jacket from Jeff's closet.

"He's always so dirty, Harold." She set Jeff's outgrown dress shoes in a paper sack and laid the folded jacket, pants, and dress shirt on top of them. "His parents don't have two nickels to rub together."

Dad's lips pressed together. "They probably don't have running water."

"The other children tease him because he smells. They act like he's stupid, but he's a smart kid. Smarter by half than most of them, but he doesn't know it. I worry about what will happen to him in the future, but I can make him presentable for the Christmas program."

Dad wheeled to their dresser and took out a few bills from what they'd been squirreling away for Christmas. His hand shook as he held the money out to Mom. "Get him new underwear and socks while you're at it. We can cut a few corners. Reuse the wrapping paper we kept from last year. Make stocking stuffers instead of buying them."

I brushed away tears with my sleeve and composed myself by taking a deep breath. Still a big mistake.

"Would you like to see some pictures of Mom? There are a bunch in the photo album beside the couch."

His face brightened. I got the album and handed it to him. Then I returned to my chair with its view of the window to wait for Velma and her posse. Russ paged through the album. When he came to a picture of Mom, he pointed at her with a grubby finger.

His lips trembled. "Are you gonna tell her what I done?"

"I don't know." It wasn't a lie. "Why don't you tell me why you did it, and then I'll decide what to tell her?"

He gave an almost imperceptible nod and began to talk. Not to me. To the picture of Mom. "I got sent to Fly Ranch for selling pot at school. I never sold much. Just enough to pay for my own and to buy groceries for my mom and little sister. The time before this last one, the judge said he'd send me away for as long as the law allowed if he laid eyes on me in court again. I shoulda believed him."

"Is the ranch a bad place to live? Is that why you ran away?"

He shut the album and spoke to me. "I have my own bed, clothes that fit, and as much as I can eat. Even school was okay." He lifted his chin and straightened his shoulders. "My teacher says at the rate I'm going, I'll finish my GED by spring. I didn't want to run."

"Then why did you?"

He picked up his fork and plucked at the tines. They emitted a low, steady hum. "My roommate framed me. He hid some pot in my mattress."

"How did he get his hands on marijuana out here?"

"He coulda scored it on a trip to the Black Hills. But I think somebody at the ranch is dealing. A counselor or a teacher maybe."

"Are you sure?"

"You sound like the counselor who found the pot. He's a jerk." The fork tines twanged. "I swore it wasn't mine, that my roommate was lying. He lied all the time. My roommate chumped me, and I don't like being chumped. Soon as the counselor left, I decked my roommate. I figured that's why he snuck out that night and ran for it. When he turned up dead—"

Edgar.

"—the jerk counselor hauled me to the office. He coulda warned me that the sheriff was there, but did he? No. He just sat there while the sheriff lit into me. I told him the truth. That Edgar left while I was asleep. The jerk knew I was telling the truth. He's the one who came in during bed check. He shook me awake, wanting to know where Edgar had gone. I said how would I know? Me and Edgar weren't best friends or anything.

"I told the sheriff everything I knew, even about getting so pissed off I decked Edgar. The sheriff was real interested in that. Asked me about it so many times, I lost count. He practically accused me of murder. The jerk sat there. Didn't back me up. What a loser."

"So you ran because the sheriff won't believe you, and the jer—um, the counselor didn't vouch for you?"

The mention of the sheriff turned him surly. "I ran because I think the drug dealer killed Edgar. I'm not stupid. I'm not waiting around for him to come after me next."

"But instead of getting as far away as possible, you've been skulking around Little Missouri in the middle of winter, eating out of garbage cans, and freezing half to death. If you're not stupid, why stick around?"

He licked his lips. "I've got my reasons."

"Tell me what they are."

He stood and began to pace. "Why should you believe me when nobody else does? I'm holding you hostage."

"For starters I found Edgar's body, and it feels to me like there's something off. Plus I'm Doris Newell's daughter. She said you were a good kid. Smart, too. This is your chance to prove her right."

He slumped into the chair and covered his face with his hands. After a long minute, he let them fall into his lap. "You'll hear me out?"

As I opened my mouth to assure Russ that he could trust me, the sheriff tiptoed in from the entryway, crept up behind him, and pinned his arms to his sides.

Russ swore. He glared at me. Footsteps sounded from behind me. Dick appeared beside me. Vince Douglas grabbed my arm and pulled me through the kitchen toward the laundry room. But not before Russ swore again.

"You liar," he snarled.

Chapter 25

"**L**et go," I hissed at Vince.

He didn't.

"Let go, or I'll bite."

That got his attention. He loosened his grasp and whispered. "The sheriff said to keep you out of danger."

"Are you seriously referring to Russ? He's scared. He's cold. He's exhausted and hungry. But he's not dangerous."

The sheriff and Russ were still tussling on the far side of the kitchen table. Dick Phillips stepped in front of me like he was trying to protect me. Why? Russ had been sitting at the table talking. Harmless. Had I looked like I needed protecting? Did any of these men know how to read a room?

Dick narrowed his eyes. "What do *you* call a kid who cuts your phone line, breaks into your house, and holds you hostage?"

"Weren't you listening before? He's scared, cold, exhausted, and hungry." I pushed past Dick. What was playing out in front of us was inexcusable.

"Why are you doing that?" I snatched away the hand-cuffs the sheriff was about to fasten around Russ's wrists.

Rick resorted to hammerlocking Russ. "He committed a serious offense."

"Oh for the love of Pete." I slid the cuffs inside my bra for safekeeping. Oh my gosh, they were cold. I bit down on my lip to keep from gasping until I could speak again. "I'll go through this one more time. He's a scared, cold, exhausted, and hungry kid. He doesn't have a weapon. He didn't look for a knife, and he never threatened me. He sat at my kitchen table and ate everything I fed him. He appreciated my cooking, and I refuse to press charges against him. It wouldn't be right."

I winked at Russ. He bit his lip to hide what could have been a smile. Or a scowl. Or a grimace of pain as the sheriff shoved him into a chair. A little harder than necessary if anyone had asked me. Which no one had done even once since entering my apartment.

I took matters into my own hands, went over to Russ, and stood beside him. "This young man is from my hometown. My mom was his third grade teacher. We were reminiscing about her when you interrupted us. You have to take him to Fly Ranch, but before you do"—I turned and spoke to him as if we were alone again—"I want you to know that you can talk to me about whatever you want. If you want me to give your mom or your brothers and sisters or anyone else a private Christmas message"—I paused to let my words sink in—"you can call me anytime."

I took the picture of my mom from the picture album and wrote my phone number on the back of it. Then I put it in Russ's hand and folded his fingers over it.

"Any time," I said. "I mean it."

He began to cry. Big, racking sobs that started in his toes and were determined to escape. I put his head on my shoulder and whispered into his ear. "Tell the sheriff everything you were about to tell me. Right now. Right here."

His gaze bounced from me to Dick and Vince, and from them to the sheriff. "Are you taking me to jail?"

The sheriff glared at me. "Since Jane isn't pressing charges, you're going back to Fly Ranch."

Dick took Russ by the elbow. "I'll get him there." He pulled him to his feet. "Let's go."

Russ's head reared back as if he'd been slapped. Terror flashed in his eyes. He didn't protest or speak because he couldn't. He cowered like a rabbit caught in a trap. He was waiting to die.

Once they were outside, Vince asked, "How do you know he wasn't feeding you a load of hooey?"

I rounded on him. "How do you know he was?"

"Kids like him. They shade the truth a little here. Twist the facts a little there. Take it from me. They can't be trusted."

A wave of tiredness hit me. I couldn't wait for him to go. I dropped into Russ's chair. "Please leave."

"Thanks for your help." The sheriff gave Vince's shoulder a man-to-man pat. "Now if you don't mind, I need to speak with Jane in private."

"Any time, Sheriff." He zipped his coat and turned up its collar. "I was glad to do it. See you, Jane."

I stared at my hands until the door clicked shut. Now to get rid of the sheriff. I was raising my head to look at him when something on the floor caught my eye. It was

Russ's hat. I picked it up and rushed outside onto the landing. "Hey Russ! You might need this."

Russ was seated in the cab of Dick's truck and couldn't hear me. So I yelled at Dick, who was going around to the driver's side, and at Vince. He was halfway to his vehicle which was in front of Dick's on Main Street. Vince jogged toward me, and I lobbed it to him when he was close enough. Vince tossed it to Dick and walked to his own truck.

Russ opened his door, and Dick returned his hat. He also took something from his coat pocket and tucked it into Russ's. Whatever it was gleamed white in the weak light of the street lamp. Maybe a sandwich in a plastic bag? It was hard to tell from where I stood.

A gust of cold slapped at me. I shivered and went inside. Rick was seated at the table scribbling in the little notebook he always carried.

"Sorry about that." I plopped into the chair across from him. My tiredness returned. I slouched down and closed my eyes.

"Returning a kid's hat doesn't require an apology. Can I make you some coffee or tea?"

"That would be lovely." I kept my eyes shut. "The tea bags are in the cupboard between the stove and the refrigerator."

A cupboard squeaked open—"Found 'em."—and banged shut. I listened as he filled the kettle. A gas burner lit with a whoosh. Only then did Rick speak again. "You can change your mind about pressing charges."

With my eyes still closed, I fished in my bra for the handcuffs and laid them on the table. The action required immense effort. I was so tired. "I'm not going to do that to a tired, hungry kid who did something stupid. Did you know Edgar was his roommate at Fly Ranch?"

"Yes. I tried to interview him, but the kid wouldn't talk."

I opened my eyes and straightened. "He's scared, Rick. That's why he ran."

"Scared of what?" Rick poured boiling water into a mug and set it in front of me, along with a tea bag.

"You arrived before he gave me the whole story. But from what he did say, he's more afraid of a who"—I blew on the tea to cool it—"than a what."

"Who then?"

I thought about what Russ had said about someone at the ranch dealing drugs and of the bag Dick had slipped into Russ's pocket. Had it been a sandwich or something else?

"He said something about a night counselor not being on the up and up."

"Did he mention a name?"

I sipped at the tea. Still too hot. "No, and I wouldn't have recognized it if he had. The only counselor I know out there is Dick Phillips." I shrugged. "Maybe start with him?"

"I will." Rick wrote in his notebook. "Thanks."

I raised my mug in a mock toast. "Here's hoping it leads to answers."

A pounding at the door made the mug jump in my hand. I yelped as hot tea splashed onto my neck and shirt.

Rick threw me a kitchen towel on his way by. "I'll get

rid of whoever it is while you clean up and change. Some of the kid's stink is stuck on you."

I took fresh clothes from my bedroom to the bathroom. After a blissful few moments in the shower, I dressed. The clothes I'd worn to Hank and Ruby's, from coat to mittens to undies and everything in between, went in the washing machine. I turned it on and went to the kitchen to move Rick along. He was gone, and Velma was sitting in his chair.

She began firing orders without so much as a hello. "You get in your bedroom and pack an overnight bag. We gotta air out yer apartment. Otherwise the stink in here'll git into the paneling, and I'll never get it out. The sheriff opened your windows before he left, and I cranked the furnace down. Merle's gonna keep watch on this place, and you're gonna stay overnight with me. Your parents called Betty and she told them your phone line was cut. I stopped Betty before she could tell them why. They're going to call you at my house in"—she consulted her watch—"about an hour."

Her words galloped past me at first. It took a minute for them to circle back and penetrate my brain. Another sleepover with Velma. At her trailer instead of here. And a phone call from my parents. I stifled a whimper.

"Don't just stand there, girl. I got a chicken in the oven and cinnamon rolls rising for breakfast. Get a move on."

Why hadn't she led with that?

"I'll be ready in five minutes." My mouth watered as I pushed past Velma and into the bedroom. "Maybe less."

Chapter 26

I threw my toiletry bag in my duffel, along with pajamas and a change of clothes.

Velma yelled from the living room. "You got something in there for church?"

"What's it to you? You don't go to church."

"But you do. Tomorrow's the last service before you head out for Iowa, and folks will want to see you. Now quit your sass and do it."

I traded my sweatshirt for a red sweater and my ratty jeans for grey wool trousers. They would have to be dry cleaned to get rid of the cigarette odor after a night at Velma's. Who was going to pay for that? Unless I missed my guess, it wasn't going to be Velma.

I joined my slumber party buddy and fashion consultant in the living room. "Let's go."

"Not until you're dressed for the weather."

Make that slumber party buddy, fashion consultant, and surrogate mother.

We stepped into Velma's trailer and were greeted by

the aromas of roast chicken and cinnamon. They almost masked the stale smoke smell, but not quite.

I sneezed.

"Gesundheit." Velma took of her coat and boots and put them in a small closet. "Put your winter gear in there. Then get a move on and help with supper."

I got a move on. Soon we were seated at her small kitchen table piling chicken, warm bread, roasted potatoes, gravy, and cooked carrots onto our plates. The smells set my head to spinning.

She watched me tear into my food. "How long since you ate?"

The answer would have to wait. Flavor exploded in my mouth as I chewed. Everything was so good I nearly cried. Only the thought of Velma's reaction to such behavior sucked the tears back into their ducts.

I picked up the salt shaker. "I had a big salad for lunch. Those calories ran out during the Fly Ranch boy's visit."

"Well that explains why you're wolfing down your meal like you ain't laid eyes on food for a blue moon." She rested her elbows on the table and laced her fingers together. "About the kid. How much of what happened this afternoon"—she raised her penciled-in eyebrows until they were even with her dyed black widow's peak— "are you wantin' your parents to know about before you talk to them?"

The salt shaker nosedived into my mashed-potato-and-gravy lake. "Nothing! Nothing at all!" My voice was shrill in my ears. I drank a little water and tried again. "What I mean is that I want to break it to them. In my own way." Which meant never telling Mom anything about it. Ever. And probably not Dad either. My fingers shook as I fished the salt shaker out of the gravy and wiped it with my napkin.

"That's kinda what I was thinking, considering what I've seen of your mother." She marched to the phone and picked up the receiver with a take-no-prisoners attitude. "I'll warn Betty so she doesn't blab it all." From what I gathered from Velma's side of the conversation, Betty protested loud and long.

Velma gave as good as she got. After a few of what Velma later informed me were suggestions, but what Betty may have perceived as threats, Velma banged the receiver into the cradle and marched back to the table. She sat, stabbed a piece of chicken with her fork, and devoured it.

I expected her to recount Betty's end of things. Instead she asked me to pass the vegetables. I held the bowl out of her reach. "What did she say?"

She harrumphed.

"You can harrumph all you want, but my parents are calling any minute, and I need to know what Betty's going to tell them."

"Oh, all right." She plunked her fork on her plate. "She's gonna keep her mouth shut about you and that Fly Ranch boy. She'll say Dick Phillips cut your phone line when he got over-enthusiastic shoveling your sidewalks and cleared a path behind the school build—"

"What are you talking about? Dick didn't shovel at the school."

Velma held her palms up and out in self-defense. "I'm just telling you what Betty said Merle told her. Only not the part about shoveling behind the building. Betty made that up. Merle said he watched Dick clear your driveway."

"Why would he do that?"

Velma shrugged. "The school janitor from Tipperary who's in charge of snow removal is a lazy old goat. He mighta got Dick to do it."

The phone rang. Velma gave me a look. "Who's gonna answer?"

I jumped up. "Me."

"Fine and dandy." She picked up her fork and skewered another piece of meat.

I picked up the receiver. "Hi Mom."

"Oh, Jane! It seems like ages since we heard your voice!"

Her voice was as highly charged as the Energizer Bunny. It would take some finessing to wear her out. I'd done it with Russ. I could do it again now.

"We talked this morning, Mom."

"I'm well aware of that, young lady, but when Betty connected me with your phone this afternoon to give you a *very* important message, there was this terrible buzzing, which Betty said could mean there was something wrong with your phone line, like it was cut or something, but that her husband—I think his name is Gus—was on another service call out in the country and it would be hours before he could check on you—"

She was on a roll. I knew better than to interrupt.

"—and what if something happened to your father while you were without phone service? What if he had been taken to the hospital? How could I let you know? I can't drive all the way to that godforsaken wilderness to tell you."

I waited a few seconds to be certain her battery had run down. "You would tell Betty. Betty would call Merle. Merle would walk over and tell me or leave a note. Gus would fix the phone line. I would call you back."

"Oh." Silence. Then a deep inhale. "But, and I've raised this concern before, every single person you named is old. And tonight you're staying with that grumpy janitor in her smoke-filled trailer—"

"She invited me to stay so you could call in case Gus doesn't get the phone line fixed until morning."

"But she's old too, not a day under seventy from the looks of her. There have to be a few young people in Little Missouri. Why aren't you friends with them?"

How had she re-energized so quickly? What could I say to power her down again? I pictured Dick in his abominable snowmobile suit. Ah, yes. He would do.

"Dick Phillips, the guy who shoveled the snow, is about my age."

"Is he the one who cut your phone line?"

"Yes."

"So you're saying that all the young people out there are incompetent."

"Not all. I haven't met them all."

"Well if this fellow—Dick Philco or whatever you called him—is any indication of the future of that little town, it's in big trouble."

This call needed to end.

"What's the message, Mom?"

"What?"

"You said you called this afternoon with a very important message. What is it?"

"Oh. That." Silence again. "I don't remember. This

phone line business drove it right out of my head. Would you like to talk to your father?"

"I would love to."

"I'll say goodbye and give your father the phone."

"Don't talk too long, Harold," I heard her say before Dad came on the line. "Our phone bill can't take it."

I gave him a brief, yet colorful synopsis of my visit with Hank and Ruby York, minus the moon boots and Hank's temper. Dad would never intentionally tell Mom about what we'd discussed about the investigation. But by evening, he usually wasn't at his best. He might let something slip. The censored version of my visit must have struck his funny bone because Mom's voice came on the line again.

"Jane, I don't know what you said to your father, but he can't stop laughing. And he can't say a word. Good-bye, dear." She hung up.

I gently placed the receiver in the cradle. I considered any night graced by my dad's laughter to be a good one. I closed my eyes and held onto the moment. My eyes flew open when a terrible racket brought Velma to her feet.

The doorknob rattled. The dishes rattled. "Let me in, Velma," a man shouted above the noise he was making. "I know Jane Newell's in there. I have to talk to her. Now!"

Chapter 27

"Quit your hollering, Gus! We're not deaf." Velma flung the door open with enough force to drag the poor man, who was still jiggling the doorknob, over the threshold. He stumbled. Velma caught him by the elbow and righted him.

"There isn't any call for yelling like that unless you're being chased by a rabid skunk or an axe murderer." She peered into the darkness as if checking to see which one was lurking there. Then she slammed the door shut.

"You gonna let go of me before my elbow falls off from lack of circulation?" Gus twisted his arm away. "You want me to be blind and one-handed too?"

Velma let go and gave Gus a stink-eye. If he could have seen it, it would have withered him. He glared right back.

How did he know to do that?

Neither of them blinked. All I wanted was to finish my supper and go to bed. But I couldn't until one of them broke their stalemate. If my recess whistle had been handy, I would have used it. Instead I cracked an artificial and very noisy yawn.

"I'm beat, Gus." I stretched my arms above my head, the effect lost on a blind man. "What do you need?"

His face crumpled. "Miss Newell, I apologize for barging in so late. It's all because of my Betty. She said not to bother coming home until your phone repair was finished on account of your parents being upset and all." He gave a little bow. "I'm happy to report the repair has been completed."

Velma exploded. "Gus Yarborough, you coulda called with that message instead of pretty near breaking down my front door. You don't got the sense God gave a pig!"

Gus held up a finger. "I would like to place a call from Miss Newell's phone to yours to test the connection, but her door is locked." He turned his back on Velma. "Could you let me into your apartment?"

No! I wanted to eat, put on my pajamas, and go to bed—not traipse through the snow in the dark. I yawned, this time for real.

I found my purse and dug out the key. "Here." I laid it on his open palm. "I trust you. Just bring it back when you're done."

He left and I finished my stone cold supper. Then I tried to help Velma clear the table. She said I should get ready for bed and showed me where the bathroom was. A few minutes later I emerged wearing my pajamas.

Velma held out a fitted sheet. "It's about time you got out here. We gotta make up the hide-a-bed." I was grabbing for one end when the phone rang. She snatched the sheet away and snapped it open over the mattress.

"It's probably Gus. You answer it."

I picked up and said hello.

"Your line is in tip top shape, Miss Newell. I'll bring back the key."

He hung up, and I rejoined Velma. We were smoothing the blankets when the metal porch steps clattered. The distance between the foot of the bed where I was standing and the door was less than a yard. I pivoted and turned the knob.

Gus held up my key. "Here you go, Miss Newell."

I took it from him. "Thanks, Gus."

"All in a day's work." He clapped a hand to his forehead. "Oh, I almost forgot. My Betty said to tell you that she let your mother know your phone's been fixed."

"Tell Betty thank you too." I stepped onto the metal porch and hugged Gus around the neck.

The cold burned on the soles of my bare feet. I pushed away from Gus and hopped into the trailer. My momentum propelled him backwards. His arms began to windmill, and his hand grasped the spindly stair railing at the last minute.

"I'm so sorry, Gus," I apologized. "That was all my fault."

"No harm done." He was breathing hard.

"Tell Betty thank you from me and pass along the hug, will you? Not the bit where you almost fell down the stairs. But the rest of it."

"For the love of my heating bill, finish your goodbyes and quit letting in the cold air." Velma stomped over and shut the door in Gus's face.

"Why did you treat him like that? You're not being very neighborly." My feet were simultaneously ice and fire. I danced from one to the other. Discreetly, I hoped.

"The Yarboroughs live two blocks away. They're not my neighbors." She stomped into the kitchen, took a saucepan from the cupboard, and banged it down on a stove burner. "What kind of fool pulls a stunt like you just did when it's cold like this? Now can you get into that bed and sit yourself up without doing anything else stupid while I make us something to drink and get a hot water bottle for your feet?"

I demonstrated that I could.

She filled the water bottle from the tap and propped it against the soles of my feet. I didn't move a muscle as she wound a scarf around my feet and the bottle to hold it in place. Then she pulled the blankets up to my waist. I leaned against the back of the sofa bed. My eyelids drooped, and I listened to Velma pour and stir, pour and stir. When she brought my cup of hot cocoa, I forgave her for being mean to Gus. I took a sip. Warmth traveled from my throat to my torso to my toes. What had she added to the milk other than cocoa and sugar?

I wrapped my hands around the cup. "What did you do after you saw me and the Fly Ranch boy in my apartment this afternoon?"

She sat on the edge of the sofa bed. "I come home fast as I could and called the sheriff. He said to tell Fly Ranch to send someone to Round the Bend to wait 'til he got there. He said to tell Betty to send an EMT to the café without the ambulance. He didn't want the whole town getting riled up about it. Once them calls were made, he wanted me to go to the café and wait with the EMT and whoever came from Fly Ranch until he could get there, too."

"Okay." I drank more cocoa. "That explains why Vince and Dick showed up."

Velma shot me a malevolent look. "Is this your story or mine?"

"Yours." What else could I say? I mean, she had alerted the rescue party. Not that I needed rescuing from Russ Hansen. Another five minutes with him and he would have turned himself in. But Velma hadn't known that.

She gave a curt nod. "Before I could so much as find a booth, Dick Phillips and that Vince fella'—I forget his last name—stormed in like they were on their way to a five-alarm fire. They were determined to bust into your apartment without waiting for the sheriff. I gave them a piece of my mind, if you know what I mean."

I kinda did.

"I told them to sit their butts down unless they wanted a taste of how I treated drunks when I was a bouncer—"

"You were a bouncer?" The look she gave me could have soured my hot cocoa. I took a sip. It hadn't. I swallowed the mouthful.

"I promise not to interrupt again."

"They took me serious and stayed quiet until the sheriff got there and laid out his plan. We would park a block north of the school and walk to the door of your classroom furthest from your apartment. I was to unlock your room"—She preened a bit here. Who could blame her?—"and leave quick as I could. Rick said they would army crawl through the schoolroom. I'da given my eyeteeth to see that. Then Dick and Vince were to take the bathroom hallway while he went through the entryway."

I had a million questions. What if Russ had heard them? What if that had made him run away again? Or grab a kitchen knife and threaten me? What would Rick have done if Russ had moved from the chair where Velma had seen him? Would Rick have drawn his gun? I opened my mouth to voice my concerns, but Velma's scorching look shut me up.

"The sheriff told Dick and Vince to wait in the hall until he hollered for them to get you outta there. We followed the sheriff's orders to a tee up to when I unlocked the door. After that I don't know." She took my empty cup. "Unless you care to tell me what happened after I left."

I picked up the story. "Neither Russ nor I heard anything until Rick came into the room and restrained him. The other two did what they'd been told. Until I threatened to bite them. Really, it was over almost before it started." I put a hand on her shoulder. "Thanks for what you did, Velma. You're a good friend."

She squeezed my hand, and the tension went out of her shoulders. Her eyes went shiny and damp. For a second, I thought she might be nice back. Silly me.

"If you're trying to soften me up so you can skip church tomorrow, don't even think about it." She pushed my hand away and stood. "It's getting late, and believe me when I say that skipping your beauty rest will not do you any favors."

I scooched under the covers while she tore around the trailer. She set an alarm clock and slammed it on the end table next to the sofa bed. She turned off the lights and ordered me to limit my morning shower to three minutes. "Now good night and I don't want to hear a peep out of you until morning."

"Good night." I smiled with all the sweetness I could muster. "And thank you again."

She stomped into her bedroom, mumbled, "You're welcome," and slammed the door so violently the entire trailer and everything in it shook.

I rolled over and yawned contentedly as the sound of pans rattling in the cupboard and the tea kettle trembling on the stove rocked me to sleep.

Chapter 28

"Darn it, Velma, all that pounding made me smudge my mascara." I spit on a tissue and rubbed at the dark spot under my eye.

"You mess around in there much longer and your oatmeal will get cold." She whacked the bathroom door again. It sounded like a yardstick. I hoped it wasn't one of those free ones from the lumberyard like Mom used for spankings when I was a kid. Those suckers hurt like the dickens.

I opened the door, caught hold of whatever she was waving at me, and pulled it away from her. It was the wooden spoon, and if the goo oozing between my fingers was any indication, she'd been using it to stir oatmeal.

"Serves you right," she gloated.

I made a big show of licking the spoon and smacking my lips. "It could use more salt."

Velma snatched the spoon and chased me to the table. I sat down and ate my porridge like a model house guest. Then I thanked Velma for all she'd done, gathered my things, and walked to my apartment. There was just enough time before the service began to close the windows—the stink had dissipated nicely—turn up the furnace, and move laundry from the washer to the dryer.

Cookie Sternquist greeted me when I walked into the church foyer. "Jane, are you doing okay? Rick told me about you and the Fly Ranch boy. And that you spent the night with Velma. What in the world was he thinking?"

"I'm fine. Don't be too hard on Rick. Knowing Velma, she didn't give him time to think."

"You're right about that." Cookie chuckled and then grew serious. "Tiege's not going to let me hear the end of this, but would you would mind if we rescheduled tonight's supper invitation? Christmas is only a week away, and our tree still isn't decorated. I have yet to wrap a single present. Tiege's getting a little worried."

"With everything that's happened in the past twenty-four hours, a day at home sounds wonderful. My presents aren't wrapped yet either."

"Maybe you could come after Christmas vacation?"

"Let's plan on it."

"Good." Cookie squeezed my hand. "Now I'd better get to the piano and play the prelude."

She dashed off. I entered the sanctuary more slowly. It was crowded, and I slid into an open spot at the end of the back pew. Too late, I realized the person next to me was Rique DuPeuss. Oh joy.

The final piano chords faded, and Pastor Petersen went to the lectern. He gestured for everyone to rise for the opening prayer. There was a seat open in the Barkley's pew two rows ahead. I made my move as the pastor said, "Would you bow—"

Someone tapped my shoulder. I yelped, shot up like a firecracker on the Fourth of July, and landed on Rique's foot. He wobbled and used the pew in front of us to steady himself with one hand while steadying me with the other. The entire congregation turned in unison to see what the commotion was.

I extricated myself from Rique's grasp. "Thank you."

Before I could make good on my escape, Dick Phillips entered the pew. I tried to push him away, but he just blushed and refused to budge.

For the next hour I was wedged between the two. I prayed for a short sermon. And to sing just one verse of each hymn and carol. And for a fast getaway. *In the present situation,* I informed God in no uncertain terms, *this is not too much to ask.*

He delivered on two of my three requests. Pastor Petersen's sermon clocked in at ten minutes. Cookie played the "Amen" chords after the first verse of each song. After the benediction, however, Dick and Rique remained where they stood. I was about to drop onto all fours and crawl to freedom when Bud Sternquist came up the aisle. He clapped a hand on Dick's shoulder and drew him from our pew. I wanted to kiss him. Bud, that is. Not Dick.

Tiege took me by the hand and led me to the corner next to the kitchen. "You got to see this, Miss Newell." He recited his Christmas program lines flawlessly. His inflections, gestures, and facial expressions would have wowed Walt Disney. It certainly wowed the congregation in the sanctuary. They applauded approvingly after Tiege finished. He ignored them, went down on one knee, and took my hand in both of his.

Was Tiege about to propose? How was I going to turn a seven-year-old kid down gently with so many people watching? The hand he was holding began to shake. Then all of me began to shake.

Tiege's face was solemn. He bit his lip before speaking. "Would you please—"

I tried to twist my hand away to no avail.

"—tell my brother that I got my part all memorized so I can go sledding this afternoon?"

My shaking turned into giggling. Uncontrollable, eye-watering, snot-inducing giggles. Tiege gave me a red bandana. I mopped my eyes and fought to regain my composure. It took a while.

Finally, I tugged at Tiege's hand. "Stand up, you crazy kid. Let's find your brother and end your house arrest." Once I vouched for Tiege and his brother sprung him loose, my favorite Christmas tree whooped and ran off.

"How you holding up?" Rick asked.

"From what? My afternoon with Russ or spending the night with Velma?"

He grimaced. "Sorry about that. When we made our plan at the café, she said she wouldn't unlock the school until I promised to notify her once the coast was clear so she could haul you to her trailer. Was it terrible?"

I let him off the hook easier than he deserved. "Not as bad as I expected. Plus it was a chance to air out the apartment. If I'd known my clothes and hair would absorb the stench of a herd of cats, I would have cut my visit to Hank and Ruby's shack short."

"What were you doing there?"

"Checking to see if the boots Hank wore to the Community Christmas par—"

The word died on my lips too late. Rick's face hardened. He put his hands on my shoulders, steered me into the kitchen, and shut the door.

"What about Hank's boots?"

I crossed my arms, hoping to wait him out.

"You can tell me, or I can charge you with obstructing my investigation."

The jig was up. "The boots Hank wore to the Community Christmas party were the spitting image of the ones Edgar Running Horse was wearing the day before he died."

"The Christmas party was two weeks ago. You should have said something immediately," he roared.

"At first I thought it was just a coincidence and didn't give it a second thought." That sounded lame, even to my ears. "I didn't think of it again until boot prints came up during show-and-tell. I was going to call you at the next recess. But Stig had a bloody nose and I forgot again. Then, when I told you about Rique and Dick, you bit my head off. I decided it was best not to mention Hank and the boots until I was more certain, which is why I took him and Ruby a casserole yesterday. My intention was to call you once I got home, but being held hostage and having my phone line cut put the kibosh on that. Is that a good enough explanation for you?"

I waited while he stood there, his expression as silent and cold as a December moon. I stalked to the door and turned the knob. When he didn't stop me, I hurried through the crowd in the church foyer, keeping my head down until I was outside.

The cold air cooled my burning cheeks and I filled my lungs with frosty air.

In one short hour, I'd been the center of attention not once, not twice, but three times. The more that happened, the greater the potential for the town gossips and Edgar's killer to get wind of my snooping around. I hurried home. When I came to the spot where Hank and Ruby's jar of beet pickles had broken open, I wished I'd taken a different route. The snow was still disturbingly blood red.

Chapter 29

I spent the rest of the day in my apartment. All doors locked. All windows closed. The phone tested and working. The record player blaring out Christmas carols to drown out the silence and to squelch the danger warnings my brain issued whenever I tried to relax.

I took advantage of my adrenaline rush and tackled the chores that had to be completed before I left for Iowa in six days. I did laundry, ironed, vacuumed, dusted, checked lesson plans, checked them again, and got out my suitcase. I wrapped and packed presents for my family, prepared a week's worth of lunches, and fell into bed too exhausted to heed danger warnings. Or alarm clocks.

The next morning light poured through the bedroom window when I woke up. I rubbed the sleep out of my eyes and squinted at the hands of my clock. Seven-thirty? Liv was coming to review the week's schedule at eight.

I leapt out of bed, scooped up my clothes, and

sprinted for the bathroom. Twenty-five minutes later, I strolled into my classroom clean, dressed, and with my hair scraped into a bun to hide the fact that it hadn't been washed.

When Liv arrived, she pulled out a schedule marked all over with crossed out sections, arrows, circles, and notes scribbled in the margins. She handed it to me, but I couldn't make sense of it. She took pity, scooted her chair next to mine, and explained it.

"Corinne comes today so she can make last minute adjustments. Tomorrow the rehearsal's here in your classroom, but you and I have to go to the church once the kids leave after school."

"Why?"

"To supervise the volunteers who are setting up the stage. You with me?"

I nodded.

"Wednesday and Thursday afternoon, we walk the kids to church for practice. Their parents will pick them up there. Friday, we have Christmas parties in our rooms during lunch. Then we go to final dress rehearsal at the church since school dismisses an hour early that day."

"So we can rest before the program?"

She burst out laughing. "Not hardly. More like so we've got time to mend torn costumes and broken props and set up the refreshment table."

I leaned back in my chair and let out a big breath. "This week is going to be a marathon. How are we going to do it?"

"Now that I've done it a few times, it's no big deal. The question is whether *you're* up for it." She gave me a

long, searching look. "I heard you had quite the weekend."

"So Betty told you?"

"Me and half the county. And we all told the other
half."

I slumped down in my chair. "Do the kids know?"

"I expect so."

"Urg!" I covered my face with my hands. "I really
don't want to start the week with a discussion about a Fly
Ranch boy being in my apartment."

The shouts of children coming from the playground
ended our conversation. I waited until Liv was in her
room to ring the bell. My students lined up and entered
the room. Their questions began before a single mitten
came off or a coat was shed.

Elva pressed a Hershey's kiss into my palm. "This'll
make you feel better."

Stig pulled a misshapen silver lump from the pocket
of his jeans. "I've got one for you, too. It sorta melted."

Cora and Bennan stood on either side of me and
hugged my legs. "Was he mean?" they asked in unison.

"Are you okay, Miss Newell?" Renny asked.

"Stop with all the questions," Tiege said in a fair
imitation of his father. "You ever think she maybe don't
want to talk about it?"

Beau stared at me with the sad, old-man expression
he wore when something reminded him of his mother's death. He hung up his coat and set his snow boots
beneath it. Then he slipped his small hand into mine.
We walked into the classroom with none of the joyful
fa-la-la-la falderal that should herald the start of the
week before Christmas. Darn Betty Yarborough and

Little Missouri's rumor mill! I wanted to strangle the lot of them.

"Miss Newell." Beau winced and twisted his hand. "You're hurting me."

I let go. "I'm so sorry."

My apology wasn't enough. He pulled his hand away. As he went to his desk, I made a decision I hoped I wouldn't regret. After the Pledge of Allegiance, I walked to the front of the room. I told the children to ask their questions. My intention was to educate them about what had happened and squelch the rumors they'd heard. As it turned out, I was the one who got the education.

Renny wanted to know if Russ was high on drugs. "My dad says to stay away from those guys 'cause they're a bunch of potheads."

"My parents say it's a crying shame how city kids get shipped out here on land we need to raise cattle," Elva said.

The discussion devolved into a gripe session. Tiege complained about Rick working overtime when boys ran away. Cora and Bennan bickered about which roads had been ruined when the stupid Fly Ranch counselors had driven busses through the Long Pines during the spring thaw.

Even Beau spoke up. "Grandpa and Grandma don't like it when Fly Ranch boys come in the store. Grandpa says they're all shoplifters. They lie when they get caught, and the ranch won't pay us back for what got took."

The children were merely parroting what they'd heard their parents and others say. Many of those parents were my friends. Every one of them would come running to my aid if I needed them. I looked from one child to the next while putting my thoughts in order and praying for the right words.

"The boy who broke into my apartment did a very bad thing. I wanted to be mad at him and to blame him, but I couldn't. Do you know why?"

"Why?" Tiege asked.

"For one thing, he was cold and hungry and tired and not much older than my own brother. If my brother had been in that shape, I would have wanted someone to feed him and help him get warm. So I made something for the Fly Ranch boy to eat, and we started talking. Then, we discovered something amazing. We grew up in the same town, and my mother was his third grade teacher. Just like I'm your teacher."

My students were hooked.

"Like I said, that Fly Ranch boy did a very bad thing. But he's not just a Fly Ranch boy to me now. Neither is the boy who died in the Long Pines a few weeks ago. They are boys like my brother. They have names. Russ Hansen and Edgar Running Horse. They have stories. The hardest part of their stories is that their parents couldn't take care of them like your families care for you.

"Every boy at Fly Ranch did wrong things, and being at the ranch is how they are paying for those wrong things. I want you to remember that every one of the boys has a name, even though you might not know what their names are. Those boys have stories, though you may never hear them. More than likely, their stories have a lot of bad and sad in them.

"When we say bad things about them just because they're Fly Ranch boys, we add more bad to their stories.

But their stories don't need more bad. They need more good. From now on, in this classroom, we aren't going to say bad stuff about the ranch or the boys who live there. Instead, we're going to say and do good things, kind things to add good to their stories. I'm not sure how we'll do it, but you are smart kids. So let's put on our thinking caps and figure it out together."

Cora raised her hand. "Maybe we could make Christmas cards for Russ when we finish our seatwork?"

Tiege sprang from his chair. "How many boys are out there? We gotta make cards for all of them."

"I'll call the ranch during recess and find out." I added "Christmas cards" to the list of assignments on the chalkboard and set a stack of construction paper on the back table. With a burst of excited chatter, the children attacked their assignments. Just like that, the fa-la-la-la falderal that had been absent earlier that morning flooded our classroom with great and childlike joy.

Chapter 30

Corinne Wentworth and I were laying out costumes in my apartment when Liv rang the bell to signal the end of lunch recess. I draped Mrs. Santa's costume on a kitchen chair. "We didn't get as far as I thought, and now I have to abandon you."

"Don't give it a second thought." Corinne scooped up two green felt trees and laid the smaller one on the arm of the couch. "Cookie called last night and offered to come early and give me a hand before rehearsal."

"In that case, I'll leave you to it." Raised voices on the playground sent me scurrying to the classroom door where my students were lined up and chatting. Except for Renny. He was at the end of the line with his back toward me and his classmates. He was yelling at Gavin Wick, who was meandering toward Liv's students who were waiting outside her door. I put a finger to my lips to silence my students so I could hear what Renny was saying.

"Stop talking about Fly Ranch boys like that. They have names, you know."

He must have sensed the quiet behind him. He turned around and looked embarrassed when he saw seven pairs of eyes trained on him. He shut his mouth, but not for long.

"Right, Miss Newell?"

I flashed him a triumphant smile and raised my voice to guarantee that Gavin would hear what I said. "Right. They have names. And they have stories. Just like we all do." I gave each of the children a high five as they entered the entryway. Except for Renny. He got two.

The entryway was a jungle of coats, boots, and flailing limbs when Cookie squeezed through the door.

I was pulling at Stig's boot, but stopped and pointed to my apartment when she came in. "Corinne's expecting you. Go on through."

"Let me help you." Cookie held Stig by the shoulders. "Give it a yank now."

It worked. The boot came off. Stig toppled sideways. Cookie stood him upright before she went to join Corinne.

Later some of the students were completing seatwork at their desks while the first graders worked on a math lesson at the front table. Corinne tiptoed in and crossed to Tiege's desk. She tapped his shoulder and whispered in his ear. He laid down his pencil and they crept out of the room without being noticed. About five minutes later Tiege returned. He tapped Elva on the shoulder, signaled for her to go to the apartment, and the process repeated itself. An hour later, every child had made a silent trip to the apartment for a costume fitting. How had Corinne and Cookie worked such quiet magic?

"Psst. Miss Newell." Cora's whisper caught my attention. She pointed at the clock. "Can we go out for recess?"

I jumped up. "Oh my goodness. I lost track of time. Children, put your things in your desks, push them against the front wall so we're ready for program practice, and go outside." They were done and out the door in a flash.

When they came back into the classroom, Cookie and I supervised as they put on their costumes over their clothes. Liv took her students to my apartment where she and Corinne helped them do the same. Then everyone crowded into my classroom. Cookie took her seat at the piano and I shouted, "Action!"

The Christmas trees marched into place. Their costumes were so wide, the trees on the perimeter of their felt forest were smashed against the walls. The reindeer, completely in character, galloped on stage and snagged the elves' hats with their antlers. Hats went flying, as did the elves when they gave chase, only to trip over their curly-toed boots.

The trees elbowed one another, trying and failing to make room, but shedding ornaments like an evergreen dropping pine cones in a wind storm. Several reindeer got down on all fours to gather ornaments. Instead, their antlers tangled like bucks during mating season. When Cora bent to pick up her hat, a reindeer rear ended her. She fell onto the floor sobbing. Mrs. Santa Claus screamed. The older girls chimed in.

"Action" had been a poor choice of words.

Cookie's hands pounded a great crashing chord on the keyboard. The clamor ceased. She spoke, barely above a whisper. "Remember the rules, boys and girls."

They froze. They were motionless as Corinne went from child to child, gathering fallen bits of costumes, removing antler headbands, and reuniting elves with their hats.

"Now," she said after she gave Cora a hankie and told her to wipe her eyes, "let's pin the bottom branches of the trees back a bit and try that again."

A few minutes later Cookie played the introduction to the first song. The children found their places on stage again. Liv and I stood in front of them, directing the singing.

"Do you feel superfluous?" Liv whispered as the song ended.

"Completely." I went to cue Mr. and Mrs. Santa to move center stage for their duet. They were already there. "Do you know anything about Cookie's rules?"

"No. Let's make her stay until she tells us."

"Agreed."

The remainder of the rehearsal went off without a hitch. The children were taking their final bows when Cookie spoke again. "You did a lovely job, kids. Now, do you remember the rules?"

Apparently they did. My students lined up in front of Corinne and Liv's in front of Cookie. They helped the first child in each line slip off their costumes and hang them up. Then that child moved to the end of the line. When every costume had been shed, the children sat on the floor. Cookie and Corinne took the costumes into

the apartment and returned carrying a box and a thermos respectively.

"You followed the rules beautifully." Cookie held up
the box. "Now, are you ready for the cinnamon rolls?"

Corinne set the thermos on the sink counter. "And
apple cider?"

Liv and I grinned. We liked these rules!

***

The children went home after school with full stom-
achs, sticky fingers, and sugar highs. Except for Tiege.
He bounced to the sink and washed his hands. Then he
bounced from one desk to the next, pushing them into
place while his mom and Corinne performed costume
triage in my apartment.

He held up the empty box that Cookie had used for
the cinnamon rolls. "What should I do with this?"

"Check with your mom. If she doesn't want it, put it
in the burn barrel."

He bounced away and was back in no time. "She said
to throw it." Tiege ran the box outside and returned.
"The barrel's full. Can I burn the trash?"

"Go for it. You know where the matches are."

He got them from my desk and bounced outside.

I surveyed the room. Tomorrow's assignments were
on the chalkboard. Seat work packets were on the students' desks. Papers were corrected and grades recorded.
I could assist Cookie and Corinne with the costumes.

I crossed the classroom and opened the door between
its entryway and my apartment. It was impossible not to
overhear Cookie.

"Rick can't say much when he's in the middle of an investigation, but—"

But what?

"—I can tell when he's got a suspect in his sights. Something happened when he found that Fly Ranch kid—"

I wanted to burst in and shout, "His name is Russ Hansen!" But I wanted to eavesdrop more.

"—and he's showing every sign of getting ready to close this case. I think it has something to do with Dick Phillips."

"Dick?" Corinne sounded surprised. "He's an odd duck, but I like him."

Cookie laughed. "Odd ducks can get themselves into fixes."

So Rick thinks Dick is up to something shady too? I bit my lip. If that was the case, the time had come to tell Rick about Dick putting the bag in Russ's pocket. I straightened, entered the apartment, and got busy. The sooner Cookie and Corinne were gone, the sooner I could call the sheriff.

After a half hour of mending, chatting, and organizing the costumes, they were gone. I made a pit stop in the bathroom and then went to pick up the phone receiver. Before I got there, someone knocked. I crossed to the door, expecting to see Corinne or Cookie back to retrieve whatever'd been forgotten. Instead I saw Vince Douglas.

I stared through the window for a long minute before opening the door. Just a crack. I had no desire to entertain another unwanted visitor, and braced to slam it shut if he tried any funny business.

"I'm on my way to supper at The Bend and thought you might like a change of scenery after what happened Sunday." Vince shoved his hands in the pockets of his down jacket. "Want to join me?"

Yes, I wanted to join him. I also wanted to call Rick. I was also starving. I looked at the phone. The conversation with the sheriff might go down better with a full stomach. I looked at Vince. He didn't appear to be up to any funny business.

"Let me get my coat."

He crooked his arm when I stepped onto the landing, and I took it. As we walked down Main Street, sparkling snowflakes fell around us. Their beauty refused to silence the thought niggling in my head. I should have caught up with Vince at the café after calling Rick.

I'll call when I get home, I told myself. *I promise.*

Chapter 31

Except for Vince and me, the café side of The Bend was empty. We slid into the booth farthest from the drafty entrance. He faced the door. I faced the kitchen.

Trudy waved. Before taking our orders, she stopped at the phone and picked up the receiver. She cupped a hand over it and shot a glance in our direction as she began to speak.

I pretended to study the menu. "I predict that in the next thirty minutes, there will be a steady influx of customers checking out the man who's eating supper with the teacher."

Vince's forehead wrinkled. "You can't be serious."

"Just you watch."

Trudy hung up, took an order pad and pen from her apron pocket, and came to our booth. "Hi, Miss Newell. What can I get for you?"

I'd eaten more than one of Cookie's cinnamon rolls, and though my taste buds screamed for a cheeseburger and fries, better judgment argued in favor of a taco salad.

"Taco salad and a Diet Coke. Hold the sour cream." I tucked the menu into its slot behind the ketchup and mustard bottles.

Trudy arched her eyebrows and tipped her head at Vince with a gossipy, girlfriend vibe. "And for your—"

"His name is Vince." I gave him a dismissive wave. "He doesn't belong to me."

Her eyebrows flattened. I almost felt sorry for her. But not quite.

Vince ordered a salad with bleu cheese dressing, a sirloin steak cooked medium rare, and a baked potato.

"Anything to drink Mr.—?"

Trudy was not a quitter. I had to hand it to her.

"Coffee'll be fine."

She pinched her mouth shut and crammed the order pad into her apron pocket as she flounced off.

The door opened and a gust of cold air swirled around my ankles. I turned and smiled at Frost and Fannie McDonald.

"Why Miss Newell, fancy meeting you here!" Fannie's words sounded rehearsed. She and her husband sat down at the table closest to our booth. "Liv says the Christmas program is coming along nicely."

"I'm glad she thinks so." I turned back to Vince without introducing him. "And so it begins," I whispered.

Trudy was setting down our drinks when Burt and Iva Kelly arrived with Beau. Dale Cunningham and his wife were the next to make an appearance. Last but not least, Velma Albright and Merle Laird waltzed in. Not one of them had a motive other than hunger, I'm sure. I didn't introduce Vince to any of them.

Merle was the last to stop by our booth for a chat.

"We-ull, I got to find me a table." He sucked air between his teeth. "Unless you're gonna mind your manners and invite me to sit with you and your—"

"He doesn't belong to me." I pointed my fork at Merle and waggled the fingers on my other hand at Velma. She waggled in return like the true slumber party buddy she was. "It looks like Velma is saving you a place." Merle gave an exasperated sigh and gimped over to join her.

After Trudy brought our food, Vince cut into his steak. "How long have you lived in Little Missouri?"

"Since August. Why?" I poured taco sauce on my salad and stirred it around.

"You've lived here four months and have this town figured out." There was admiration in his voice as he eyed our fellow diners. "That's impressive. I think there's more to you than meets the eye."

He scrutinized my face. The attention made me as uncomfortable as the possibility of Velma jimmying the lock on my file cabinet and snooping around. I gave my food my complete attention.

"You know how to handle people."

I batted away the compliment. "School teachers are like that. We specialize in steering kids toward what needs to be done instead of what they want to do."

"Too bad Dick Phillips didn't pick up on your abilities. He thinks you filled that Fly Ranch boy's head with a bunch of hooey."

My response was slow and deliberate. "The Fly Ranch boy has a name. Russ Hansen."

"Point taken. I know better." He paused. "Anyway, Dick wasn't happy to be the one who had to bring Russ back to earth again."

"Dick Phillips is a jerk and a liar." I slammed my glass down. Diet Coke splattered the worn Formica. I grabbed a wad of napkins and sopped up the spill.

"I didn't fill Russ with false hopes. I talked him into telling me why he ran right before the three of you barged in. A little less enthusiasm on your part would have gone a long way with Russ. You scared the crap out of him."

Vince winced. "You're right about that. Dick stood outside the school and argued with the sheriff about the best way to capture Russ. The sheriff wanted to look in your apartment window to see if the boy posed a threat. Dick said the kid had a volatile temper and a history of violence. My toes nearly froze while they sniped at each other. I'd never seen Russ get violent. But Dick's the one with access to the files so I stayed out of it. He can be real persuasive, and he won the argument."

"What else did he say?"

"Do you mean Saturday or since then?"

"All of it."

"He gave me an earful yesterday about you. Didn't mince his words any." He laid his fork on his plate. "You sure you want to hear it?"

"I can deal with it."

"He said you ask a lot of questions."

That wasn't bad. It was true. I took a bite of taco salad.

"He also said that you like to stick your nose in where it doesn't belong."

That was bad. But also true. I stabbed at a piece of lettuce.

"He said he's keeping an eye on you because you like to string men along and can't be trusted."

My fork dropped into my salad. An eruption of lettuce, taco sauce, and cheese sent Frost and Fannie scooting their chairs out of range.

"Oops!" I apologized and snatched more napkins from the dispenser. "I guess I don't know my own strength."

Once they started eating again, I hissed at Vince. "How can he say that? He hardly knows me."

"That so?" Vince poured steak sauce onto his plate. "He made it sound like the two of you were an item. Until you dumped him."

An indignant retort sprang to my lips. When Vince looked at me, his face awash with admiration and empathy, I swallowed my angry words.

"What Dick said didn't jibe with my impression of you from the Christmas party. You could kinda say I had an ulterior motive for inviting you to supper tonight." He dabbed his meat in the steak sauce. "To see who was telling the truth. You or him."

My appetite vanished. I wadded my dirty napkins into a ball and dropped them on my plate. "Have you made your decision?"

He put a piece of steak in his mouth and took his time chewing and swallowing. "There's not a doubt in my mind, Wonder Woman." He held up his cup in a mock toast. "It's you."

Vince's faith in me was gratifying, but what he'd said about Dick's version of things creeped me out. The man had fabricated a relationship with me. No doubt he had shoveled the school sidewalks so he could spy on me. And followed me home from the Yorks' for the same reason. I shivered.

"You getting cold?" Vince motioned to Trudy. "Coffee for the lady, please."

It was a nice gesture, but hot coffee wasn't what I needed. What I needed was to go home and call the sheriff. To come clean about what I'd learned about Dick Phillips and to reiterate my suspicions about his involvement in Edgar's death. When Vince finally finished his meal and we paid our bills—I told him we had to go Dutch or Trudy would be on the phone again as soon as we left the café—he struggled to keep up with me on the way to my apartment.

His boot hit a slick patch and his arms windmilled as he fought to regain his balance. "What's the hurry?"

My pace didn't slacken. "I need to take care of something that I should have done before supper." I pointed to where his truck was parked. "Why don't you wait here until I'm in my apartment? I'll switch the porch light on and off once I've locked the door."

I hurried inside and blinked the light. He honked and drove away. I picked up the phone and asked Betty to ring the sheriff's office. No answer. I asked her to try his house in Tipperary. No answer there either. Betty suggested calling the Nine Pins in Tipperary to see if he was eating supper there. He wasn't. I suggested ringing the sheriff's parents. Cookie did pick up, but she didn't know where her son was.

"Do you want me to keep cawwing his office and his house?" Betty asked. "When he answers, I can put him through to you."

"That would be wonderful. Thanks, Betty."

I tried to read while waiting for the phone to ring, but all I could think about was Dick Phillips spying on me. I got up and peered through the window. Thankfully, there was no sign of him. I checked all the locks and pushed furniture against the doors. Then I took a basket of clothes from the dryer to the kitchen table to fold them. Next to the phone. So I could snatch up the receiver when Rick called.

He didn't call.

What good was a sheriff who showed up when he wasn't wanted and disappeared when I needed to talk to him? I picked up a pair of socks I'd folded into a neat ball and lobbed it at the phone. "Take that, Rick Sternquist!" I yelled. The action was so satisfying, I threw another pair. And another. And another until the floor under the phone was drifted with socks.

I shoveled everything into the laundry basket and turned to the living room window. "You're next, Dick Phillips!" I took aim and lobbed socks at the window until the basket was empty. Then I reloaded it and aimed at the window again. If Dick was watching, I wanted him to think that in addition to asking too many questions—*lob!*—being generally nosy—*lob!*—stringing men along—*lob!*—and lying—*lob!*—I was on the crazy side—*final lob!* Maybe then he would leave me alone.

I gathered the socks and put them in my dresser drawer. Then I locked myself in the bedroom and slid my nightstand in front of it. Just in case.

Chapter 32

The sheriff dropped by the next morning before school. "I hear you've been trying to find me."

None too gently, I set down the lesson plans I was reviewing. "Where were you yesterday evening?" After a night spent tossing and turning, I sounded whiny and immature. I didn't care.

He removed his hat and clenched its brim. "That isn't public knowledge. All I can say is that I was working on the murder investigation. Is that enough to pacify you?"

"Rick!" Tiege shouted from the landing. "I'm turning into an ice cube. Can I come in yet?"

"No, you may not." Rick shouted as he went to the door. He opened it a crack. "Go to the truck and wait there like you were told in the first place."

Tiege trudged to the truck after a good deal of foot stomping and huffing. Rick resumed the conversation. "Now, what did you want to see me about?"

I was itching to blast twin barrels of anger and frustration at him. The bags under his eyes and the lines on his forehead stopped me cold. He looked as tired as I felt. I gave up the fight and led him to the table at the front of the classroom. "What time did you get to bed last night?"

He sank into one chair with a sigh and propped one foot on top of the other. "I haven't yet." He closed his eyes.

"Are you closing in on a suspect?"

"More like eliminating them." He rubbed his temples. "Hank and Ruby swear up and down that they spent from Thanksgiving morning until early Sunday with relatives in the Black Hills. The only time Hank wasn't with his family was when he kept a doctor's appointment at the VA hospital in Sturgis on Friday. He says that they drove home Sunday after the roads were plowed and that he found the boots at the dump the same afternoon you discovered Edgar's body."

"Do you think he bullied Ruby into backing him up?"

He opened one eye and studied me. "You caught that vibe, did you?" He closed it again. "I've interviewed their family members and Hank's doctor. They all vouch for him, and I believe them. Hank's not the killer."

I tapped my pen on the table. "Have you checked into any other leads?"

"I really can't say." He slurred the words, like Dad did when he was tired.

I wanted to be angry with him, but couldn't. "I suppose you can't. Actually, I feel like you deserve an apology. There is something I forgot to mention the last time we talked."

He opened his eyes and swung his feet to the floor. "Go on."

"On Saturday, Dick Phillips slipped something into

Russ's coat pocket after escorting him to his truck. I thought it was a sandwich in a plastic bag and didn't give it a second thought until yesterday."

"What changed your mind?"

"A couple things." I fiddled with a cuticle on my thumbnail. "Vince Douglas and I went to supper at the café last night. According to him, Dick Phillips thinks my talk with Russ made the boy's situation worse."

The sheriff raised an eyebrow. "So you no longer have the power to make him blush?"

"Not according to Vince. It's more like Dick doesn't trust me. He keeps fabricating ways to keep tabs on me."

Rick took out his notebook. "What do you mean?"

"Well, more than once he showed up to shovel the school sidewalks without being asked. On Saturday he followed me home from the Yorks."

I chose my next words carefully before relaying what Cookie had said to Corinne. I didn't want to throw either woman under the bus.

"From what I've gathered, some people around town think he's got a knack for getting into predicaments."

"Was anything specific mentioned?"

"No. It's probably gossip without a shred of truth attached to it. Even so, it got me to thinking about what Russ said about the night counselor not being on the up and up. I think his exact words were that he thought a counselor or a teacher was dealing drugs at the ranch. Now I wonder if the little bag Dick put in Russ's pocket contained drugs and not a sandwich." I glanced at the clock. "Oh my word, it's time to ring the bell."

The sheriff rose. "I'll get out of your way." He walked to the door, swaying like a sloppy drunk.

I hurried over and took his elbow. "You're dead on your feet."

"I need to get to Tipperary"—a yawn split his face—"and put out some feelers about Dick."

"You need to get some sleep first. You're not fit to drive." I marched him into my apartment and ordered him to lay on the couch. "I'll have Betty call your parents and ask one of them to take you to Tipperary. You can nap here until they pick you up."

I pressed Betty into action. Then I collected Tiege from where he was sitting in the truck and took Rick's keys from the ignition. Tiege rang the bell while I put the keys on my kitchen table. Rick was sound asleep, snoring loud enough to make the windows rattle. A thin line of drool inched down his chin and pooled on his collar. I put a wad of tissues under his chin to limit the damage and tucked an afghan around him. Then I rushed to welcome my students to school at the door.

Tiege beat me to it. He was standing in the entryway, reminding his classmates to hang up their coats and arrange their boots along the wall.

"Go straight to your desks," he instructed his fellow students, "and take out your reading books."

"You've been a great assistant, Tiege. I can take it from here."

"I don't mind." He trotted to my desk, flipped my grade book, and took a pen from my desk drawer. "I'll take attendance for you."

The kid was about to stage a coup. I closed the grade book and steered him to his desk. "You're the only student who hasn't started his reading lesson."

He handed me the pen. "Maybe I'll be a teacher when

I grow up. Bossing kids around is fun." He frowned. "But I want to be a sheriff and solve crimes, too. Can I do both?"

I almost replied with "It's not working out well for me," but replaced it at the last second with "Of course you can."

He plopped into his seat and took out his reading book.

I waited for him to open it. "Your brother can show you everything you need to know to be a sheriff. I'd be happy to fill you in on what it takes to be a teacher." I pointed to the story he had turned to. "But for now you have a reading assignment to finish."

"You sound just like my mom," he grumbled.

"Thank you for the compliment, Tiege. Your mom is a good woman."

The good woman removed the snoring lawman from my apartment as I was showing the first graders how to count by twos. A couple car doors slammed. I stepped to the window and saw Bud was driving Rick's truck north on Main Street. Cookie followed in her truck, with Rick sitting in the passenger seat.

The rest of the school day rolled by without incident. I had ample time to speculate on how long Rick had slept at his parents, to wonder if he'd put out any feelers about Dick yet, and to obsess about how little time remained to find Edgar's killer before Christmas break.

Liv stopped in my room while I corrected papers at my desk. She eyed my wool blazer and dress pants. "You might want to change into work clothes before you drive to the church. Putting up the stage and moving pews gets pretty dusty."

Geez Louise! My memory was as full of holes as Dick Phillips' opinion of my character. I dropped my pen and stood. "I'll change and meet you there in twenty minutes."

I rushed into the church with two minutes to spare. I was not surprised to see Liv, Velma, and several parents moving pews and setting up the stage. I was surprised to see Rick trading stories with Rique DuPeuss, Henry York, and Dick Phillips in a corner of the foyer. From the looks of the sheriff, his day of rest had given him a second wind.

My early morning empathy for the man, my kindness and concern disappeared. While the sheriff had napped, all warm and cozy at his parents' house, I'd taught seven Christmas-crazed students their daily lessons. All the while, I'd imagined Rick springing out of bed and into the investigation with renewed vigor, resolutely determined to follow up on the information I'd provided. And this was how he put out feelers and eliminated suspects? Not on my watch!

I conscripted my meager store of energy, marched over to Rick, and thumped his shoulder. "We need to talk." I jerked a thumb over my shoulder. "Now."

CHAPTER 33

The room went silent as we crossed the foyer and entered the kitchen. I closed the door to shut out the curiosity seekers watching us. Then I crossed my arms and lit into him. "Is this how you run your murder investigations? You respond to a good lead by inviting the suspect to join you for a story swap? Is that the best you can do?"

Rick hoisted himself into a sitting position on the counter of an ancient metal kitchen cabinet. The cabinet wobbled and creaked as he crossed an ankle over one knee. I held my breath, afraid his weight would send the cabinet crashing to the floor.

He waited until it stilled. "You have anything more to say?"

I glowered and shook my head.

"First of all, I oughta thank you for stepping in this morning when I was too tired to think straight. I'm in much better shape now. Second of all, I didn't invite Dick to anything. He was here when I showed up."

That took a little wind from my sails, though I didn't let on. "In that case, why aren't you taking advantage of the situation and questioning them one by one?"

"Well, when I called around this afternoon, every one of them had the same story. They'd volunteered to help you build the stage and didn't want to renege. I decided to reward their community-minded spirit by giving them a hand." He scratched his forehead. "Do you mind telling me how you rounded up such a committed work crew?"

A sneaking suspicion replaced my indignation as Rick spoke. "I didn't, but I have a good idea about who did." I turned the doorknob and then paused. "I'm sorry for getting on your case. It's just that I keep thinking about how hard this Christmas will be on Edgar's family. Finding his killer would give them some closure. I don't think I can enjoy Christmas with my family otherwise."

For a long minute Rick gazed at me with compassion and perhaps some regret. "I'd like to wrap it up, too. But not by rushing the investigation and arresting the wrong person. All I can say is that things are happening. There's progress, but it's slow. You can believe me. Or not." He slid off the counter. The motion set the sink to rattling like a pair of loose dentures. The cabinet swayed in protest but refused to crumple. "Now if you don't mind, there's a bunch of work to be done and a foyer full of interesting characters doing it. Mind if I join them?"

"After you, sir." The door swung open towards us.

Rick and I took a few steps backward. The interesting characters Rick was eager to rub shoulders with had erected the stage platform while we'd been in the kitchen. It blocked the lower three feet of the doorway.

Dick Phillips loomed over us holding a set of portable wooden steps in his hands. Even without a parka and snowmobile suit adding bulk to his frame, he looked like the abominable snowman's long lost brother.

He handed the steps to the sheriff. "Velma says they go down here."

Velma. The very person I needed to interrogate. Once the steps were in place, I climbed onto the stage and began hunting for her. My pace slowed to a shuffle when I realized the planks were still loose. When I reached the front edge I sat and slowly scooched along on my backside until my feet touched the floor. I spied Velma and Merle in a corner surveying the room, emanating smug satisfaction.

I headed for them, passing Liv on the way. She was showing Rique DuPeuss and Vince Douglas—what was he doing here?—how to turn the pews so they faced the stage. She left the two men to the heavy lifting and intercepted me.

"This is going to be done in no time." Her delight was unmistakable. "I'm going to get home in time to eat with Axel and the kids. I expected a few parents would make it, but not the rest of this crowd. Where did they come from?"

"That's what I'm about to find out. Follow me." Liv and I zigzagged past people hammering nails into planks and moving pews on our way to Velma and Merle.

They exchanged a brief glance. He lifted his gaze to the ceiling and rubbed his ear. She studied the floor and tsk-tsked at the puddles of melting snow on the linoleum. They couldn't have looked guiltier if the word had been stamped on their wrinkly foreheads.

Velma tsked again. "I should give the floor a swipe with the mop."

Merle sprang into action. "Let me haul the bucket. It's on the heavy side."

"Oh no you don't." I clamped a hand on each of their forearms. "You're not leaving until you tell me what gives. Why are there so many people here?"

Velma accentuated her tsking with sputters and squawks.

"Let me be more specific," I hissed. "Why are there so many unmarried men here?"

Merle sucked a prodigious amount of air between his teeth. "I mighta said something about it to Reek when he come for breakfast this morning."

"Why would you do that?"

He resumed his examination of the ceiling. "We-ull, he mighta inquired into where he might find you in order to strike up a conversation."

Velma twisted her arm and let out another tsk.

I tightened my grip. "Spill it, you."

"Betty mighta mentioned that your mother thinks you aren't around young people enough, and I mighta said you would be here tonight, and she mighta rung up all the young men on the list we put together, and they mighta listened when she told them you would like to get better acquainted with the young people in the county."

Every unmarried man in this church thinks you are hunting for a husband, Jane Newell.

"How dare you!" The force of my anger felt strong enough to lift the two old yentas off their feet and pin them to opposite wall.

Liv burst out laughing. She clapped a hand over her

mouth, but giggles escaped through her fingers. She doubled over, unable to quell her laughter. Her shoulders shook.

I stared at her in horror. "Fat lot of help you are. People are starting to notice."

"I'm sorry," she burbled. Eventually she straightened and wiped her eyes with her sleeve. A new bout of giggles erupted. She pinched her nose to stop it.

"Everything okay?"

I nearly jumped out of my skin before whirling around to snap at the sheriff. "Why did you sneak up on me?"

He focused on Liv. "Whoa! I thought she was choking."

"I'm fine," she gasped. "It's just that—" She laughed through her nose. It wasn't pretty.

I narrowed my eyes at Rick and then at the matchmakers. "Are you here because of these two yahoos?"

He eyed Velma and Merle, then shook his head. "I already told you why I'm here."

Liv dissolved into giggles again.

"What's so funny?" Rick asked.

"These two"—I glared at Velma and Merle—"can tell you where this work crew came from."

Vince called from where he and Rique were setting down a pew. "What can we do now, Liv?"

She fled like a convict released on parole. Rick looked at Merle and Velma. They studied the ceiling and floor respectively.

I addressed the sheriff. "Could you leave now?"

He fled almost as quickly as Liv had.

I spoke in a low tone, fighting to control the shaking in my voice. "Let me make this perfectly clear. I am young and I have a lot to learn. But I am an adult, and contrary to what my mother would have you and Betty believe, I can manage my own life. I know you care about me, and I care about you. But if either of you pull a stunt like this again, I will no longer be your friend. Do you hear me?"

I didn't wait for them to answer. Instead I marched to the stage, picked up a hammer, and began nailing boards in place.

I. *Whack.*

Can. *Whack.*

Manage. *Whack.*

My. *Whack.*

Own. *Whack.*

Life. *Whack.*

The hammer clattered to the floor. I clutched my thumb and hopped from one foot to the other, squelching the urge to howl in pain.

I *could* manage my own life. Just not right now.

Chapter 34

Merle and Velma acted like they hadn't noticed the meeting of my thumb and the hammer. Unlike the half-dozen single men who rushed over to see what had happened.

Dick turned my hand toward the light and inspected my injury with grim intensity. "You're going to lose your thumbnail."

"Is anything broken?" the sheriff asked.

"Don't think so." Dick dropped my hand without warning.

A ribbon of pain shot up my arm and sucker-punched my gut. I gasped.

"She's turning green." Vince eased me onto the edge of the stage. "Breathe." He pushed my head between my knees and yelled, "Is there ice in the kitchen?"

"It won't help."

I breathed in Dick's gloom and breathed out fire.

"It might. I'll make a cold pack."

I breathed in Rique's accented optimism and

breathed out calm. Shortly thereafter, a soggy coldness engulfed my thumb. I sat up slowly and squinted at my hand. "What is this?"

"My ski mask. Stuffed with snow."

It was a very Daniel Boone thing to do. Having the trapper's ski mask, which very likely had microscopic bits of dead animal skin stuck to it, wrapped around my thumb was gross.

Then again, the improvised ice pack was doing a bang-up job. My thumb throbbed less by the second. So instead of dropping it to the floor like it was crawling with cooties, I burrowed my hand deeper into its wintery depths. I gave Rique the smallest possible smile to communicate gratitude without the possibility of a dinner date.

"My thumb feels much better." Then I frowned at Dick. "You might want to let your EMT buddies know that applying cold to hand injuries reduces pain significantly."

He had the decency to blush.

I scanned the circle of eligible do-gooders. Had Rick seen the flush on Dick's face? No, he had not. He was at the other end of the stage nailing planks into place. For Pete's sake! My first graders had longer attention spans than the county sheriff.

I stood. Admirers hurried to assist me.

"I'm fine." I held my thumb above my head, out of harm's way, and pushed through the forest of hairy hands and manly forearms. "We'll never get the stage finished if you keep fussing."

One by one they picked up their tools and resumed their tasks. I went to the kitchen. Rique's ice pack was melting faster than Frosty the Snowman come spring. I fashioned a twentieth century version with ice cubes, a zippered bag, and a tea towel. I slid Rique's ski mask in another bag and tucked it in my purse.

If Rique asked for it, my response was at the ready. I wanted to mend and wash it before returning it to him. Neither of which would happen until I'd thoroughly examined and documented its fiber content, construction, and tear patterns. Or until I was as adamantly convinced as the sheriff that Rique had played no part in Edgar's death. In other words, he might as well kiss it goodbye.

I hid my purse on the top shelf of the battered metal kitchen cupboard. Then I went into the foyer and found Liv. "What do you want me to do?"

"Stay away from hammers."

"Very funny."

She tapped her index finger on her chin. "What's a one-handed job that needs doing?" Her head swiveled this way and that. "I know! You can get a rag from the cleaning closet and dust the pews. Be sure you straighten the hymnals and throw away any old bulletins you find, too."

I got right to it. The amount of dust lurking in the pews' nooks and crannies was astounding. I dirtied several rags in rapid succession and piled them on the kitchen counter. They would go home to be laundered for real. Unlike the ski mask.

Putting the hymnals in order was a bit of a challenge. They were piled every which way and in need of dusting, too. It was slow work since every now and then, I had to run to the kitchen to refresh my ice pack.

Merle blocked my way during one such trip, then eyed the ceiling as he spoke. "I got a pot a soup on the stove, and seeing as it ain't easy to cook with only one hand, maybe you'd like to stop in for supper after this." His gaze shifted in my general direction. The corners of his mouth turned up a fraction of an inch. It was as much apology as he was likely to give.

"Thanks, Merle. I'll come as soon as we're done here."

By the time the dusting and hymnal stacking were almost done, the stage was finished. Liv and I were the only people still at the church.

"I'll help you." She glanced at her watch.

"No need." I ran a rag across the final pew. "This is the last one. You go home."

"Thanks." She put on her coat and gloves. "Turn off the lights on your way out."

"Should I lock up?"

"Nah. The key's been lost for years."

I waved my rag in farewell and straightened the stack of hymnals before scooping up my coat in the foyer and switching off the lights. That way, I could leave through the door at the back of the kitchen after retrieving my purse and the dirty rags.

I was in the kitchen zipping my coat when the door at the front of the church squeaked. Footsteps padded into the foyer. I assumed someone was returning for forgotten tools or gloves. But the footsteps receded toward the sanctuary instead of coming toward where everyone had been working. I tiptoed to the kitchen door, turned off the light, and peeked out.

Yellow light from the street lamp streamed through the sanctuary windows. The glow backlit a figure crouched in the nearest corner of the sanctuary. Whoever it was straightened and moved to the window closest to the foyer. The light illuminated the face. It was Dick Phillips. I could see what he was holding, too. A hymnal. I'd rooted out every last one of those suckers. Dick must have squirreled this one away. And why would he do that unless he had something to hide?

He opened the hymnal. I inhaled with a soft hiss.

Dick's head snapped up. He glanced around.

I stood stock still. Thank God I'd turned off the kitchen light. Still, the next few seconds aged me.

Finally Dick lowered his head. He took something out of the hymnal. I couldn't see it, but it crinkled like a plastic bag. He put it in the pocket of his parka. Then he reached inside the other pocket and brought out a white envelope. A thick envelope. As in big stack of money thick. He put the envelope inside the hymnal. When he closed the hymnal, the front cover lay flat.

Like in the black and white movies on late night television. Not that I watched anything after the ten o'clock nightly news at home. Mom wouldn't allow that. But when I babysat the neighbor kids on weekends, I'd watched my fair share of B-movies. The ones where convicts escaped using tools smuggled into the prison in hollow books like the one Dick Phillips was carrying back to the corner of the sanctuary where I'd first seen him. His body blocked my view. I couldn't see what he was doing, but when he stood again, his hands were empty.

I waited while Dick crossed the foyer and left the

building. Then I waited some more. He had come back once. He might come back again. Or he might be waiting outside to follow me. I counted to a thousand before creeping out the back door and into the alley next to the Yorks' shack. I took an indirect way home, first walking to the highway in the opposite direction of the school. Then I went east to Main Street, turned north, and hurried the two blocks to my apartment.

When I was inside with the door locked, I picked up the phone and asked Betty to ring the Sternquists. Cookie picked right up.

"Is the sheriff there?"

"Rick." Cookie raised her voice. "It's Miss Newell, and it sounds urgent."

His voice came down the line calm and professional. "Jane, what is it?"

He listened without interruption to my account before asking, "Did you find where he hid the hymnal?"

"No. I came home and called you."

"Well done, Jane."

I beamed. "Thanks."

"What are your plans for the evening?"

"Merle invited me to supper, but I can cancel."

"No, I can call you there if you're needed." He paused. "This could be the break we've been waiting for."

I hung up and boxed at the air. Dick Phillips was in the hot seat now. I jabbed the air a few more times before the absence of pain in my thumb registered.

I flexed my hand. Still no pain. I squeezed my thumb gently. That hurt. But not much. I wrapped a Band-Aid around it and headed toward the light spilling from

Merle's windows. Silent laughter bubbled inside me. Dick Phillips was about to get what he deserved. I laughed out loud and twirled in a circle.

"What's so funny?"

I lost my footing and slammed into the dark outline of a human, blacker than the night around us.

Chapter 35

"Would you pipe down?" Velma growled, her hand a claw as she steadied me.

"I didn't think anyone was out here."

"The way you're hootin' and cacklin', everyone in town can hear you with their windows closed."

"How handy for the men you and Betty sent to build the stage at church. They can keep tabs on me without assistance from the two of you." Cold seeped through my coat. I began walking to Merle's again. "That should make your life easier."

Velma fell into step beside me. The paper grocery sack she was carrying crinkled. As she shifted it from one arm to another, it began to rip.

She stopped. "Oh dear."

"Let me carry it." I took off my coat and wrapped it around the sack. "Where are you going?"

"To keep you from getting food poisoning." She tromped toward Merle's house. "This time a year, he starts a pot of soup on Saturday and leaves it simmering on the stove all week. He's been doing it so long, he's got an iron stomach. One spoonful will give the likes of you the scoots from now 'til the new year."

Merle's apology to me had been an invitation to supper. Velma's was to rescue me from his cooking. I accepted it without a word as we walked quietly through the silent night. Velma barged into Merle's mudroom without knocking. I followed her into the kitchen where an aroma akin to gym socks gone bad greeted us.

"Put my sack on the table," she ordered.

I eased it down gently, then took off my coat and hung it on a hook.

Merle was at the stove. A soup pot sat on the back burner. He stuck a spoon in it and gave it a stir. Foul steam rose from the pot. My eyes watered.

He brought the spoon to his lips and sampled his cooking. "That's good." He dipped up a second spoonful and offered it to Velma. "Want a taste?"

"You tryin' to kill me?" She snatched the spoon from his hand and lifted the pot from the burner. "It smells like you been boiling roadkill again. Take the whole mess outside and get rid of it. I got chili and cornbread for the three of us."

Merle picked up the pot without argument. He turned away from Velma and gave me a wink and a grin.

The wily old codger! I bit my cheeks to keep from grinning in return. I didn't want tip off Velma about how easily she'd been played.

The kitchen was, as per usual, covered with a thin layer of grease and grime. I washed three sets of dishes, glasses, and silverware while Velma unpacked and heated up our meal. Merle returned to the aroma of chili and cornbread, and soon we sat down to eat. Neither of them bothered saying grace. I made do with a silent prayer of gratitude at being spared death by diarrhea. Then we all got down to the business of eating. One taste of Velma's chili and cornbread and I was begging her for the recipe.

She accepted the compliment by batting her eyes. "I've never written one down for the chili, so that'll take some thinking."

Merle spoke around a mouthful of cornbread. "This tastes like Hilda Strider's recipe."

"It is." Velma drizzled honey on hers and took a bite.

"I got Hilda's recipe over here." He licked his fingers and went to the windowsill where he picked up a piece of paper. He wiped it on his overalls before handing me the spotted and stained index card.

I set it beside my napkin. Copying it could wait until after supper. "I haven't met Hilda yet. Does she live around here?"

"Not far." Merle split open a second piece of cornbread and buttered it. "She and her husband Henry live about ten miles south of here on the Montana side of the river."

"Why don't their names ring a bell?"

Velma blew on a spoonful of chili. "They never had kids, so they don't come to much school stuff. They may come to the program Friday though, what with Dick showing up to build the stage." She spooned chili into her mouth.

I did the same and swallowed before asking, "What does Dick have to do with them?"

Merle took a third piece of cornbread. "He's their

nephew. Been living with 'em since he got hired at Fly Ranch. Henry says he's a good worker and they're glad to have him around. They're not gettin' any younger."

I helped myself to more cornbread before Merle could take the last of it. "Did Dick grow up around here then?"

"No." Velma shook her head. "He grew up in Alaska. His parents are still there."

"Alaska?"

"Yup." Merle drew a whistling breath between his teeth. "According to Henry and Hilda anyway. I ain't been able to get Dick to string more than three words together. And believe me, I've tried."

"Hilda says he's real shy." Velma scraped the last of the chili from her bowl. "He couldn't hardly meet her eye for a month after he moved in. She says he pretty near lost his job because he just stared at them boys and never said a word. Gave them the heebie-jeebies and they complained something fierce. She says he got some better after he went through EMT training, but some of the boys still don't take a shine to him."

"I can see that." I pressed the tines of my fork into the cornbread crumbs on my plate. "In my experience, he has the warmth of an ice cube."

"Well"—Velma's tone indicated the reason for that was obvious—"that's to be expected. Mary Borgeson got to know him during EMT training. According to her, he's tongue-tied around women."

Merle rose and began clearing the table. "You ever seen him blush?"

"Only every time I see him." I carried my dishes to the sink. "It makes him look guilty."

Merle took them from me. "Guilty of what?"

Of murder.

I swallowed the words at the last second. The sheriff was finally investigating Dick. I wasn't about to tip off the town gossips and send him scurrying to Alaska.

"It's too bad he doesn't make a better impression." Velma wiped the honey jar with a damp rag. "Hilda goes on and on about what a good man he is. She and Henry make no bones that they trust him with their lives."

The weight of what I'd seen Dick doing in the church pressed against my heart. I wouldn't trust him with a wooden nickel, yet he'd won over his aunt and uncle. If the sheriff couldn't make an airtight case against him, the Striders could well be Dick's next victims.

"I need to go home." I took my coat from the hook. Merle and Velma looked put out, but I didn't care. The sheriff might already know about Henry and Hilda, but I didn't dare leave anything to chance. I zipped up my coat and put on my mittens. "Thanks for supper."

Merle picked up the recipe card. "I thought you was gonna write this out."

"I'll do it at home," I hollered. I snatched the card and barreled out the door.

That was a lie. I had no intention of copying Hilda's recipe. It would be a reminder of Dick Phillips, and I wanted no trace of him in my life. As soon as he was under lock and key I would erase him from my memory.

I ran home and phoned the Sternquists. Cookie picked up and I asked to speak to Rick.

"He took off right after you called earlier, Jane."

"Will you tell him to call me when he gets back?"

"Can it wait until morning? He's on an all-night stakeout."

Rick was on another stakeout?

"I assume it has something to do with what you two talked about."

"In that case, morning will be fine."

"I'll let him know."

"Thanks, Cookie. Bye."

Giddy with relief, I changed into pajamas and crawled into bed. I closed my eyes and envisioned Rick parked in the shadows outside Henry and Hilda's house. He had his binoculars trained on Dick's bedroom window, waiting patiently for Dick to make his move. I drifted off imagining Dick's arrest, trial, and conviction. After eight hours of blissful, uninterrupted sleep, I woke up smiling.

Chapter 36

I sang *Rockin' Around the Christmas Tree* while getting ready for school. I left the bathroom door open a crack while fixing my hair. I didn't want to miss Rick's call and hoped to weasel some details out of him while he was too sleep-deprived to be on guard.

The call didn't come before my students arrived. That could be a sign of the investigation progressing rapidly. Evidence being gathered. Search warrants being issued and arrests being made. That sort of thing.

A blast of icy air whooshed into the entryway along with sunshine and students. The cold made my eyes water. The sheriff could be dealing with frostbite after a night in these elements.

"Good morning, kids!"

Bennan tossed his stocking hat into the air. "Only two days until our Christmas party!"

His announcement popped the children's excitement like a champagne cork. I attempted to quell their high spirits, but the bubbles kept coming. The effervescence rubbed off on Liv's students. Though they were old enough to consider the program more embarrassing than festive, even they sparkled during rehearsal.

"Way to go!" Liv applauded enthusiastically after the children took their bows. "You're gonna knock your parents' socks off Friday night!"

Tiege pinched his nose. "That'll be kinda stinky."

Cookie swiveled around on the piano stool and glared at him.

He whipped his hand to his side. "Sorry."

Cookie's evil eye had no effect on Liv's students. They whisper-chanted "kinda stinky, kinda stinky, kinda stinky" as they followed their teacher out of the room.

After school, I created my own chant to jazz things up while correcting papers. "Two days 'til the program. Three days 'til Iowa. Whoo!"

I was about to repeat it for the umpteenth time when I noticed a stack of bills that should have been mailed two days ago. I put on my coat, grabbed the bills, and hoofed it to the post office.

I was out of breath when Dale Cunningham greeted me. He clapped his hands and rubbed them together. "I've been hearing good things about the school program. Me and the missus are coming early to nab front row seats."

"The kids are getting into it." I slid my bills across the counter."

"How many children are in the program? We want to have enough goody bags for everyone."

"How thoughtful of you." I counted in my head. "Nineteen."

"We'll bring two dozen to be on the safe side."

I unlocked my box and collected my mail. He prattled on about the pattern his wife was using to make the cloth bags they would fill with candy and trinkets. The door squeaked open and cold swirled through the lobby. I turned to see who it was.

Rique DuPeuss.

He stood there looking at me. I stood there looking at him, casting about for small talk and came up empty.

Dale's voice sliced through the silence between us. "Rique, let me introduce you to Miss Newell."

Rique made an odd little bow. "We've met."

"Then you know she's a teacher at our little school?"

"I do."

"Can you imagine how tired she is from wrangling kids this close to Christmas?"

"I can."

"So why haven't you asked her to supper at the café yet?"

I wanted to crawl inside my post office box and shut the door. Rique looked at me. I looked at Dale. Dale looked at Rique.

"Come on, man," Dale said as the air grew thick with social ineptitude, "what's taking so long?"

Rique bowed again. "Miss Newell, can I take you to supper at the café tonight? Perhaps at six o'clock?"

My reply was honest to a fault. "I thought you'd never ask. I'll meet you there."

I went home and readied my classroom for the next day. There was enough time before supper to wrap my students' presents. I had even appliqued their favorite animals under their names on their book bags. In other words, horses for all of them, though a variety of breeds—quarter, appaloosa, mustang, Morgan—and colors—paint, dun, chestnut. The things I'd learned living in cowboy country.

Once the presents were wrapped, I rummaged through my supply of paper and bows for old-fashioned red curling ribbon, the kind Mom had always used on our presents. I found the spool, but it was nearly empty.

I ran through my options. Burt and Iva? They didn't carry wrapping paper or ribbon at the store. Merle might have some. My students might not appreciate ribbon adorned with cat hair and grime. Mary Borgeson? Pam Barkley? Cookie Sternquist? It didn't feel right to ask my students' parents. Velma? Only if I was okay with her telling the town how she had rescued me. Shop in Tipperary after school tomorrow and eat supper at the Nine Pins? Now that was a good idea. So was being sure to buy enough ribbon.

I rang up Betty and asked her to connect me to Mom. "Do you need the number?"

"No. I know it by heart." She put the call through but no one picked up. "Do you want to try again in a few minutes?"

I glanced at my watch. Five forty-five. "No, I'm going to sup—" I swallowed the end of the word "—I'm going somewhere."

"I can caww and give her a message. We're due for a chat."

Of course they were.

"Ask her how much curling ribbon to buy for my students' presents."

"Got it."

"Thanks, Betty."

"My pweasure."

I walked to The Bend. Rique DuPeuss was already in a booth. I scooted in across from him. Trudy waited to call the Miss-Newell's-latest-date hotline until after she took our orders. To say that the conversation lagged after Trudy delivered my Diet Coke and his hot tea would be a gross exaggeration. We had yet to say a word to one another.

"Well," I said after Rique spent considerable time bobbing his tea bag in hot water. Granted, a tea bag could be more scintillating company than an elementary teacher preparing for a Christmas program. But what would Trudy have to report to the hotline if Rique paid less attention to me than to Earl Gray?

"Well," I said again. "Your quick thinking after I hammered my thumb paid off. It's good as new" I opened and shut my hand several times to prove the point. "What other natural remedies do you recommend?"

Rique dropped the tea bag like it was old news. "I boil tree bark down into tinctures for pain." Trudy brought our food. He paid her no mind. "And to eliminate worms."

"Worms?" I asked.

"Yeah," He slathered his burger with ketchup and mustard. "It cleans out stomach parasites slick as a whistle. Want me to bring you some?"

What I wanted was to ask Trudy for a doggy bag so I could take my food home and eat in peace. To my dismay Trudy was taking orders from the influx of customers who arrived after she'd gotten off the phone. Rique's prattle—he was describing how he'd once slit a doe's throat to drink its blood to ward off anemia, which if you asked me sounded like a recipe for a nice crop of belly worms—continued unabated. Just when I thought the evening couldn't get worse, Dick Phillips came in.

What was he doing here? Why hadn't the sheriff arrested him? Or had he been arrested and then posted bail? What was going on?

Dick's eyes locked onto mine. He didn't look away. He didn't blush. Instead he positioned himself at a table where he knew I could see him and stared. Unblinking. Unwavering. Unnerving.

As unappetizing as Rique's dinner conversation was—I tuned in and then out seconds later when he began to describe how a hot onion and horseradish poultice brings a boil to a head—I had to wait for him to finish his meal and walk me home. I wasn't about to venture outside alone after dark with Dick on the loose.

Trudy circled round and dropped off our bill. "You didn't eat much." She gestured at my untouched burger and fries. "Want me to box up your food and put your drink in a to-go cup?"

"Please."

I kept an eye on Dick while Rique took my money and his to the cash register and paid the bill. I listened patiently on the walk home while he gave instructions about how to make soap from bear fat and wood ash. When he offered to come inside and write down the recipe, I drew the line.

"It sounds fascinating, but—"

I paused, searching for a convincing excuse. Washing my hair was out. He might volunteer to whip up a batch of shampoo.

"—I have a lot to do between now and the Christmas program." I whisked inside and waved goodbye through the window.

I locked the door and rang Betty, peering out the window while waiting for her to answer. A pickup truck rumbled past the school, turned west at the corner, and parked halfway down the block. The driver cut the engine and lights, but didn't get out. The vehicle was just outside the pool of light cast by the streetlamp, so I couldn't identify it. Whoever had parked it knew what he—or she—was doing.

"Answer the phone, Betty." I moved away from the window. My hand shook as it hunted for the cord and closed the curtain with a snap. "Please, Betty. Answer the phone."

CHAPTER 37

"**Y**our mother and I had a nice chat." Betty spoke faster than Tiege Sternquist on a roll during show-and-tell. "She says two spoows of curwing ribbon with the smaw center cores should do the trick. I checked with the hardware store in Tipperary, and they have them in stock. But watch out and don't grab the ones—"

"Thanks, Betty. I need to talk to the sheriff right away. Can you connect me to him?"

"No."

"How about his parents? Do they know where he is?"

"No."

"You're sure?"

"As sure as I can be since me and Cookie just got done tawking. She said she don't know where Rick is, but I was to give you a message from him."

She paused. Knowing Betty, she was going for dramatic effect. Her effort backfired. All my pent up nervous energy shot out and landed in her ear. "For crying out loud, Betty, give me the message!"

"Weww, if you're going to be that way about it." She sniffed. "The sheriff says everything is going wike it shouwd. He knows you saw Dick Phiwwips at the café, and you're not to worry. I don't know why anyone would worry about Dick. He wouldn't hurt a fwy. He's a very nice young man. Why he—"

I broke in again. "Was that last bit part of the sheriff's message?"

"Uh,"—she cleared her throat,—"no. The sheriff said he's keeping tabs on Dick and the stakeout is going fine. You shouwd just stay put untiw he gets back to you."

"Did Cookie mention when that might be?"

"I asked her the very same thing, and she said she quit guessing when Rick wiww show up anywhere because it turns her hair grey. She said to caww her if you want her to stay with you tonight. Her bag is packed."

The offer was tempting, but Cookie was already spending her afternoons at program practice. With the sheriff watching Dick, there was no need to inconvenience her further.

"I'll be fine."

Once the doors were barricaded and the butcher knife was within arm's reach, I was fine. More than fine. My appetite returned while I bustled around the apartment. I switched on the oven, arranged my burger and fries on a cookie sheet, and slid it into the oven to reheat. All that remained was to freshen up my Diet Coke with some ice. I opened the freezer door and was pleased to see the one freezer meal I was saving for supper on the day school resumed after Christmas vacation. That pleasure was quickly replaced by a feeling of unease. The sense of a detail overlooked. A rote action not completed.

The list of suspects! I slammed the freezer door, dragged over a chair, and scrambled up. The paper was gone. Maybe it had fallen to one side or the other. I slid my trembling fingers up and down the gap between the refrigerator and one wall, then the other. Nothing. I dropped onto hands and knees, pressed the side of my head to the floor and squinted. No paper.

I cursed my carelessness and ran through other possibilities. It could have fallen behind the refrigerator. Not likely since I'd set the sheet of paper near the front of the fridge. Which left one remaining option. Someone had taken it.

Who had been in my apartment since I'd laid the paper on top of the refrigerator? Corinne and Cookie had worked in here during dress rehearsal. Velma, Rick, Vince, and Dick had been here the day Russ was apprehended. One of them must have taken it. But who?

I discounted the women and the sheriff immediately. The thought of Corinne and Cookie stealing anything was ludicrous. Velma and I had practically been joined at the hip while I packed for the night at her house. The information I'd given Rick about Hank's boots had taken the sheriff aback. If he'd seen the list, my revelation would have been old news.

That left Russ, Vince, and Dick. Russ could have seen the list while he was in my apartment before I got home. Maybe he saw Dick's name and took it hoping to use it against his least favorite counselor. Vince and Dick had both stayed in the kitchen as far as I knew. Then again my back had been toward them when I argued with Rick about handcuffing Russ. Which one of them would have taken it? Vince's name wasn't on the paper but Dick's was. That fact alone made him the likelier culprit. Throw in his threatening behavior in the past week—the glowering and the brooding and the lurking—and it was hard to believe he hadn't taken it.

What a fool he'd been! Along with a matching ski mask and murder weapon in his possession, this was a damning turn of events. Passing this bit of information on to the sheriff was going to be a pleasure.

A faint acrid odor set my nose to tingling. I sniffed. My food! I sprinted to the stove and pulled out the cookie sheet. Other than a few charred french fries, the meal was salvageable. I threw out the french fry briquettes, transferred the rest to a plate, and ate. Afterward I put on my pajamas and took the butcher knife to my bedroom. I slept fitfully, dreaming of curling ribbon with a butcher knife before using it to cut worms out of Dick Phillip's intestines. Absolutely bizarre and absolutely bloody.

When I woke on Thursday morning I felt absolutely unrested and unrefreshed.

Chapter 38

The sun was bright and the air felt warmer when the children tromped into the entryway. That boded well for shopping in Tipperary after school. However, I predicted six long hours of pre-Christmas craziness until then based on the frenzy among my students as they shed their winter gear. Their behavior was to be expected, but what Elva announced during her turn at show-and-tell was not.

She stood stiff and straight as a holiday nutcracker. "Santa mailed this to my mom." She held up a small notepad. "His letter says it's for Miss Newell. He wants her to write our names under naughty or nice today while he loads his sleigh." Every hand shot up. Elva called on Renny first.

"Why didn't Santa send the letter straight to Miss Newell?"

Elva didn't bat an eye. "He was afraid she wouldn't get to the post office 'cause she's busy with the Christmas program." She called on Cora next.

"How will he get it from her by Christmas Eve?"

"She's supposed to tape the list to the window of her apartment after the program tomorrow. He'll stop here before he delivers our toys."

Elva glided over and presented the notepad to me. I sucked in my cheeks to keep from laughing and accepted it. I solemnly tucked it in my shirt pocket, making sure it peeked out a bit. In college, the developmental psychology professor often said that young children are concrete thinkers who attend to visual reminders. Boy, was he right.

By the time we walked to the church for program practice, every child's name was on the nice list. By the end of practice, I'd added each name several more times. At dismissal time back at school, they waited patiently while I locked the trailer, put on my coat, and shouldered my purse.

I led them outside and waved at Mary, who was waiting for Elva and Stig in her truck. I cupped my hands around my mouth. She rolled down her window. "Thank you!" She gave a thumb's up.

I hopped into the Beetle, drove to Tipperary, and parked in front of the hardware store. Dusk was falling, but the temperature was balmy for December. Light poured from the store windows. The aisles were busy and I hesitated before going in. I hadn't been around a crowd for months and wasn't sure I remembered how to behave.

As it turned out, my etiquette still functioned. "Excuse me, excuse me," I murmured while weaving through the aisles. I found the curling ribbon and took it to the cash register. I took my place in line and made pleasant small talk with the woman behind me as we inched our way forward. We were deep in conversation about the wonderfulness of her first cousin Cookie Sternquist when the man ahead of me turned and gestured toward the register.

"You're up." He did a double take. "Jane?"

"Vince?" My surprise matched his. "Nice to see you."

He hung around while the clerk rang up my purchase and handed me a paper bag with the ribbon and receipt inside. We walked out together.

"Are you doing last-minute Christmas shopping too?" I asked.

Vince held the door, and an icy cold blast hit my face. I shivered, surprised at how the temperature had plummeted during the short time I'd been shopping.

"Nah." He juggled the bags he was holding and turned up his collar. "I had a tire go flat, and I've been killing time while the gas station patches it. I'd better see if it's ready before I buy anything else I don't need."

"Where'd you leave it?"

"At the station south of town."

I felt around in my purse for my keys. "That's a frigid hike in this weather. My car's right here. I'd be happy to give you a ride."

"I'm happy to accept one."

I stowed my things in the VW's back seat. Vince set his bags on the floor between his feet. The cold had seeped into the car, and my teeth began to chatter. I started the engine and turned up the heat before backing out. "Brrr."

Vince tapped on the window as we passed the Nine Pins. "You ever gone bowling there?"

"No," I answered through chattering teeth. "But I've eaten at the café."

"Is the food decent?"

"Decent enough to treat myself to supper there before driving back to Little Missouri. You can join me and decide for yourself if you like." I pulled into the gas station and parked in front of a pump.

"You're full of good ideas." Vince rested his fingers on the door handle. "And yes, if the tire's ready, I'd like to have supper with you."

"I'll fill my tank while you find out."

When I finished and came inside to pay, the attendant at the counter was counting change into Vince's hand. I blew on my hands while they finished up. "Does this mean the tire's fixed?" I asked.

"It does." Vince pocketed his change.

I took out my checkbook. "The car's unlocked, so you can get your things. I'll meet you at the Nine Pins in a few minutes."

At the café I was pleased to see that Vince had claimed the interior corner booth. The temperature had dropped further, and sitting next to a cold window would have been miserable. Even though our booth was the farthest from the entrance, cold air blasted our legs whenever another customer entered.

Despite the cold, there were plenty of customers. I recognized two of the town teachers and a clerk from the Tipperary Super Value. I thought one man might be the sheriff's deputy though he wasn't in uniform. I'd only seen him in passing a couple months ago, so I wasn't sure.

The waitress, an older woman, brought menus. "Sorry for the delay. You'd think we're running a jack rabbit convention the way this place is hopping. I'll be back in a jiffy to take your orders."

Vince's eyes sparkled with amusement as he watched her trot away. "What can you tell me about jack rabbit conventions?"

"From my limited experience"—I indulged in some over-the-menu eye twinkling of my own—"they are on the hairy side."

He groaned. "Very punny."

"No, very bunny."

His eyes lit up again. "You win! This must be the result of being shut up with small children five days a week."

"More like the result of having a father whose entire skeleton was composed of funny bones."

Vince laid his menu on the table. "Was? Has he passed away?"

"No." I set down my menu too. "He's had multiple sclerosis for a long time. Little by little, it's taking a toll on him."

"Where does he live?"

"In Sioux City."

Vince whistled softly. "You're a long way from home."

"Little Missouri is my home. But it'll be a long drive from here to Sioux City on Saturday. I'm spending Christmas with my family."

Our waitress scurried over and clicked her pen. "Okay, kiddos. What'll you have?"

I exchanged chagrinned looks with Vince and picked up my menu. "Um, let me see."

"You need more time?" She clicked her pen and stuck it behind her ear. "I'll catch you in a few."

When she returned, we placed our orders. Tomato soup and grilled cheese with hot tea for me. Beef stew and cornbread with coffee for him.

"What could be better than stew on a day like this?" Vince rubbed his palms together when the waitress set a steaming bowl in front of him.

"Everybody else is thinking the same way." She set my soup and sandwich on my side of the booth. "You got the last bowl of this, buckaroo. Enjoy it."

Vince tasted his stew. "Mmm. That's good." He ate more and wiped his mouth. "Don't look now, but our waitress is pointing you out to some guy two booths over. He's scowling like you put his nose out of joint."

"What did I do to him?" I picked up half of my sandwich and turned around to look. "I don't even know the guy."

Vince nodded at my bowl. "You beat him to the last of the tomato soup."

I dipped the corner of my sandwich in the creamy liquid and took a bite. My eyes closed as tomatoey tang and cheesy goo tangoed on my tongue. Oh the deliciousness! No wonder the guy in the other booth was out of sorts.

I leaned over and curled a protective arm around my bowl. If he or anybody else decided to fight me for it, they'd better be ready. I intended to win.

CHAPTER 39

We ate steadily until our food was gone. I wiped my chin, and the white paper napkin came away covered with pink polka dots. To think that Vince hadn't said a word. The man was a prince if ever there was one.

I crumpled the napkin and dropped it onto my empty plate. "How long have you worked for Fly Ranch?"

"I don't."

"But somebody said—"

"Yeah. I know. Most people in Tipperary County think I work there. I can see how they get that impression. I have my own company and do freelance jobs for organizations and companies in the west and southwest."

"So you're a consultant then?"

"Small plane pilot." He set his silverware in his soup bowl and placed the bowl on his cornbread dish. "I bring Fly Ranch's big wig donors out for fundraising events a few times a year. Sometimes the ranch pays me. Other times the donors do. More than a few celebrities and CEOs hire me to bring their kids out here after they get in trouble with the law. Their daddies and mommies make deals with a judge to send their boys to here to keep their names out of the news. And because they hope a dose of good old-fashioned hard work and social isolation will turn them around."

I raised my eyebrows. "Are you telling me that their idea of living with the consequences of their choices begins with flying in a private plane?"

"Uh-huh."

"How often do you do that?"

He considered the question. "I'd say once a month or so."

"Do their parents come with them?"

"Not a one."

I thought of the day Uncle Tim and Mom said goodbye after they'd moved me to Little Missouri. I was an adult who chose to live here. I had been thrilled about starting my first job. Even so, watching Uncle Tim's truck vanish into the distance had been pure torture. My experience was a walk in the park compared to these boys who'd been sent packing by their parents and dropped off by a complete stranger.

"That's so wrong." I blinked back tears. "Does it get to you, leaving the boys at the ranch like that?"

"Only if their parents don't pay up."

His tone was light, but he didn't meet my eye. Ah, he was softer than he let on. I changed the subject. "Did you grow up around here?"

"Nah, though my parents are ranchers. Their home spread is in Arizona. They have a second place in

Mexico, more for fun than anything else. They shuttle between them so often I can't keep track of them."

"Do you see them often?"

"We're celebrating Christmas at the ranch in Mexico." Anticipation lit his face. He rubbed his hands together and blew on them as if they were chilled. "I'm flying out early tomorrow afternoon. As soon as my business around here is finished." He rubbed his hands together as if they were chilled. "All I want for Christmas is to be warm again. However many layers of clothing I wear in this country, I'm always cold."

"What brought you this far north in the first place?"

"I played football at the University of Nebraska with a guy who grew up south of Little Missouri."

My hackles rose. "That's why you hangar your plane at the Wentworths'."

"It is. Do you know Junior?"

There was no point in telling Vince that I knew Junior better than I wanted. "Corinne sewed the costumes for the Christmas program. What do the Wentworths have to do with Fly Ranch?"

"I've been flying Junior's hunting clients out here since he started his guide business. Somebody at Fly Ranch approached me when they heard there was a pilot familiar with this area." He grimaced. "Now that Junior's out of business, it's not worth flying out here. I told Fly Ranch to find themselves a pilot who likes freezing his butt off. From now on, I'm heading south of the border and staying there."

I imagined sitting underneath a palm tree beside a pool. A margarita in one hand and a warm breeze ruffling my hair. I could go for that. Frigid air whipped at my ankles. I turned to stare at the offender who'd let in the cold wind and ended my daydream.

"It's nasty out there," he said to the waitress as he brushed snow off his shoulders. "Visibility's bad and getting worse."

"That's no good." Vince stood and dug his wallet from his pocket. "Let's settle up and caravan to Little Missouri together."

We left cash at our booth to cover the bill. We wound scarves around our necks and zipped our coats. I crammed my hat low over my forehead and ears before putting on my mittens. Vince wriggled his fingers into thick gloves and turned his coat collar up and over his ears. Thus prepared, we went outside.

Cold burned my throat with every inhale. The wind hurled snow in my face and turned Vince's hair white. He turned his back to the wind and shouted. "Who should lead the way? Me or you?"

"You."

We minced across the slippery parking lot, started our vehicles, and brushed the snow off of our windshields.

"We'll be okay if we take it slow." The wind flung his puffs of frosty breath in every direction. "Hug my bumper and lay on the horn if you fall behind. Blink your brights when you catch up."

"Got it."

He drove slower than a second grader writing her name in cursive for the first time. I pictured him bent over the steering wheel, his tongue hanging out as he concentrated. An icy patch sent the Beetle fishtailing. I slowed and fought the steering wheel as the car's tail end swung violently from side to side several times. By the time I regained control, the taillights of Vince's truck had disappeared into a wall of snow. I honked the horn until his taillights reappeared. Then I flashed the blinkers. He increased his speed a tiny fraction, and we continued our slow creep down the highway. At this rate, Santa would get to Little Missouri before we did.

About five miles west of Tipperary, we drove out of the snow squall. Vince increased his speed from five miles an hour to fifteen and then to thirty. He topped out at an astonishing forty-five miles an hour. We arrived at Little Missouri, flushed with triumph. The trip had taken three times as long as it did in clear weather. But we had made it and I was grateful.

Vince led the way to the school and waited to leave until the Beetle was parked. Then he tooted his horn and went on his merry way. I wondered where his merry way would take him, but my thoughts moved on to what I needed to do before calling it a night. I carried my purse and the sack with the ribbon inside and shed my winter things, leaving them on the entry room floor. I took the ribbon to the kitchen and finished decorating my students' gifts, curling and adding ribbons until the wrapping paper underneath was barely visible.

I carried the seven packages into my classroom and placed them under the tree. The excess I was lavishing on my students would have shocked my mother. She never dreamed of wrapping our Christmas gifts so extravagantly. Then again, she never dreamed of sending me off to Little Missouri alone. Her advice and meddling were aggravating, but her love for me was unwavering.

The certainty of it wrapped around me like a cozy blanket.

A yawn split my face. It was time for bed. I went back to the apartment, pausing in the entryway to hang my coat on one hook and my scarf on another. As I laid my hat and mittens on their spot on the shelf, a thought flitted into my consciousness. I tried to hang on to it, but another yawn sent it skittering away.

Too tired to chase it, I changed into pajamas and climbed into bed with a grateful sigh. By this time tomorrow, school and program would be over and Christmas vacation would begin. Once again a thought, as precise and ethereal as a snowflake, twirled on the edge of wakefulness. It teetered there a moment, daring me to capture it. Instead, I tumbled into the sweet abyss of sleep and the thought melted away.

Chapter 40

The phone woke me bright and early. The only person with the nerve to call at six in the morning was my mother.

Something's happened to Dad.

I threw back the covers, raced to the kitchen, and answered on the third ring.

"Mom?" The word came out breathless and bleary. "What's wrong?"

"I told Harold that calling now was a bad idea, but he insisted. I waited as long as I dared. But with you being in a different time zone and me going to school early to get things in order I had to call now. I want to walk out of my classroom this afternoon as soon as school's out and enjoy having my family here during Christmas vacation without giving work a second thought."

"So Dad's okay?"

"He's fine and dandy, and he's the instigator of your early morning heart attack."

"And you're calling because?"

"Oh listen to me going on and on like this phone call doesn't cost a cent. I'm not sure what your father wants to say, but I want to wish you well at your Christmas program tonight. It's a big undertaking for a brand new teacher, and you've worked hard to make it a success."

There it was again. Her love creeping in and wrapping me in delicious warmth. If only it would reach my bare feet. The kitchen floor was cold and my feet were going numb.

"Ah Mom, that's about the nicest thing you've ever said. Thanks."

"Also, I called the National Weather Service, and they said a high pressure system in central South Dakota guarantees good weather for driving for tomorrow. It's going to be cold, so throw some extra blankets in the car just in case. And don't let your gas tank go below half full."

"You called the National Weather Service?"

"I did. And you're welcome. Now, just one more thing. Betty mentioned a young man she thinks is very, very nice. She said you've met him, and she wishes the two of you had hit it off because he's the kind of man she'd want her daughter to marry if she had one. I'm trying to remember his name. I'd have asked Betty to repeat it, but she was fixing breakfast for Gus. Maybe it was Rick."

"Rick's the sheriff."

"Then it's not him. Thank goodness because you'd use dating him as an excuse to break your promise and start snooping around again. I am thanking my lucky stars that you're done with that."

Oh, boy.

I rallied. "Are you sure it wasn't Rique, the state

trapper? He's French Canadian and spells his name R-i-q-u-e."

"Betty didn't say this young man was French Canadian, but that could be interesting. Do you like him?"

"He kills animals, lives in a pickup camper that's propped up on cement blocks, deworms himself with tree bark, and dresses like Daniel Boone."

"Hmmm. I must not have understood what Betty said. Might the nice young man's name be Dick instead of Rick?"

I should have seen that one coming. In my defense it was early in the morning, and my toes were turning blue. At least dashing her hopes didn't require forethought.

"A guy named Dick lives around here. I can tell you unequivocally, beyond the shadow of a doubt that he is not nice. Despite what Betty says he is not the kind of man you want your daughter to marry."

"Then he's not the young man you ate supper with at the Nine Pins last night?"

At which point the warm blanket of my mother's love grew unbearably hot. "That was Vince Douglas."

"Is he nice?"

"He is."

"Ooo."

"He's moving to Mexico."

"Are all the nice young men in Little Missouri foreigners?"

I leaned against the wall. "When did you say you wanted to leave for work?"

"Oh my land, Jane, I have to go. I'm handing the phone to Harold and dashing out the door."

"Hi Dad. Mom said you're the brains behind this call."

"Always." He snorted.

"I have to admit, my curiosity is piqued. What couldn't you wait to talk about until tomorrow?"

He snorted again. "We'll have plenty to cuss and discuss when Doris is around. But I don't want to bring this up when she's around or she'll worry herself sick about you being involved in the murder of that dead boy. How's about you bring me up to date now?"

Ten minutes later, Dad knew as much about the case as I did. "And as far as you know," Dad asked, "the stakeout is ongoing?"

"That's right. The sheriff said he'd get back to me, but I haven't heard a peep out of him since Wednesday night."

"Either he's trying to set a record for the longest stakeout in South Dakota history or he wants the evidence against the boy's killer to be indisputable. Which one of the suspects did you say is the killer?"

"Dick Phillips. The guy Mom and Betty Yarborough think should be my next hot date. You should be ready to scrape Mom off the floor when she hears he's arrested. Her disappointment is going to be legendary. I don't understand how he's managed to pull the wool over Betty's eyes so completely. He's bamboozled his aunt and uncle, too."

"Well." Dad paused. The receiver picked up the sound of his breathing.

Had his multiple sclerosis caused him to lose his train of thought again? It did that far too often. Or was he simply considering his next words? I prayed it was the second.

"Well." He sounded decisive, like he knew what he wanted to say. "We all wear masks so other people see only what we want them to know. It sounds like Mr. Phillips wears a different mask when you're around."

"Right now, I'd like nothing more than to rip it off and expose what he did to Edgar."

"Can you wait until after Christmas vacation to do it?"

I laughed and then sobered. "That shouldn't be a problem. The sheriff is in no hurry to wrap up the case."

"Pinky shwear?"

I knew two things about my father. He slurred his words when he got tired, and he was crooking his little finger like he used to do when we made promises to each other.

I crooked my little finger in return. "Pinky swear."

"See you t'morrow," he mumbled. "Drive shafe."

I stayed on the line until his receiver crashed into the cradle. As I hung up, I considered our conversation. Everything Dad had said rang true, save one small detail.

My father didn't wear masks. He couldn't. The relentless fatigue of his illness stripped him of the energy required to hide his emotions or motives. I hated how it denied him the ability to choose what to reveal about himself as much as I hated Dick Phillips' choice to end Edgar's life.

I wasn't proud of the hatred and the deceitful mask I'd slipped on during our pinky swear. If a chance arose in the next twenty-four hours to expose Dick, I'd do it in a heartbeat. I uncurled my fingers which had balled into fists.

I'd not only do it, I'd enjoy it.

Chapter 41

I stood in the shower until the stream of water, as hot as I could make it, thawed my cold, stiff feet. Then I ate a quick breakfast and dressed in a bright green sweater over red wool pants before donning the Santa hat Corinne had given me. I trotted over to my classroom and crawled under the Christmas tree to plug in the lights.

"There has to be a better way to do this." I backed out, grumbling, and snagged my hat on a branch. Someone banged on the door while I tried to work the hat free. "Be right there," I called.   The tree refused to loosen its grip no matter what I did. The banging resumed, more insistent this time.

"Hold your horses! I'll get there as quick as I can." I gave the hat a hard tug and it came free. I scrambled to my feet and hurried to let in whoever was making the racket. On the way, I pinned the hat in place at what I hoped was a festive angle.

Rick Sternquist stood on the landing. He was carrying two large, flat boxes. I held the door wide to let him in.

"Where have you been?" I demanded as he came inside. "Is the stakeout done? Have you arrested Dick Phillips? When do you want me to make a statement? You know I'm leaving early tomorrow."

"Hang on a sec." He raised the boxes higher. "Can I set these in your kitchen?"

"What's in them?"

"Treats Mom made for the Christmas party. When she heard I was stopping in to see you, she asked me to drop off everything that needs to go in the refrigerator. She'll bring the rest when she comes."

"There's more? This looks like enough to feed an army."

"She's been known to go slightly overboard in the food department at Christmas."

"Come on through." I led the way and opened the fridge. "Well," I said once he slid the boxes inside, "what's going on? Why didn't you call when the stakeout ended?"

"It's ongoing." He stood and straightened.

I felt vindicated when the refrigerator door grazed his nose as I slammed it shut. "Then what were you doing at your parents' house, and why are you running your mother's errands? Why are you here instead of following up on what you said, and I quote, 'could be the big break we've been waiting for?' "

"First off, there's three of us running the stakeout. We've been rotating shifts since you called Tuesday. The logistics have been on the complicated side, and they kept me tied up. I'm sorry you've been in the dark for so long. What you reported was a big deal, and I should have made time to call you."

Sakes alive, he was acting decent. He'd even apologized. How could I nurse a grudge when he was being reasonable? Then again, he'd kept me waiting for days. He could wait a few more seconds.

I relented once he looked sufficiently uncomfortable. "Apology accepted." He opened his mouth to speak, but I had more to say. "There's no way Edgar's killer is going to be arrested before I leave, is there?"

Before he could answer, the classroom door squeaked open. Bennan and Cora tromped inside calling for me, their voices high and insistent.

Rick shrugged. "If they're half as excited as Tiege was this morning, you better go. I'll catch you later." He was out the apartment door and gone before I could protest.

I punched a fist at the empty space where he'd been standing and asked, "How *much* later?" Then I hurried into the cloakroom. The second they saw me, Cora and Bennan thrust a small package into my hands.

Cora hopped from one foot to the next. "Open it!"

Bennan jumped up and down. "Mom said you might want to wear them for the party."

I peeled off the wrapping paper and held up a garish pair of earrings. "Oooo."

Cora twirled around me. "They're beautiful, aren't they?"

"That they are." They followed me to the mirror above the sink in the back of the classroom and watched while I exchanged my understated gold studs for the tiny green and red Christmas balls dangling from silver hooks.

Bennan's eyes widened. "The earrings match your clothes."

Footsteps sounded in the entryway, and we went to see who had come inside. My other students stood shoulder to shoulder and thrust more Christmas presents into my hands. Each child echoed some variation of what Bennan had said earlier. "Mom said you should open it right away."

"As soon as your winter things are where they belong and you're seated at your desks, I'll open them," I promised. In a flash, they were in their seats, and I began opening gifts.

Renny's was a necklace of battery-operated Christmas lights. "Put it on," he begged. I slipped the necklace over my head and flicked its switch.

Elva and Stig gave me a jingle bell bracelet. I slipped it on without being asked. Tiege's gift was a belt of green and red chains which soon replaced my black leather one.

A giggle bubbled up from my toes when I opened the last present. "Oh Beau, did you pick this out yourself?"

He nodded and his eyes shone when I held up a tiara studded with green and red plastic jewels. I unpinned my Santa hat and stuffed it in my pocket. My students watched, spellbound, as I fastened the tiara into place. I felt like Queen Elizabeth wearing the crown jewels. The day couldn't get any better than this. But it did.

Iva Kelly, Pam Barkley, and Cookie Sternquist arrived midway through the morning, their arms full of decorations, games, and more food. Once they quit laughing at my finery, Iva escorted me to the front of the room with great pomp and circumstance. I didn't lift a finger

while she transformed my chair into a sparkling silvery
throne, and Pam led the children through a host of
activities and party games. Afterward Cookie served, not
so much party treats as a party meal of cocktail weenies,
egg casserole, hot apple cider and cocoa. For dessert we
ate the fruit pizza which Rick had left in my refrigerator.

After we finished stuffing ourselves the children went
outside for recess supervised by Pam. Bless that woman!
I laid my students' gifts on their desks. Then I removed
my Christmas finery and put on my coat and hat and
loaded the Beetle with what hadn't yet been hauled to the
church for the program. Once that was done, it was time
for the children to come inside again. They traipsed in
smelling of cold and fresh air.

"Carry your coats and backpacks to your desks. Then
sit down and put your hands on your heads." I had to
repeat the directions twice. "Now you can all open your
presents," I said when they were seated.

Tiege unwrapped his first. He swung his book bag
over his head like a lasso. "It's a roan on it just like I got
at the ranch!"

"Mine's a paint." Cora rushed over and hugged me.
"Thank you, Miss Newell."

The other children echoed her thanks and there were
hugs all around. After Stig squeezed me, he poked at my
pants pocket. "What's in there?"

"My Santa hat." I pulled it out and put it on Stig's
head.

"It hurts." He took off the hat and stuck his hand
inside. "What's this doing in there?" He held up a pine
needle.

At the sight of it, the elusive spark flashed from where

it had been trapped in my thoughts since the night before. It was about to break free when Elva took the hat from Stig.

"It's ripped." She poked a finger through a hole in the fabric. "My mom can mend that easy."

I was about to tell her that wasn't necessary when Renny, Bennan, and Beau scampered into the bathroom hallway. That was a recipe for trouble if ever there was one. I was getting ready to go after them when they returned bearing a large shirt box topped with a gigantic silver bow.

"This is your real gift," Beau explained as they brought it to me. "Gramma said what we gave you this morning was to make you gag."

It took me a minute, but I got there. "Did she maybe call them gag gifts?"

"Yeah." Beau chewed his lower lip. "But this is the real one."

Tiege clarified. "From all of us."

Renny clasped and unclasped his hands. "You should open it now. So you can wear it tonight."

I removed the lid and gasped at what lay nestled in the cloud of tissue paper. It smelled faintly of Corinne's sewing room. Bennan held the box as I lifted out a green velvet dress trimmed with antique lace and held it to my shoulders.

"Oh, Miss Newell." Cora's body trembled as she touched the soft material. "It's a princess dress."

"It's beautiful," I agreed as the children crowded in to stroke the soft fabric. I waited until they were done admiring it to return it to its bed of tissue paper and cover the box.

The wonder of Christmas lit Bennan's eyes, and he asked, "Will you wear it tonight with the crown Beau gave you?"

The children gazed at me. Their eyes reflected the Christmas tree lights and glittered brightly. Again something sparked inside my mind. Two unrelated thoughts lit up briefly. I strained to connect them.

"Please?" Elva begged.

The inner spark dimmed. I closed my eyes and the light grew stronger. I almost had it.

"Pretty please?" Tiege added.

My eyes opened. Seven small children waited for my answer. "Yes."

They cheered.

I shut my eyes again and willed the spark back to life. It flared briefly. But as the children's cheers grew louder, the spark wavered, dimmed, and died.

Chapter 42

"Miss Newell? Are you all right?"

My eyes flew open at the sound of Corinne's voice. Her question displaced the wonder in my students' eyes and replaced it with alarm.

"I'm fine." I smiled at each child in turn. "Just surprised." I gestured to the dress. "It's beautiful. And you were in on it, weren't you?"

"I was." She held her hands out, palms up. "I can take it to your apartment and hang it up so it's ready for tonight."

I was about to accept her offer, but the knowledge that Corinne at least had the opportunity to take my suspect list held me back.

I picked up the box. "Would you mind waiting here with the kids while I hang it up?" I whispered. "I know right where the padded hangers are." When she nodded her agreement, I asked the children to go to their desks and hold up their book bags for Corinne to see.

Corinne was walking from student to student and

admiring their presents when I returned. A glance out the window confirmed that others had arrived for the final dress rehearsal.

"Children." I spoke in a low, calm voice. "Zip your gifts inside your book bags." Once that was done, we put on our coats and lined up at the door. "Corinne will lead you outside and make sure you all have rides to the church. I promise to get there first and meet you."

With that I locked up, grabbed my purse, and beat a path to my car. I arrived at the church with time to spare and used it to carry an armload of props and costumes into the Sunday school rooms we were using as the boys' and girls' dressing areas.

I was gathering a second load when Liv and Cookie parked on either side me and got out.

"Let the kids bring the stuff in so we can sort it out," Liv suggested.

Cookie agreed. "Yes, you two go inside. I'll help the kids haul everything. I'll send Corinne to help you when she gets here."

Liv and I went inside and began putting the dressing rooms to rights. The students practically derailed our progress. They dumped antlers here and costumes there, until the dressing rooms looked like the North Pole after a tornado.

"Cookie said to tell you this is the last of it," Corinne called from the stage. She popped her head in the dressing room. "Oh my," she said as she surveyed the storm damage. "Let me take care of this while you start rehearsal."

We left her to it and lined the students up on stage to practice the opening song. Cookie played the opening chord and the refreshment committee members walked in. They carried Tupperware containers and platters filled with Christmas cookies.

"Are those for us?" Gavin shouted from the back row.

The children burst into a cacophony of questions.

"How many can I have?"

"Can we eat them now?"

"I want a snowman cookie!"

"I want a star."

Gavin ran to the edge of the stage and beat his chest. "I want to eat my brother. Give me a reindeer!" He stood poised as if ready to leap off the stage and raid the refreshments.

If this kid thought he could hijack the program, he had another thing coming. I moved directly in front of him and slammed down my clipboard. "You jump off that stage," I said with the authority of Santa ordering the reindeer to let Rudolph join their games, "and you'll spend the program sitting beside your parents. Good luck explaining to them why I'm the lead reindeer and you're not."

"You don't have the guts to do it," he sneered.

I put my hands on my hips and glared at him. "Try me."

Liv came to stand beside me. "She'll do it, Gavin."

He slunk to his place in the back row.

Cookie played the introductory chord again. The children came in on cue, their singing sweet enough to melt the hardest heart. How could they be the same children who moments ago had nearly mounted a cookie insurrection?

"Well done," Liv said when the song ended. "Now

that you're warmed up, go put on your costumes, and we'll run the whole program."

I told Liv I would pair up with Cookie, who was supervising the boys. She looked at me like I'd lost my mind. "You sure?"

"I want Gavin to know I've got my eye on him."

"In that case, I'd better see what Corinne needs done with the girls."

Cookie had the boys arranged into groups according to the parts they played. She watched the elves and Christmas trees, Santa took care of himself, and I supervised the reindeer.

I tapped Gavin on the shoulder.

He flinched at my touch. "I'm not doing anything."

"Good for you." I gave him his costume and sent him to change behind the sheet we'd strung up as a privacy curtain. When he returned I handed him the bag of antlers. "You pass these out to their owners once they're in their costumes. I'll be watching you."

He lowered his head. "I won't mess up." He did his job carefully, even waiting until the other boys put on their antlers before putting on his own. His pair refused to stay in place. They fell over one eye and then the other with every step he took toward me.

"These are too big." He shoved them into place again. "I don't think they're mine."

"Let me take a look." I slid them off his head and examined them. "You're right. This is the pair that was made wrong. Corinne made a new set. They must still be in my car. For now let me bobby pin these—"

Gavin took a step back. "I'm not using bobby pins. They're for girls."

"This is just for rehearsal. As soon as it's over, I'll get your pair from my car."

"What if you can't find them?"

"I'll go home and make you a new pair. I promise you won't need bobby pins tonight."

He relented. I fastened his headpiece in place and he took his position at the front of the reindeer lined up against the wall of the dressing room.

After a final costume check, Cookie and I left. She went to the piano and I sat in the front row. Gavin cracked open the dressing room door and winked at me.

I stared at him and mouthed, "I'm watching you."

He dipped his head in what I hoped was heartfelt repentance for his misbehavior. Then again, it could have been an attempt to shake off his antlers and the bobby pins he detested. His intentions weren't clear until Cookie played the opening strains of the first song and the reindeer made their entrance. Gavin's antlers stayed in place as he and the other reindeer pranced onto the stage like they'd taken lessons from the Radio City Rockettes.

The elves and the Christmas trees followed in perfect order. They found their places and burst into song right on pitch and with perfect rhythm. I beamed at Liv and we exchanged a thumbs-up.

We had ourselves a show!

Chapter 43

Mr. and Mrs. Claus exuded jolliness. The elves scampered about Santa's workshop, singing as if their holiday bonuses depended upon it. The Christmas trees waved their boughs in perfect time to the music. The littlest of their number took advantage of every opportunity to ham things up. His antics, however, didn't steal the show. The reindeer's did, as they jingled their bells and stamped their hooves. Under the direction of the lead reindeer, they formed two merry lines in front of Santa's sleigh and heave-hoed with whole-hearted, holiday cheer.

Liv and I leaped to our feet shouting, "Bravo! Bravo!" She put two fingers in her mouth and whistled. The members of the refreshment committee whooped and clapped. Cookie reprised the final song for the curtain call. The children joined hands. As they bowed in unison as they'd been taught, Gavin's antlers fell onto the stage.

He clutched his head with both hands. "Youch!" he yowled. "That hurt like sh—"

Cookie banged down on the keyboard to drown out the end of his sentence, though the gist of it was lost on no one. Including the first graders, Bennan, Stig, and Beau, if I was reading them right.

Liv's voice boomed above the giggling chaos. "Gavin, take your antlers to Miss Newell. Everyone else sit down right where you are."

Liv reviewed what the kids were to do with their costumes and when to arrive for the program. I took the antlers and the bobby pins, furry with tufts of Gavin's hair, from him. "Youch is right." I shuddered as I inspected the patches above his ears where tiny bits of his scalp used to be.

"It's nothing," he replied, recovering some of his customary swagger.

"It's something," I countered. "I want to walk home with you in a little bit and tell your parents what happened. Hand your costume to Mrs. Wentworth, and we'll go as soon as I'm free."

He objected, but I didn't budge. Once the other children were dismissed, Gavin and I put on our coats. We crossed the street to his house north of the church. While he went down the hall in search of his mother, I waited just inside the front door and stared out the window. Rique DuPeuss' truck camper sat a short distance away in the side yard. I wondered if he was teaching Gavin and his brothers how to be mountain men.

His mother looked none too pleased when she and Gavin returned. I explained what had happened, and she parted the hair above his ears, tipping his head from side to side. She squinted at the bald patches and gave him a sour look. "I think you'll live." She let go of his head and encircled the back of his neck with a scrawny hand. "Me and his dad know he's got a mouth on him. Has he been giving you any guff?"

Gavin went completely still. The look on his face was pure terror. His eyes, large and wordlessly pleading, met mine.

I put a hand on his shoulder. His mother let go of his neck. "I can't say enough about the leadership he showed during today's rehearsal. You're in for a big surprise at the program tonight."

The boy lit up like the star that topped the littlest Christmas tree. "Do you mind if I take your son to the church to look for the missing antlers?"

"It'll make my life easier if you do. Keep him as long as you like." Without giving her son the tiniest compliment, she plodded off. Her callousness broke my heart. A tiny piece chipped off and shattered when I saw the pain etched on Gavin's face.

He shoved his hands in his coat pockets. "How come you didn't tell her the truth about how I acted?"

"Everything I told your mom was the truth—just not all of it. She doesn't have to know everything unless I believe it's necessary. Is that okay with you?"

He nodded.

We crossed the street, and I opened the Beetle's passenger door. "Unless my guess is way off, the missing antlers are in here somewhere. There's a flashlight in the glove box if you need it to see under the seats. You can keep any spare change you find. Bring any paper money you find, the antlers, and anything else you unearth into the church when you're done. That's where I'll be. Got it?"

He unlatched the glove box. "Got it."

I went inside and helped Liv and Corinne put the costumes and props where they belonged. It didn't take long, and they left as Gavin came in. He brandished the missing antlers like he'd found Santa's favorite pair of wool socks.

"I found a bunch of stuff." He dumped his entire haul on the lip of the stage.

"You're a lifesaver, Gavin." I handed him the antlers. "Now, try these on."

He did as instructed and jumped onto the stage. He pranced around, shook his head, and made a deep bow. Only when he was convinced the antlers would stay put did he show me the fifty-five cents he'd found. "It was in the crack where the back of the passenger seat meets the bottom." He pocketed the change. "Along with that." He pointed to a crumpled piece of paper.

"You outdid yourself, young man. Guess who I'm going to call when my car needs a good cleaning?"

"I'm your guy. See you tonight." He bounded to the door like a puppy after his master said he was a good boy.

I laid the paper, blank side up, on the stage and smoothed out the wrinkles. Then I turned it over. The writing on the other side was as familiar as my own handwriting. Because it was my handwriting. I was staring at my missing suspect list. I had no recollection of putting it in my car. The only explanation that made any sense was an option I'd not considered yesterday. I'd seen it on the fridge when I was in a hurry to get somewhere and unthinkingly shoved it into my purse. The note had fallen out when I'd thrown my purse onto the seat. I couldn't afford to be that careless again.

Relieved, I folded the note and zipped it into the pocket of my parka. I couldn't afford to be careless with it again. Then I poked through the rest of what Gavin had piled on the stage. A lot of it was garbage. Candy wrappers. Old store receipts. Used tissues. I threw them in the waste basket. All that remained was a paper sack with "Merry Christmas from your friends at Tipperary Hardware Store!" printed under a manger scene.

I turned the sack upside down and shook out its contents, expecting a spool of curling ribbon to fall out. A ski mask landed on the stage with a soft plop. A camouflage ski mask. I reached out a fingertip.

No, Jane! Don't touch it!

I snatched my hand away as if burned and reached for the sack instead. It crinkled as I turned it inside out and put my hand inside the bag. Using it as a makeshift glove, I picked up the mask and turned the bag right side out until it once again held the mask. I put on my coat and went outside, the bag in one hand and my purse in the other. Gavin and his brothers were building a snow fort in the front yard. I crossed the street and held up the bag.

"Gavin," I called. "Where was this lying when you found it?"

"Under the passenger seat. Why?"

"Just curious. Thanks."

That was not exactly true. The minute I laid eyes on the mask, I knew where he'd had found it and the bag it was in. With my hunch confirmed, I needed to tell the sheriff, but not until I'd examined it. I drove home and went straight for my microscope. I slid the mask onto the table and lifted the jagged edge of the hole with two craft sticks to examine its underside.

At the sight of the twig and pine needles snared in the yarn, the spark my brain had been chasing for two days flared and connected. The reason Vince hadn't put on a hat during last night's snowstorm was that he didn't want me to see that his was ripped.

Vince was the reason the suspect list was in my car. He had taken it from my house when the sheriff apprehended Russ because he was Edgar's killer. It must have slipped out of his pocket when I gave him a lift to the gas station. It had been dark when he gathered the packages he'd piled on the floor of the Beetle, and he'd overlooked this one. Later, when my car fishtailed on the drive to Little Missouri, the sack slid under the seat so I didn't see it either. Did he know the note and the hat were missing? If he did, he wouldn't care. He was leaving for Mexico any minute if he wasn't gone already. He thought he was home free.

I ran for the phone and shouted into the receiver. "Betty!" I cut her off before she settled in for a chat. "Put me through to the sheriff's office. Now!"

Chapter 44

Rick answered on the first ring. "Sheriff's office."

"I have definitive proof that Vince Douglas is Edgar's killer. He's flying to Mexico this afternoon. He may be gone already. We have to try to stop him, or he'll get away with murder."

"Is he leaving from the Fly Ranch airport?"

"No, the Wentworth's airstrip. That's where his plane is hangared."

"I'm on my way. And Jane?"

"What?"

"Stay where you are. Don't leave your apartment."

I jerked the receiver away as a horrible racket came down the line. Rick must have thrown the receiver at the cradle and bolted out of the office at the same time. Did he really expect me to stay home and twiddle my thumbs until he arrived? Well, he had another thing coming.

"Are you going to wisten to the sheriff and stay put?"

"I'm a rule follower, Betty. It's one reason I became a teacher. Don't you breathe a word of what you just heard to another soul!" I hung up, grabbed my keys and coat, and raced to the Beetle. I hopped in, started the car, and backed out, spraying snow and gravel on the way. Once I turned onto Main Street, the car hit a patch of ice. I checked my rearview mirror as the Beetle fishtailed and saw a pickup truck about a block behind me. I pumped my brakes and slowed down. The truck kept its distance. When I reached the bridge, its surface was clear and dry so I hit the gas. The Wentworths' lane came up quickly. I cranked the steering wheel to the left. The Beetle fish-tailed again. The pickup driver had every reason to lay on his horn—I hadn't used my blinker—but the truck zipped by noiselessly.

I bumped down the lane, searching for a place to hide the Beetle without getting it stuck in a snowbank. My choices were limited. I couldn't leave it out in the open where Corinne might see it and come outside. That would be bad.

Worse yet, Vince would see it and the element of surprise, the only card I had to play, would be lost. I continued down the lane until a huge snow pile appeared beyond Corinne and Richard's cleared driveway. I circled the mountain of snow until it blocked my car from view of both house and lane. I cut the engine and got out. The barely audible click of the door closing was nearly drowned out by the sound of a vehicle slowing on the highway and turning down the lane.

If that was Vince, there was no time to lose. I edged along the snow pile and poked my head around it to see down the lane. I could hear the vehicle, but couldn't see it yet. It was now or never. I crouched low and hurried along the plowed path that I guessed went to the airstrip. I guessed right. The hangar loomed up before me, but there was no sign of Vince's pickup truck. Either he'd parked it in the hangar or he was driving down the lane. I crept over to a small door next to hangar doors, turned the knob, and pushed it open. I stepped inside as the engine noise from the approaching vehicle grew louder. Now I could hear the squeak of tires on packed snow. I pulled the door shut behind me and darkness surrounded me.

Far too slowly, my eyes adjusted to the gloom. Once they did, a scan of the hangar made my heart beat faster. Vince's truck wasn't there, but two small planes were. One had to belong to the Wentworths. The other, I hoped, belonged to Vince. About halfway along the closest wall, a workbench jutted out at a right angle.

A vehicle door slammed. My heart hammered. My feet refused to cooperate. I put a hand out until it touched the wall. I willed my feet to move and tiptoed toward the workbench. I was nearly there when the hangar door slid open. A thin stream of winter light appeared. It grew wider and wider, threatening to expose me. I dropped to my knees and crawled behind the bench. I pressed my body into the shadows and waited until my ragged breathing slowed, and I could hear above the pounding in my ears.

I peered through the slats of the workbench. The hangar doors were wide open now. Vince walked over to his plane. Any hope I'd had of creating a delay by slashing his tires or punching a hole in the plane's gas tank—where was a plane's gas tank anyway?—before the sheriff came faded. Vince climbed into the cockpit. The plane roared to life, but it didn't compete with my ominous inner drumbeat.

You're too late, Jane. Too late. Too late.

Vince drove the plane through the hangar doors and onto the runway. I couldn't bear to watch him put his plane in position for takeoff and be another step closer to his escape. I just couldn't. I lowered my head and buried my face in my arms. I intended to stay like that until the plane took off and the sound of the engine faded away.

The engine noise ceased abruptly. I lifted my eyes and peeked through the slats again. Vince climbed out of the cockpit with a clipboard clamped between his teeth. Once he was on the ground, he took the clipboard in his hands and began to walk around the plane. I had no idea what he was doing, but if there was any chance of stopping him, this was it.

I rose slowly, positioning myself to remain hidden from view behind the workbench. I ran a hand along its surface, looking for a weapon. A hammer. A screwdriver. A pair of needle-nose pliers. I wasn't picky. My hand landed on a wrench. It felt like a big one. I lifted it up and tested its weight. Yes, it would do quite nicely.

With the wrench in hand, I crept to the front of the hangar, staying in the shadows as best I could. I still hadn't worked out how to stop Vince, so I prayed for divine intervention. Or inspiration to strike. Or opportunity to knock. Again, I wasn't picky. Any one of them would do.

Opportunity showed up first. It came knocking when Vince pushed the plane over to the gas drums at the edge of the runway. He positioned a ladder beside the near wing and then took the fuel hose from the drum and proceeded to climb the ladder, dragging the hose with him. He stuck the nozzle in the top of the wing—*that's where a plane's gas tank is?*—and waited until it was full. He descended the ladder, moved it to the far side of the plane and repeated the process. But this time, once he put the nozzle in the tank, he climbed down and jogged over to his pickup truck which was also on the far side of the plane.

This was my chance! I jammed the wrench into the waistband of my trousers, ran to the plane, and climbed up to the cockpit door. It took several nerve-wracking minutes to figure out how to unlatch it. I got inside and was crawling into the back seat when Vince's footsteps approached the plane again.

I eased the wrench out of my waistband. Before curling into a ball behind the pilot's seat, I risked a peek out the window on the side where Vince was fueling. The hose was gone and Vince was hauling the ladder away. A dark flash near the snow pile caught my eye. I squinted to get a better look, but saw only white. It must have been a bird.

I heard a clatter as the ladder landed on the ground and then Vince's footsteps drew closer. I ducked down and made myself as small as possible. The plane rocked and I felt it inching forward. Vince had to be pushing it away from the gas tanks. The movement ceased, and I peeked through the crack next to the seat where I had stowed away. The cockpit door opened. Vince slid into the pilot's seat and latched the door shut.

I had no way of knowing what Vince did as seconds stretched into minutes. My legs went numb. I strained my ears for the shriek of a siren and the squeal of brakes. I heard nothing.

Rick, you ought to be here by now. What is keeping you?

The engine sputtered and caught. The plane crept forward. It was time to make my move.

I uncurled my body and grasped the wrench. Needles of pain ran up my legs when I shifted my weight and got on my knees. I bit my tongue to stifle a scream, raised the wrench, and aimed it at Vince's head.

Chapter 45

The plane swerved. The sudden movement knocked me off balance and the wrench slid onto the padded seat behind me.

Vince cursed. "Where did you come from?" His voice was venomous.

I shrank down behind his seat and waited for him to stop the plane and kill me. He'd killed before. He could do it again.

"You got a death wish? Get off the runway!" he bellowed.

The runway?

I inched up until I could see above the cockpit dashboard and tried to process the scene outside the window. Dick Phillips stood about fifty feet in front of the plane holding out his arm like a cop directing traffic. The man was the biggest nut job in Tipperary County. Except for Vince. A sane person would have slammed on the brakes and swerved to save the nut job's life. Vince aimed straight for him.

I was not inclined to leave them to their game of chicken. Not as long as there was a chance to make Vince pay for killing Edgar. I felt around on the floor for the wrench. It wasn't there. I twisted my arm and ran my hand along the seat behind me. My fingertips brushed against hard, cold metal. I took hold of it and raised it high just as the plane lurched to a stop. The momentum pitched me forward. My head bounced off of Vince's shoulder. The wrench flew from my hand and skittered to the floor.

Blast it! My timing could use some work.

Vince's head whipped around. "What the—"

Violent pounding drowned out his words. Dick's face pressed against the side window next to the pilot's seat. He tugged at the door. His voice rose above the sputtering engine. "Get out of the plane! Both of you!"

Vince's face went slack. He shifted in his seat.

He's giving up! Hope flared within me. *We've got him!*

Quick as a blink, Vince's expression tightened. He turned toward Dick, brought his right leg up, and kicked at the latch beneath the window. The door flew open. The force of it sent Dick tumbling. As the door swung toward the plane again, Vince's arm snaked out and fastened the latch. He taxied to the end of the runway again and turned the plane around.

I beat on his shoulder with my fists. "What do you think you're doing?"

He kept his gaze fixed on the airstrip. "Taking you to Mexico. Unless I come up with a way to get rid of you before then." He bent his arm and jabbed my left temple with his elbow. The impact snapped my head to the side and I fell to the floor. "I'll do worse than that if you touch me again."

I obeyed. Not because of his threat. Because I didn't want him to look out the side window and see what I'd glimpsed outside it when he hit me. Dick was sprinting down the runway toward the right side of the plane. I rose up and took another peek. The nut job was nearing the plane. I had to hand it to him. He was persistent. By golly, so was I.

I dropped down and hunted for the wrench. It was the least I could do in light Dick's fall and his crazy race with the plane. As my hands felt along the floor, I caught a glint of metal from the corner of my eye. The wrench was wedged between the seat and the side of the plane.

"There you are, my pretty!" I cackled soft and low and took hold of it. I tugged with all my strength until it came free. Then I stood on my knees and lifted the wrench just as the plane began to pick up speed.

A movement on the runway made me glance out the passenger window again. Dick took a flying leap and managed to grab onto a wing strut. The extra weight threw the plane off balance, tipping it to the right. Vince fought to pull up the wing. The plane wobbled and threw me off balance. The wrench slipped out of my hand and crashed against the passenger window.

Vince turned in the direction of the noise. "What was that?" At the sight of Dick, his face red and teeth gritted, still dragging on the strut, Vince howled. "If you're gonna do stupid, I won't stop you." He worked the controls. I held my breath as Dick clung to the strut.

"You're going to kill him!" I leaned over the back seat, determined to pry his fingers from the lever he was pulling. Before I reached his hand, the plane began to spin. The dizzying motion slammed me against the side window and pinned me there. The plane spun in a tight circle. Dick was at its center hanging from the wing.

Any second now, he would fall onto the runway. Given half a chance, Vince would angle the plane and run over him. Pinned against the side of the plane by centrifugal force, I couldn't stop him. My dizziness increased tenfold. I closed my eyes to stop the whirling. That was a mistake. Nausea convulsed my stomach and I opened my eyes.

Desperately, Dick clung to the strut. Desperately, I breathed in through my nose and out through my mouth. The contents of my stomach interrupted my efforts. Too late, I tried to clamp my lips together. Vomit spewed from me like lava from a hot volcano. Thanks to the spinning plane, it boomeranged and drenched my face, my clothes, and my hair.

"What's that stench? Did you just—" Vince's complexion went dead white. "I'm gonna be sick." And he was. All over the control panel. All over the levers he'd been working furiously up until now. Thanks to that lovely centrifugal force, all over himself, too.

Blindly he tried to grasp the controls. They were slimy with vomit, and his hands slid off one lever after another. The plane shuddered and its spinning slowed. Its grip on me loosened, and I slithered onto the seat. My tailbone hit something hard and lumpy. I scooted forward and pulled out the wrench. Before Vince could recover and take off again, I took the wrench in both hands and whacked the back of his head. A direct hit!

Yes!

He slumped forward. The plane quit its drunken reeling. Before I could begin rejoicing, it charted a more direct course along the runway and headed straight for the hangar. The wing, not the one Dick was attached to, hit the hangar wall and crumpled. The impact sent me sliding across the seat. Again. I looked up and, with an arm, shielded my head to avoid banging it against the window. Again.

"No!" I screamed as Dick sailed through the air, fell onto the runway, and landed in a heap.

"No!"

Chapter 46

The plane wobbled and threatened to keel over when I began to move. Gingerly, I crawled through the gap between the front seats, turned off the ignition, and put the key in my pocket. Then I unlatched the passenger door. I climbed down, the plane shifting with every step, and jumped onto the runway. Dick's unmoving body lay in a crumpled heap a few yards away. Fear propelled me, and I skidded to a stop in front of him.

I bent down to check his pulse. His head jerked up and hit my eye socket with a pop. It hurt like nobody's business. My hand flew up to shield my eye and I fell backwards onto the icy ground.

Dick got to his feet with a groan and rubbed his head. "That was a direct hit. Let me look at your eye."

"I don't want your help." I warded him off with my free hand. "At this rate, it's going to kill me."

He ignored my protests and bent for a closer look. I had to get rid of him. His quick recovery after being thrown to the ground had been astonishing, but so was his ability to inflict bodily harm, perhaps even permanent damage. A broken nose, a scarred cheek, missing teeth. With him, nothing was impossible. I wanted no part of it.

"Why don't you check on Vince?" I asked as he came too close for comfort. "I whacked his skull pretty hard."

Dick reversed course and ran for the plane. He ran faster than I would have gone considering the snowpack and ice on the runway. Then again, maybe he would fall on the frozen ground again and get some sense knocked into him.

With him out of the way, I examined my most recent injury. It hurt more than I wanted Dick to know. I ran tentative fingers over the eye socket. The lightest touch sent needles of pain into my forehead and across my cheek. It was swelling too. Taking a page from Rique DuPeuss's book, I took a glove from my pocket. Then I scooped it full of snow and held it to my eye. I felt like an arctic pirate making a fashion statement as I wound my scarf around the glove to hold it in place. Then I ran to the plane. The cockpit door was open and Dick was sitting in the passenger seat.

The distance between us was reassuring. "Should I go to the Wentworths and call an ambulance?" I yelled.

"Nah. You didn't do that much damage. Surface wounds look worse than they are. I just need you to open this first aid kit"—he tossed it to me—"and then climb up and hold it open."

The kit was coated with vomit. I had to scrub it with snow and dry it with my remaining glove before I could grip it hard enough to pry it open. Perhaps that was a delaying tactic since moving closer to Dick was the last thing I wanted to do. When I could delay no longer, I zipped the open box inside my coat so my hands were free as I climbed up to Dick. I braced one leg on the side of the plane and the other on a wing strut. Only when I surmised that Dick and I were far enough apart to protect me from an accidental shove that would send me tumbling to my death four feet below, did I remove the open first aid kit and hold it out to him.

I smiled as brightly as an arctic pirate can. "If you so much as think about ordering me to give you a scalpel, you're on your own."

Dick glowered. "You're not very funny." His nose wrinkled. "And you stink." He plucked several alcohol swabs from the kit, ripped them open, and dabbed at the gash behind Vince's right ear. He threw used swabs on the cockpit floor like they were candy wrappers.

Bright red candy wrappers. Bloody candy wrappers that reminded a country school teacher teetering on the side of an airplane of why she became a teacher and not a nurse. My ears began to buzz and the vision in my good eye turned green.

"Hold the box still, please." Dick spoke from far away. "Jane, I said—Jane!"

In a swirl of green haze, I watched the first aid kit plummet to the ground. I tried to dive into the haze to rescue it. Something jerked me out of the dive and closer to consciousness.

"Jane!" Dick's voice was closer now. More insistent.

I forced my eyelids open. *Holy moly!* His voice wasn't the only thing that had come closer. His arm was looped around my torso. My forehead was crammed against his cheek. My feet dangled in thin air as he shook me. Permanent bodily harm was imminent.

"Stay with me, Jane! Can you hear me?"

"Of course I can! You're yelling in my ear." I stretched a leg until my foot touched the wing. My free hand clamped onto the grab bar beside the door. I pulled away from him. "Let go of me. Now."

He kept a firm grip on my coat sleeve. "Are you sure?"

"I'll be fine as long as there's no more blood." I inhaled great gulps of air until my lungs were filled with it and my vision was as clear as the sky over Little Missouri on a cold winter day. "It's never been my favorite thing."

"Yeah. You good?" He let go of my coat.

I inched away and tested my footholds. "I'm good."

Vince groaned. Dick leaned toward him. The motion made the plane sway, and I discovered that my footholds were as good as I'd said. To be on the safe side, I wrapped my arms around a strut and clutched it tight.

Vince croaked. "What?" He touched the wound behind his ear. "Where?"

I clambered down before he could wave his bloody fingers for the world to see. As my feet touched the ground, a faint siren wailed in the distance. "Dick, did you hear that? It must be—"

"The ambulance." Dick's words were forced and unnatural, as if he were reading from a script. "Thanks for calling that in, Jane." His tone became calm and kind when he spoke again to Vince. "You had an accident and hit your head. Do you want to get out by yourself or would you rather wait for a stretcher?"

Vince opened his door and swung his legs out. "I can do it."

"Hang on!" Dick leaped out of the cockpit and

ducked under the plane. "Now, easy does it. You might feel dizzy. Let me grab hold of you."

They came out from behind the plane. Dick had an arm around Vince and gently led him to the edge of the runway. I followed behind them. Dick lowered Vince slowly to the ground, propped him against a snowbank, and drew a penlight from his coat pocket. As he knelt and shone the light in Vince's eyes, the siren grew louder.

Vince looked around. His head reared back when he saw me standing a few feet away. "You ambushed me. From the back seat of my plane."

He closed a fist over Dick's penlight and shoved it away. He stared at him, then squeezed his eyes shut. When he opened them, he snarled at Dick. "And you're the reason I crashed. You knew what would happen when you took hold of that wing." He twisted the penlight away from Dick and threw it at his face. Then he lunged and knocked Dick to the ground.

Sirens wailed. Tires squealed. The revving of an engine signaled the approach of a vehicle. The sheriff was finally going to put in an appearance. Better late than never. From the looks of the two guys duking it out, he might arrive too late.

I scaled a snowbank and flagged down Rick. When he slowed, I hopped inside the patrol car, and pointed to the spur that led from the driveway to the runway. "Down there. And hurry. Vince isn't going down without a fight."

The patrol car reached the runway. "Go left," I ordered.

Rick turned the wheel and there they were, about fifty feet away. Vince lay sprawled on the snow. Dick sat on top of him, dodging Vince's flailing arms as he tried to land blow after blow. Rick screeched to a stop and shouted, "Wait in here," as he got out.

Ignoring his command, I got out. "You've got a lot of nerve saying that," I yelled as I ran to catch up with him. "I'm the one who kept Vince from leaving while you took your own sweet time getting here. What held you up?"

"Cattle on the road. And you had help." He pointed at Dick. "I sent him to assist you."

I stared at the scene before us as the sheriff's words sunk in. It couldn't be Dick. It simply couldn't be him. I didn't want it to be him. But who else could it be? Certainly not Vince.

"Dick Phillips?" I whimpered.

"One and the same." Rick went to give him a hand.

CHAPTER 47

Vince looked at the sheriff and then at Dick, and the fight went out of him.

Dick clamped his hands around the prone man's wrists. "Got your handcuffs, Sheriff?"

Rick took them off his belt. "Would you like to do the honors?" He held them out to Dick.

I was done being ignored by the sheriff. I rushed over, intercepted the hand off, and dangled the cuffs out of his reach. "Don't mind if I do."

"Wait a minute," Rick protested.

Dick came to my defense. "If it wasn't for Jane, Vince would be halfway to Mexico by now. She's earned the right."

It was the longest sentence he'd uttered in my presence before. And the first nice thing he'd had to say about me. Dick held Vince down while I cuffed his left wrist. For a wisp of a second, I considered letting Dick secure the other. Then I came to my senses and fastened the other cuff around his right wrist.

It felt good. So good I wanted to get in Vince's face and crow, "You're busted, sucker!" Just then Vince revived, perhaps indignant at being cuffed by a woman, and began kicking wildly. Never a glutton for punishment, I moved out of the way.

The sheriff and Dick got on either side of Vince and hoisted him to his feet. "Vince Douglas," the sheriff intoned, "you are under arrest for the murder of Edgar Running Horse."

Inside I was running around in circles, fists raised high in victory. "Yes!" I screamed internally while the outer me stood stern and solemn as an old-fashioned country schoolmarm. "Yes, yes, yes!"

The sheriff and Dick kept a firm hold on Vince while they escorted him to the patrol car. I followed at a safe distance, and was glad I did. Vince twisted and fought as they shoved him into the back seat. Dick ran to the other side and restrained Vince while the sheriff strapped him into his seat belt.

"That should hold him." Rick straightened.

Dick did, too. "Want me to go to Tipperary with you?" he asked.

"No need. My deputy's waiting at the end of the lane and can ride with me." He gave a short nod in Dick's direction and, like an afterthought, an even shorter one in mine. "Thanks for your help."

Dick ducked his head into the back seat again and laid a hand on Vince's shoulder. "I'm sorry I had to sit on you like that. I didn't mean to hurt you."

Vince bared his teeth, lunged, and bit down on Dick's ear.

Dick's head reared up and hit the car roof. He backed

out, shut the rear door on his side, and cupped a hand over his ear. Rick slammed the other rear door, climbed in, and drove off. When Dick took his hand away from his ear, blood dripped and stained the snow red.

I ran to the plane and knelt on the runway, picking through the contents of the first aid kit for what Dick needed to doctor his ear. I took my haul over to him.

"Here." I thrust a handful of antiseptic swabs at him. "I'd clean the wound myself, but you know me and blood."

He took the swabs.

I looked away and winced. "Does it hurt?"

"No."

"Do you want a gauze pad and tape?"

"Yes."

Still looking away, I handed them over. "Anything else?"

"No."

I waited for what seemed like long enough to bandage an elephant. "You're fine then?"

"Yes."

"Is your wound bandaged?"

"Yes."

I risked a glance in his direction. No blood, and his ear was swathed in gauze. I looked him in the eye. "In that case, why don't you tell me about how long you and the sheriff have been in cahoots on this case?"

He crossed his arms.

I crossed mine. "Since Edgar's body was found?"

Head shake.

"Since the community Christmas party?"

Another shake.

"When you confronted me about visiting the Yorks?"
Shake.

"When the three of you burst in on me and Russ?"
Suspicious-looking eye squint.

I wasn't there yet, but getting close. "But during that weekend, right?"

Tiniest of nods.

"Enough with the twenty questions." I uncrossed my arms and took a step toward him. "Tell me what you've been doing. Preferably in complete sentences."

To my astonishment, he obliged. In less than two minutes, he summarized his part in the investigation in short, succinct sentences. After Dick had returned Russ to Fly Ranch, the sheriff had asked his opinion of Vince Douglas. Dick said he believed Vince was selling drugs to the boys and offered to feed information to the sheriff. That was all he did until word spread that Vince and I had been seen together at Round the Bend. Then the sheriff set up round-the-clock surveillance.

"I had it all wrong," I burst in. "I thought the sheriff was surveilling you and all along Vince was the one he was watching?"

"Not Vince." Dick looked over my shoulder in the direction of the hangar.

Why was he avoiding my gaze? Unless—

"Me? He was spying on me?"

"Only because he knew Vince knew you were snooping around. So Rick asked a bunch of us—"

"Who?"

"His deputy."

So it had been him at the Nine Pins.

"There was, um, me." He swallowed.

I narrowed my eyes. "Who else?"

Dick cleared his throat. "Rique DuPeuss."

I narrowed my eyes. "Who else?"

Dick cleared his throat. "Dale Cunningham."

That explained Dale's matchmaking. And why Rique had agreed without hesitating.

"And?"

"Uh." He still couldn't meet my eye. "Merle. And Velma."

Of course Merle and Velma. Why not Merle and Velma?

"Betty Yarborough too, I suppose?"

"No. Then everyone in town would have been in on it and somebody would have leaked it to Vince, and he'd a been gone before Rick had enough evidence to arrest him."

Thank God for small favors. Still, enough people were in on the secret to make me the town laughingstock. How would I face them at the program tonight?

Oh no! I pulled at my coat sleeve and looked at my watch. It was four o'clock. I had to meet Liv at the church in two hours. I had a goose egg on my forehead and most likely a black eye. My clothes and hair were covered with vomit. If I wanted to be a presentable laughingstock in front of everyone, I needed to get cracking, and quick.

"I have to go."

"Want me to drive you?" He waved a hand in the general direction of my trussed up head and soiled coat. "You're kinda beat up."

"So are you." I waved specifically at his palm, which was scraped raw, and his bandaged ear. "If you want to be useful, tell the rest of the Little Missouri spy ring to stand down. And from now on, leave me alone!"

I turned on my heel, and with as much dignity as my battered being could muster, I walked away from him with slow and measured steps. At least until I was hidden by the snow piles. Then I ran full tilt for my car and dove in. With the reckless abandon of someone who knows that every law officer in the county is otherwise occupied, I hit the gas and drove like a maniac into town.

Chapter 48

Two hours and ten minutes later I rushed into the church, shedding my coat while entering the foyer. "Sorry I'm late, Liv!"

"Let me put your coat in the kitchen with mine." She whisked it away from me and whistled when she saw the green velvet dress. "I heard talk that Corinne was sewing something special. I have to say she outdid herself. The tiara is a classy touch."

"Beau made me promise to wear it."

Her forehead wrinkled. "How come you're wearing glasses?"

"With leaving early tomorrow morning, I decided to take out my contacts and rest my eyes tonight." The half-truth came out smooth as fresh cream. I had no business telling Liv how the glasses masked the layers of concealer and foundation that were hiding both a goose egg and black eye. If I did, she would want to know what happened and that would lead to a conversation best left closed until after Vince's arrest was made public.

She examined my face for what felt like an eternity. I prayed that the poorly lit church foyer hid what the makeup didn't. "When you leaving?" she finally asked.

My clenched teeth relaxed. "Four-thirty."

She chuckled and headed to the kitchen with my coat. "Only five months in Tipperary County, and you're already keeping rancher's hours."

The door opened. A gust of wind accompanied Cookie as she rushed inside. Corinne arrived on her heels. They came in and saw my dress.

"Jane Newell, you are a vision. Twirl around, dear."

I obliged.

"One more time," Corinne said. "I want to see how it fits."

"It fits beautifully. Corinne, you did a wonderful job." Cookie wagged a finger at me. "And Jane, tonight you're going to turn heads right and left. Betty says there's been a string of them making eyes at you all month."

So Cookie didn't know the whole story. Which meant I would not be a laughingstock in her eyes. That was reassuring, but still, it was past time to divert their attention away from me. And my face. Especially my face.

I glanced at the clock and feigned surprise. "Will you look at the time? We'd better get cracking or we won't be ready when people start arriving."

Cookie bustled to the piano, Corinne to the costume room, and Liv to the props table in the kitchen. I ducked into the ladies' room. This might be my last chance to touch up my concealer and foundation. I studied my reflection with a critical eye. No repair job was required. I downed several aspirin to dull the headache I'd been ignoring it since Dick and I had bonked heads. Then I returned to the foyer.

The students began arriving soon after that. The next half-hour was a blur. There were children to herd to the costume room to get dressed. There were children bouncing off the walls with excitement. There were children nervous about forgetting their lines. Somehow, five minutes before showtime, they were all present, dressed, and ready to go.

I peeked out. The church was packed. Every seat was taken, and several people were standing behind the back row. I signaled for Cookie to begin the overture. The crowd quieted as she played an enchanting medley of holiday tunes and Christmas carols. When she finished, I grinned at the children. They had gone still and were wide-eyed.

"Break a leg," I whispered.

"Don't tell the littlest Christmas tree to break a leg, Miss Newell." Tiege's high voice sailed above the crowd as I went out to greet them. "Tell it to break a branch!"

The room filled with whoops of laughter. Once they died down I welcomed them. "Thank you for joining us for this rendition of *The Littlest Christmas Tree*. You've already heard from the tree"—more chuckles—"and rumor has it that Santa will put in an appearance during the cookie and punch reception afterward, so please stay if you can. Now, on with the show and Merry Christmas!"

I took my seat in the front row, flanked by Merle on my left and Velma on my right. I cued Cookie and we were off.

The performance had its flaws. The Christmas trees

sang off key. Two elves collided during the workshop scene and rolled off the stage. The reindeer games were on the rowdy side. When Liv turned off the overhead lights and the children's faces were illuminated by their tiny electric candles, the imperfections were forgotten. Our students began to sing into the darkness.

Silent night, holy night,

The audience stilled as holiness came to dwell among us. Not a rustle or whisper was heard.

All is calm, all is bright.

Calm reigned within my heart. The brightness of a baby born in a manger eased my aches and pains. The bright promise of God come to earth as a baby touched me as it never had before. I opened my mouth and sang with the children.

Round yon virgin, mother and child,

Merle and Velma joined me, their voices cracked and vulnerable and strong. The people on either side of them, then behind us, entered in. Before long everyone in the room was singing. Some in tune. Some out of tune. All of them lovely and broken.

Holy infant so tender and mild.

My heart swelled with joy and hope and wonder as I saw, in the children leading the song, the Child who was sent to lead us to God.

Sleep in heavenly peace, sleep in heavenly peace.

Peace, palpable and penetrating, invaded the room and burrowed into my bones. I put a hand to my cheek and it came away wet with tears. And smeared with foundation.

I pulled out a tissue and covered my face. "It's so beautiful."

I buried my head on Velma's shoulder and sobbed.

"I need some time to pull myself together. Can you think of something to say to the audience until I get back?"

She patted my back, but I didn't wait for an answer. I grabbed my purse from under my chair and scurried to the bathroom. I repaired the water damage in short order and slipped into my seat again. At least I thought it was my seat. It was hard to tell because Merle was nowhere to be found, and Velma stood on the stage, backlit by the glow of electric candles. The older children held theirs still. The younger ones, as in all of my students except for Elva, waved theirs around like sparklers on the Fourth of July.

"Now"—Velma put her fists on her hips and glared at the audience—"I'm cleaning this church tomorrow before the Christmas Eve service. I've already gotta mop the floors 'cause none of you bothered to stomp off the snow on the extra rug I laid out for that express purpose. When you help yourselves to cookies and punch in a few minutes, I expect every one of you to make good use of your napkin so I don't have to get on my knees to scrape crumbs off the floor. And you'd best fill your punch cups only halfways so I don't have to bleach stains out of the linoleum."

Her impression of the Grinch was spot on, but she wasn't going to steal Christmas if I had my way. Apparently Liv was of the same opinion. We mounted the steps to the stage together. She flipped on the lights and began gathering candles.

I put an arm around Velma's shoulders and faced the crowd. "Let's give Velma a hand for her hard work."

A mere smattering of applause.

"And now"—I looked over my shoulder—"it's time for the kids to take your bows."

The children snapped into curtain call formation and the applause swelled. The audience whistled, shouted bravo, and gave them a standing ovation. The children accepted the accolades as their due, which they most certainly were. I directed the audience members to the cookie table. Then Liv and I herded the children back-stage to where Corinne waited to gather their costumes. She had collected all but a few when we heard a faint "Ho, ho, ho!"

Tiege cried, "Santa's here!" and led a stampede across the stage to where the jolly old elf had just entered the church. The children swarmed around him and tried to peek into the bag slung over his shoulder.

They pelted him with questions. "What's in your bag, Santa? What did you bring us?"

My first instinct was to charge over and tell them to mind their manners. Instead, I burrowed into the peace that had begun with the singing of *Silent Night*. The small bags of candy Santa gave the children would last a day or two. The gift I'd received tonight, the gift I intended to spend the rest of my life unwrapping, would last for eternity.

The children pressed in closer, and Santa began to tip over. I set my musings aside and inserted myself between him and his small, but rabid fans. It was time to save Santa Claus.

Chapter 49

"Santa needs room to breathe." I shouted above the children's high, excited racket. "He needs to be in good shape when he climbs in his sleigh tomorrow."

The children pressed closer in. "Bring me a doll," one clamored.

"I want a horse," shouted another.

"A BB gun!"

"A bike!"

"New cowgirl boots!"

"A sad—"

"Will you look at that?" I pointed at the refreshment table. "I think they're running out of Christmas cookies!"

The kids abandoned Santa like yesterday's newspaper. The moms handing out cookies paled as the onslaught approached, then rallied and filled trays as quickly as the children emptied them.

Santa winked and mouthed "Thank you," through

the white curls of his impressively authentic beard and mustache.

That Merle! He deserved combat pay and an Oscar for his performance as Santa. I walked over to tell him as much. Laughter rang out behind me and I turned to see what was so funny. There stood Merle, not in a Santa suit, regaling a small group of people with one of his stories.

Who was in the Santa suit? I resumed my march toward the guy hiding behind the beard, mustache, and bowl full of jelly belly. His eyes tracked my progress. I had the feeling he wanted to talk to me. I'd gone fewer than five steps when Gavin Wick and Rique DuPeuss blocked my way.

"The program was a pleasant surprise." Rique patted Gavin on the back. "And this young man outdid himself."

"He's very talented." I beamed at Gavin. Then, because I wasn't in the habit of being rude on the night before the night before Christmas, I beamed at Rique too. "And Merry Christmas to the both of you. Now, if you'll excuse me, Santa and I have urgent business to discuss."

I made it two more steps when the Barkleys intercepted me. They were chock full of effusive praise for the program, and Pam went on and on about my dress. After the Barkleys, the Bertholds, the Sternquists, the Borgesons, and several perfect strangers stopped to chat. Santa waited patiently, though I can only vouch for the waited part. His patience was hard to gauge, what with the fake facial hair masking his expression and his identity equally well. But when I disentangled myself from a long and awkward conversation with the perfect strangers, who treated me like an old friend though I'd never laid eyes on them before, Santa had vanished. Dang it!

Maybe he'd gone out for some fresh air. I rushed outside to see. "Santa? Are you out here?"

"He said to tell you he had to get back to the North Pole." Rick answered.

"You can be such a smart aleck, Sheriff."

"Taking a murderer to the jail in Sturgis has that effect on me."

"That excuse won't fly with Tiege. Your little brother was counting on you making it to the program." The velvet dress was no match for the cold. I crossed my arms and rubbed them with my hands.

"I nipped in as the lights went down."

"That's good." Needles of icy pain pricked my legs. "I'm going inside."

He spoke to my retreating back. "What's a good time to take your statement tomorrow?"

"It'll have to wait." I kept walking. "I'm leaving for Iowa in the morning."

"It can't wait, Jane."

I stopped moving.

His next words were gentle but firm. "We have to finish it before you go."

"No." My throat constricted and my words came out thick and slow. "I want to leave by four-thirty or I won't be home for supper with my parents before their Christmas Eve service." I dug a tissue from my pocket and blew my nose.

He exhaled, his breath a frosty, shimmering billow in

the light streaming from the sanctuary window. "Could we do it now? At your apartment?"

"How long do you need to take my statement?"

"An hour. Maybe more."

I fought against my brimming tears and inclined my head toward the foyer. "It'll be at least a half hour before people leave and we can tear down the stage. I've got a long drive tomorrow and was counting on a good night's sleep."

"If that's the only thing worrying you, I will guarantee we'll be done by nine o'clock." He batted away my objection with an excess of Christmas cheer. "Come inside." He took my elbow and we were in the foyer before I had a chance to protest.

"Attention everyone." The crowd immediately complied. "I need to take Miss Newell's statement regarding the arrest of a suspect in the Edgar Running Horse murder case. Liv, can you spare her for the rest of the evening?"

"Yup."

"Thank you." He looked at me. "You've got five minutes to get your things and tell your students goodbye."

It took me ten. Even so, we arrived at my apartment by eight-fifteen. The afternoon's events were seared in my brain, and I made short work of the statement. Next, I went to my office for Vince's ski mask and the note he'd stolen and left in my car. Both items were bagged and labeled.

Rick turned the bags over and admired my handiwork. "Very professional!"

I was tempted to gloat, but in the spirit of Christmas, chose to glow in the wake of his compliment instead. He took down my parents' address and said he would mail a typed copy to their house. I was to sign and mail it back as soon as it arrived.

"Now it's my turn to ask some questions."

"Go ahead."

"When did Vince become your chief suspect?"

"After I couldn't break Hank York's alibi. Vince still wasn't a serious suspect until after the Fly Ranch boy broke in. I didn't like how eager Vince was to take the kid down. It rubbed me the wrong way, so I started digging into his background. The results of that investigation, along with his sudden interest in you—"

"Sudden interest? What are you insinuating?"

"He took you to Round the Bend on Monday. He showed up at the church on Tuesday." Rick ticked off the days on his fingers. "Later that same evening, you called about what Dick had found at the church. I knew then that Vince had hidden the stash and he was our man."

"How did you know it was Vince and not Dick?"

"Dick is the most honest person I have ever known, and I've known him a long time. Also he phoned the sheriff's office as soon as you hung up. He left nothing out. As a matter of fact, both he and Vince arrived at the church Tuesday before anyone else. Dick got there first and was in the kitchen when he heard Vince come in. He peeked out the door, like you did later, and saw Vince stash something in a hymnal and hide it. Dick waited until more people were milling around and Vince was occupied to leave his hiding place and join the work crew. He sneaked in later and found the bag Vince had put in the hymnal. He took it, called me from the pay phone by the garage to report, and hand delivered the bag to the sheriff's office.

"I've had my eye on Vince since a year or two after Fly Ranch first contracted with him. Drugs started showing up in Tipperary County shortly after that. I suspected it wasn't a coincidence, so I contacted law enforcement in the places where he's previously lived and done business. Their reports heightened my suspicions. Still I had no proof until you and Dick reported what you'd seen. Dick and I took that information to Fly Ranch. The director had no idea of Vince's past history, but their records confirmed a persistent influx of drugs that began soon after he began ferrying people to and from the ranch. Dick and I started keeping an eye on you that night."

"Why me? Why not Vince?"

"His behavior indicated that he was fishing for information and that he thought you were in possession of it. By watching you, we could keep tabs on him without tipping him off. We could get what we needed to not only arrest him, but convict him of drug smuggling and murder."

"Why didn't you tell me what was going on?"

"The reports about Vince revealed a disturbing pattern. He seems to sense when law enforcement is closing in and gives them the slip. We wanted your interactions with him to be completely genuine so his alarm bells wouldn't start ringing. If I had thought that decision would put you in danger, I would have chosen differently. I owe you an apology."

He looked miserable. Not as miserable as my pounding head, aching goose egg, and throbbing temple. But miserable enough. I let him stew in his own juice for a little longer and then said, "Apology accepted."

"I don't deserve it."

"You're right about that." I shrugged. "But it's almost Christmas and I'm feeling magnanimous."

The sides of his mouth twitched, and he glanced at the clock. "Do you have any more questions?"

"Just one. Do you have what you need to make a murder charge stick?"

"I think so."

I gazed at the wall. The movie reel of Edgar and me began to play. First, Edgar very much alive as we sat together in the cab of Dick's truck. Then, him furiously shoveling snow away from my Beetle. Next, him clearing the school sidewalk and then tromping through the snow in his ridiculous, electric-blue moon boots. Edgar sitting at my table eating an entire package of Oreos. Finally, his pale face in a circle of snow stained red with his blood. I'd banished my tears earlier in the evening, but now they coursed down my cheeks. Rick pressed a tissue into my hand, then another and another. I swiped at my tears, but they kept flowing.

"Holy cow!" His eyes grew wide. "How did you keep that shiner hidden?"

I pinched a soggy tissue smeared with make up between my thumb and forefinger. "I have my ways."

"Does it hurt?"

"Only when I cry."

He began to laugh. So did I.

"I bet that hurts too."

It did. Like the dickens. I bit my lip to displace the pain. His eyes danced. My lips twitched. He snorted, and our laughter escaped with unstoppable force. The tension and grief I'd harbored since stumbling upon Edgar's

body a month ago vanished with a giggle and a sigh of
joy.

When our laughter was spent, Rick rapped his
knuckles on the table top. His expression was a strange
mix of gravity and hope. "Before I go, I want to ask you
something."

I froze. Was he going to ask me out on a date?

"How did you learn to bag and label evidence?"

Not a date. Whew.

"Let me show you something." He followed me into
the guest bedroom and watched as I took the box from
its shelf in the closet and carried it back to the kitchen
table. I opened the lid. He examined the magnifying
glass, the sketch pad, the microscope, and the other
items I'd brought from Iowa.

"Where did you get this stuff?"

"I wanted to major in forensics at college and completed several courses when I was a freshman and sophomore. Mom found out and flipped her lid. She refused
to pay my tuition unless I majored in either nursing or
education. The fastest way to get out from under her
thumb was to become a teacher and get a job as far away
as possible. I couldn't bear to part with this stuff and
brought it with me."

"What would you think of being a forensic consultant
for Tipperary County?"

"Are you serious?"

"You saw how long the state lab in Pierre took to
analyze evidence after Twila Kelly. I went to Pierre to
ask about how to expedite the process. They suggested
we set up a lab out here. Even gave me a printout of basic
equipment and supplies. I stuck it in my pocket and it's

been there since. Without someone trained in forensics, what use is—"

"Yes." The flurry of mental cartwheels I'd been holding could be contained no longer. "I'll do it."

He grinned and took the printout. Together we made lists of what he would order and what I would purchase in Sioux City. Then he checked his watch and said, "It's nine o'clock. Time for me to go."

We stood and I walked him to the door rather stiffly, as my muscles had seized after sitting still for so long.

"Drive carefully tomorrow." He zipped his coat. "Have a Merry Christmas."

"You too, Rick."

"Be sure to save your shopping receipts and hide them from your mom." He grinned.

I did too. We both started laughing again. This time I didn't hold back. Even though it hurt.

Chapter 50

Rick left, and I shook out and swallowed four aspirin. My headache was killing me. Then I added some last-minute items to my suitcase, closed it, and set it next to a box of Christmas gifts to carry to my car in the morning. I was packing fruit and sandwiches for the trip when someone knocked at the door.

Two someones, as it turned out. Merle and Velma stood on the landing, their arms too full to let themselves in. I opened the door and Velma thrust a metal thermos with a tattered bow stuck on the side at me. "You got a long trip tomorrow, so fill this with coffee every chance you get. That's an order."

"I was just wishing for a thermos." I took the gift from her. "How did you know I needed one? Come in!"

She marched inside. "I wasn't snooping. But it's hard not to see what's in your dang cupboards when you leave the doors hanging open and where did you get that shiner?"

Before I could answer Velma, Merle shuffled in

behind her and laid a gallon jug of milk and two cartons of eggs on the table. Then he pulled a quart jar of cream from his pocket and set it beside them. "These is for your family. I 'spect they might appreciate 'em."

"Thank you both. Hang on a minute."

"You're the one who oughta be hanging on a minute, young lady." Velma wagged a finger under my nose. "How'd you get that shiner and how did you hide it tonight?"

The second question was easy so I tackled it first. "Concealer, foundation, and eye shadow."

"That's enough of your sass." More finger wagging from Velma. "How you got that goose egg and black eye is what I want to know."

My answer required some truth-shading. In my opinion it was more selective use of facts and creative name-changing—such as replacing the phrases "airstrip" with "bathroom" and "Dick Phillips' head" with "doorknob"—than lying. Also, my tactics were totally necessary as Rick had cautioned against divulging what had happened at the airstrip until my statement was signed and the details of Vince's arrest were released to the public. My story seemed to satisfy Velma's curiosity. Since I would be telling my parents the same tale in less than twenty-four hours, I considered it to be a good sign.

I went to the freezer and took out two foil-wrapped packages. "These are for you."

Velma peeled the foil from a corner of hers and raised an eyebrow. "Caramel rolls?"

"They're a variation on your cinnamon roll recipe, Velma."

She simpered. Merle bristled.

"Made with eggs from Merle's hens and Snippy's cream."

That smoothed his ruffled feathers. He set down the package and picked up the box of gifts next to my suitcase. "Can I put that in yer car?"

"I was going to take everything out in the morning."

"A woman who smacks into the bathroom doorknob and gets a black eye like you got can't be too careful." Velma picked up my suitcase. "We'll take care of it."

She could be such a softy.

"Okay then. Thanks."

"Don't just stand there," she growled. "You still gotta come out and pop the trunk."

Not all that soft.

I snatched my keys and coat and we tramped to the car. Merle loaded everything in the trunk and tested the latch after shutting it. After that I peered at Merle and Velma as I shifted from foot to foot, shivering with cold. I didn't want them to leave, but was eager for them to go so I could return to my warm apartment and finish preparing for my trip.

"We-ull." Merle sucked air through his teeth. "You need your beauty sleep—"

"Beauty sleep isn't gonna touch that black eye. It needs ice packs, beef steak, and about a month." Velma snorted. "Mark my words you'll be wearing that shiner into the new year."

"You're probably right." I yawned. "But I'm so tired that ugly sleep is as appealing as beauty sleep." I yawned again. Louder than was necessary. "Good night."

"Good night," they said in unison. Instead of turning toward their respective hugs, they stood on either side and wrapped me in a strange embrace. It felt more like tug-of-war, me being the rope surrounded by equally matched teams, than a hug. Still, it was endearing. And suffocating. I was about to push them away and gasp for air when they released me.

"You drive safe." Velma whirled around and stomped off.

"What time you leaving?" Merle asked.

I told him.

Merle held out a hand. "Gimme your keys, and I'll start your car before you leave."

I dropped them into his palm. "That would be wonderful."

He turned on his good leg and limped away.

They crunched through the snow, Velma taking three steps for every one of Merle's. I watched them go and waited until they were out of earshot to repeat what they'd just told me. "I love you, too," I whispered at their retreating backs.

Their footsteps faded to nothing. The silence and the crisp air, so icy it made my eyelashes crackle and so fresh it felt like breathing spring water, pressed in close. The stars hung brilliant and frail, shining hope into the black night. I half expected angels to appear as they had to the shepherds outside Bethlehem. Though in this corner of South Dakota, the angels would be bundled to their eyeballs as they announced Christ's birth to sheep ranchers checking their flocks by night.

I didn't see any angels. I couldn't hear them either. Even so, I sensed that the truth they had proclaimed to me during the Christmas program a few hours ago had drawn near to my soul and moved into my heart for good and forever. A stinging wind numbed my cheeks. My feet, thinly clad in dress shoes and nylon stockings, were blocks of ice. My coat and velvet dress were no match for the cold on a dark December night.

Still I was loath to move from where I stood next to a scruffy schoolyard in a town as unlovely and inconsequential as Bethlehem. Eventually, as the cold sent me stumping along the sidewalk on frozen feet, I was certain of two things. This night, I was embarking on a great and unknown, lifelong adventure. Also, that the adventure would have to wait until after a long, hot shower to keep my toes from falling off. Because if I landed on my parents' doorstep with a black eye *and* frostbite, an entirely different adventure would commence. Knowing my mom, it would not be pretty.

Once inside my apartment, I yanked off my shoes and counted my toes. All ten were present, accounted for, and firmly attached. I filled my Dutch oven with warm water and soaked my feet until they began to tingle. Then I hobbled into the shower and stood under a stream of hot water until my feet howled in protest. I didn't leave until they quieted to a pathetic whimper. Then I turned off the water, toweled dry, and wiped the steam off the mirror.

The injured eye in the reflection was less swollen than before, but more colorful—an intense shade of purple not found in nature until now. This was what I had to hide from my parents for two weeks. I went to my bedroom and set my alarm for ten minutes earlier than I'd previously planned. It would take that long and then some to paint my face before hitting the road in the morning.

I got into bed and gazed out the window. The stars glittered and pulsed in the night sky. The largest of them hovered over Merle's barn where Snippy lay next to her manger. An otherworldly warmth enveloped me. My complaining toes hushed and stilled. My heart quieted. I drank in the star's beautiful song until I grew drowsy. The star winked, blinked, and disappeared.

Chapter 51

My alarm rang in the morning and my feet didn't scream even once when they hit the floor. Still, during the short walk to the kitchen, I felt like an old woman. I walked like one, too. Sleep had stiffened my body and magnified every indignity it had suffered during the plane ride with Vince. If today wasn't Christmas Eve, if my family wasn't waiting to greet me at the other end of this day, I would have downed as many aspirin as my stomach could handle, plugged in the heating pad, and crawled under the covers again.

I started the coffee maker. Then I shook four aspirin from the bottle, washed them down with water, and stuck the bottle in my purse. I dressed and fixed my hair while the coffee brewed. Then I hid my black eye under a thick layer of makeup, filled Velma's thermos, and got into my coat and boots. Last of all, I packed Merle's eggs, milk, and cream into a box along with several packages of frozen caramel rolls.

I locked the apartment and got into the Beetle. As I

backed it onto the street, the lights in Merle's mudroom switched off and on. I blinked my headlights in return, put the car into first gear, and drove away.

The Beetle, as warm as my heating pad, though not as comfortable as my bed, putzed along Main Street. When I passed Velma's trailer, her lights blinked on and off. At the end of the block, Frosty and Fannie McDonald's did the same. Next up were Gus and Betty Yarborough, followed by the Barkleys and their neighbors in the other Forest Service houses. Lights blinked in the houses of people I knew, and in those of people I hadn't yet met.

A tear rolled down my cheek. *For crying out loud*, I told myself—perhaps not the most accurate word choice since that single tear hadn't made a sound—*it's only four-thirty in the morning and you're already crying? Get it together, woman!*

My tears—again not accurate—my *tear* dried on my cheek, and its friends did not come out to play. Not even when I turned onto the Norwegian cut-across and a full moon appeared low in the sky ahead. It transformed the winding gravel road into a magical, frost-strewn path and kept pace with me as my speed increased. A few miles later, a pair of headlights blinked on and off, on and off in the distance. What in the world? Anybody on the cut-across this early in the morning had to be crazy. Present company excepted.

My incredulity turned to apprehension as I approached the blinking lights. What if this yahoo had broken down and needed a lift into town? I would have to take him. That would put me behind schedule with my journey barely underway. The lights kept flashing. I braked and pulled over, as far away from the vehicle as possible on the narrow road. Whoever it was better have a legitimate reason for being here.

I rolled down my window just a crack and spoke into the darkness. "You need some help?"

A figure walked into the beam of my headlights. A ski mask hid its face. I gasped, rolled the window shut, and gripped the steering wheel. Blood pounded in my ears.

Calm down, Jane. It can't be Vince. He's under arrest.

The figure's gloved hand removed the mask. Dick Phillips waved it in my direction and smiled.

Not funny. Not at all. I unrolled the window and stuck my head out. I didn't care that the sheriff held Dick in high esteem. This bozo was about to get a piece of my mind.

He trotted around to my window and thrust a package through it. It was wrapped in Christmas paper and topped with a shiny red bow. "This is for you." He looked as happy as I'd ever seen him.

I threw it on the passenger seat without so much as a thank you. "Why in the world would you think this is a good place for gift exchange?"

His smile faded. "Don't you recognize where you are?"

"Are you crazy? It's dark outside! And why were you wearing a ski mask?"

"It's cold." He sounded baffled. "You really don't know where we are?"

I wanted to bite his head off. "No."

He pointed to the side of the road. "Imagine being stuck in a snowbank about right there."

My indignation drained away. "Is this where you and Edgar found me?"

"Pretty close."

I stared in the direction he'd pointed. The moonlight revealed an indentation in a snowbank. "Over there?"

"Yup." He nodded at the package on the seat beside me. "It's something you can use on your trip."

"Well then, I'd better open it." I removed the bow and picked at the tape.

"Your mom saves paper, too?"

"She does." The paper came off in one piece and I opened the box. It was a thermos, identical to the one Velma had given me. That one was half hidden by my purse on the passenger side floor.

I lifted Dick's thermos from the box. It was heavy, so I gave it a shake. "What's in it?"

"Coffee. Good and hot."

"How thoughtful." I laid the wrapping paper over Velma's thermos and wedged Dick's on the passenger seat. "I wish I had something for you."

"That's okay."

"Wait a minute." I unlatched my seatbelt, got out, and flipped my seat back forward. I rummaged around in the box with the milk and eggs and found what I wanted.

"Here." I gave him a package of frozen rolls.

"Did you make these?"

"Yes."

"Then they'll be good." He smiled and his eyes crinkled. "Thanks." He bent and put the seat back into place again. "You need to get going."

I climbed in and fastened the seatbelt. He closed the door and leaned down until our heads were level. A shaft of moonlight caught his face and illuminated a thin, white hair caught in the stubble on his chin. The hair dangled from his chin and danced in the breeze.

Dick patted the door. "Drive carefully. Call Betty when you get there."

"Consider it done." I began to roll up the window and then stopped. "Merry Christmas, San—um, Dick."

"Merry Christmas, Jane."

Before I could do something impulsive that I might regret later, I shut the window. Tight. While Dick crossed the road to his truck, I unscrewed the lid from the thermos flask and poured some of its steaming, fragrant contents into the cup. I settled the cup between my knees and beeped as I drove away. I waved until the lights of Dick's vehicle were no longer visible in the rearview mirror. Then I took a long sip of the coffee he'd made for me. It was the best I'd ever tasted.

Cookie and Velma's Caramel Rolls

Rolls

3 1/2 to 4 cups unbleached flour

1 package active dry yeast

1 cup milk

1/8 cup sugar

1/4 cup shortening

1 teaspoon salt

2 eggs

1. *In large mixing bowl, combine 2 cups of flour and the yeast. In saucepan, heat milk, sugar, shortening, and salt until mixture is warm (just begins steaming) and shortening is melted. Add to flour in the mixing bowl. Add the eggs.*

2. *Beat on low speed of electric mixer for 30*

*seconds, scraping sides of bowl constantly. Beat
3 minutes at high speed. Using dough hook on
mixer, stir in as much of the remaining flour as
possible. Turn out onto a lightly floured surface. Knead in enough of the remaining flour
to make a moderately stiff dough. Continue
kneading until dough is smooth and elastic (8
to 10 minutes). Shape into a ball.*

*3.   Place ball of dough in lightly greased bowl,
turning once to grease surface. Cover. Let rise
in a warm place until double (45–60 minutes).
Punch dough down. Turn out onto lightly
floured surface. Continue as directed below.*

Caramel Topping

3 tablespoons butter, melted
2 tablespoons brown sugar
1 teaspoon ground cinnamon
1/2 cup brown sugar
1/4 cup butter
2 tablespoons light corn syrup
1/2 cup chopped pecans

*4.   Combine 1/2 cup brown sugar, 1/4 cup
butter or margarine, and corn syrup in a
saucepan. Cook, stirring constantly until butter
is melted and mixture is blended. Distribute
mixture evenly in two 9×1 1/2 round or two 8×8
square pans or one 9 x 13 cake pan. Sprinkle
with chopped pecans.*

5.   *Roll sweet dough into a 24×16 inch rectangle. Brush with melted butter. Combine 2 tablespoons brown sugar and cinnamon over dough. Starting from long side, roll up dough jelly-roll style. Seal seam. Slice into 24 rolls.*

6.   *Place rolls, cut side down, in prepared baking pans. Cover and let rise in a warm place until double (about 30 minutes). Bake at 375° for 18–20 minutes. Cool about 30 seconds. Invert onto racks covered with foil and remove pans. Makes 24 rolls.*

About the Author

Jolene Philo discovered Laura Ingalls Wilder and Encyclopedia Brown in elementary school and has been fascinated by the prairie and mysteries ever since. She's a voracious reader of fiction, biography, and creative non-fiction. Imagine her surprise when she became the author of several non-fiction books for the special needs and disability community. The *West River Mystery Series* combines her love of mysteries and northwest South Dakota's short grass prairie, where she and her husband Hiram lived for seven years when they were first married. Jolene and Hiram live in central Iowa with their daughter, son-in-law, and their two children. Jolene instills book love into her grandchildren by reading to them as often as she can. You can keep up with her reading and writing adventures at her website, www.jolenephilo.com.